WILLING

WILLING

LUCY MONROE

BRAVA

KENSINGTON PUBLISHING CORP.
http://www.kensingtonbooks.com

BRAVA BOOKS are published by

Kensington Publishing Corp.
850 Third Avenue
New York, NY 10022

All Kensington titles, imprints and distributed lines are available at special quantity discounts for bulk purchases for sales promotion, premiums, fund-raising, educational or institutional use.

Special book excerpts or customized printings can also be created to fit specific needs. For details, write or phone the office of the Kensington Special Sales Manager: Kensington Publishing Corp., 850 Third Avenue, New York, NY 10022. Attn. Special Sales Department. Phone: 1-800-221-2647.

Brava and the B logo Reg. U.S. Pat. & TM Off.

ISBN 0-7582-0875-8

First Kensington Trade Paperback Printing: January 2006
10   9   8   7   6   5   4   3   2   1

Printed in the United States of America

For my new daughter, Sabrina.
I love you very much and
thank God for your being in my life!

And with thanks to the Oregon State Police
for answering hours worth of questions
and being so incredibly helpful with the details
on this book. Any errors found within
these pages are mine and mine alone.

Prologue

Josie's chest felt like someone had tied a rope around it and was pulling at the ends.

She didn't want to disappoint Daddy. Not again. She tried to breathe shallow, to be quiet so he couldn't find her, but he always did and he always told her what she did wrong so he could. She tried so hard to hear him moving among the trees, but she never could. He would just appear, and he would be frowning.

"You broke a twig on the other side of the tree."

She jumped, even though she'd been expecting the sound of her dad's voice. Spinning around to face him, she fell into the fighter's stance he'd taught her on her eighth birthday.

His pale green eyes, just like hers, narrowed, and without any warning one of his feet shot out toward her. Leaping as high as she could, she avoided the kick. Bringing her fist down on his extended leg, she swung her own foot in a high arc to connect squarely with his side.

Air rushed out from his lips, telling her she'd made good on the kick to his kidney, the one he told her even a little girl could use to hurt an attacker.

His hand came up to where she'd kicked him as he stepped back from her before she could make another pass at him with her hand or foot. "Good job. You're fast Josie-girl."

Standing tall, his thin lips smiling, his eyes warmed, and the tight feeling in her chest disappeared.

"Thank you, Daddy." She loved it when her dad smiled at her. "But how did you know I'd broken the twig? It could have been a deer, or something."

He picked her up and squeezed her. "I just knew. You'll learn to rely on your instincts, too, one day."

She hugged him back, feeling happy and warm, but she didn't think she would ever be as good a soldier as her dad. She tried, though. It made him happy, and since Mama died, there wasn't much that did. She tried very hard not to think of Mama or how it felt to be tucked into bed with a gentle kiss and a bedtime story.

Mama had been soft, but Josie had to be hard. Daddy said so. He said she was ten years old now and too old for bedtime stories, but he let her read at night. Once a week he took her to the library in town at the bottom of the mountain and let her check out as many books as she wanted.

She liked the old fairy tales—the ones without pictures—but they were all wrong because the princesses never knew how to fight. Girls had to know how to fight. Daddy said so. Josie figured *she* could beat some of those evil knights and dragons easy, but she liked reading the stories anyway.

"It's time for dinner, Josie. We'll go back now." Daddy set her down and ruffled her hair. "All right?"

She nodded and smoothed her hair with her fingers. It was short because he said all soldiers wore their hair short. She thought sometimes she'd like long golden hair like a princess, but her hair was dark, and she wasn't a princess anyway. She was a soldier. Not as good as Daddy, but better than some of the men that came through his mercenary school.

She put her hand in her dad's and walked beside him, trying to match her stride to his. "None of your men found me." She was proud of that fact.

Daddy smiled again, squeezing her fingers. "No, they didn't."

Then he got serious and mean looking. "They'll hear about that tonight."

She shivered, glad she was just his daughter and not one of the soldiers who paid him to teach them how to fight. Daddy might get mad at her for being sloppy, but he never yelled at her, or made her crawl facedown in the mud, or march in the icy stream that ran behind the compound, like he did the men he trained.

She was going to be the best soldier that ever lived when she grew up, but she was going to learn how to do it before Daddy figured she was old enough to be disciplined like the other soldiers. By the time she was grown up, she was never going to make mistakes, and even Daddy wasn't going to be able to find her when she hid in the forest.

Chapter 1

"So, why isn't Josie taking on the partnership?"

Daniel Black Eagle didn't like incongruities, and Tyler McCall's desire to take on a partner for his mercenary school in the Oregon Coastal Range didn't add up. Not when his daughter was more than qualified to run the school on her own.

Tyler ran his hand over his salt-and-pepper crew cut, a frown wrinkling his brow. "She's not interested. Thought one day I'd leave the school to her, but she says she's spent enough of her life living like a soldier."

"You're not ready to give it up." And probably never would be.

Men like Tyler knew one thing, warfare. Whether training soldiers or fighting, they lived for combat and usually died the same way.

"Not yet. There are still some good years left in this old body."

Daniel didn't doubt it. The Vietnam vet was in better shape than a lot of Daniel's contemporaries, and there was no arguing with the fact that he was still a damn fine trainer. "You've run the school for a long time without a partner."

"Times change. Josie's ready to move on, and I'm ready to let someone else do some of the grunt work."

Daniel didn't smile, but he felt like it. Kids would be out of school for a snow day in Hawaii before the man sitting across from him stopped training soldiers in hand-to-hand combat. "My specialty is explosives, not grunt work."

"That's why they call you Nitro."

It wasn't. Daniel had gotten the tag long before he learned how to build and diffuse a bomb, but he wasn't about to explain what had prompted his Army Ranger nickname. It came from a time in his life he never talked about and wished he could forget.

"So, what does Josie want to do?" He couldn't see her as anything but a highly skilled, highly paid warrior.

"She's got some idea about becoming a computer expert, or something, working nine-to-five in an office like *normal people.*" The way the older man said *normal people* made it clear he didn't think much of his daughter's idea. "She took computer classes on-line for over a year. I didn't even know about them. Now she's moved to Portland so she can go to PSU and finish getting her degree."

The man sounded baffled by such a plan.

"You don't want her to move on?" Most fathers would be relieved, not upset, if they found out their daughters didn't want to be professional soldiers.

But Tyler McCall was not typical in any sense.

"Don't get me wrong. I've never been all that excited about her going into the field." For once the other man's expression was easy to read. He looked haunted. "That's not why I trained her like I did. I thought she'd teach soldiers how to fight, not go out and do the fighting herself. But this computer stuff is no better."

"How so?"

"Josie wasn't raised to fit into a normal environment, and maybe that's my fault." Tyler's jaw hardened. "Hell, I know it is, but facts are facts, and my baby girl is going to fit in an office environment about as well as a forty-four slug in a twenty-two rifle."

At twenty-six, the highly skilled female warrior was hardly anybody's *baby girl*. "She'll be fine."

Tyler's face creased in a frown. "I wonder."

"What do you wonder, Dad?"

The softly feminine voice traveled along Daniel's nerve endings straight to his sex, and he got as hard as a pike between inhaling and exhaling. Damn, how could a woman who dressed, acted and fought like a man sound so much like a woman and have such an impact on his libido?

She wasn't exactly standard wet dream material, being on the short side of average with small curves. And her chin-length, reddish brown hair gave her a perky air, not a sexy one, but it didn't matter. She made him react like a horny teen getting his first glimpse of Marilyn Monroe-style cleavage.

He wanted Josie like hell on fire, and she'd shown him six ways from Sunday that she wasn't interested.

Tyler's green gaze settled on his daughter. "I wonder how well you're going to fit into the normal world."

The smile she'd been wearing when she walked into the austere room that reminded Daniel of army quarters slipped right off her face. "About as well as I fit into this world, I guess."

There was something in her voice that confused him, a bitterness he wouldn't have expected. She made it sound like she didn't belong, but he'd met few mercs as capable as she was.

Tyler grunted. "You fit in just fine with other soldiers."

"But I'm not a soldier, Dad." She sat down on the edge of a twin-size army bed pushed up against one wall and put one foot on the mattress, then looped her arms around her knee. Swinging the other leg, she gave her dad one of those serious looks that always caught at something inside Daniel he didn't want to deal with. "I've never been enlisted. I don't owe my undying allegiance to any world government."

"You're a better soldier than ninety-nine percent of the armed forces."

She shrugged and turned to face Daniel, her small but tempting breasts outlined by her khaki tank top. "How are Wolf and Lise?"

It took him a second to respond to her words rather than the seductive force of her body. "They're expecting a baby."

Primal male tension filled him as he waited for her to ask about Hotwire. She'd shown a definite preference for the other man's company on their last mission.

Oblivious to his tension, her pixie face lit up, and her smile made her seem too damn sweet to know as much about bombs as she did. "Hotwire didn't tell me. They must have just found out."

What the—"You keep in touch?"

Her pale green eyes warmed in a way that made Daniel want to hit something. "He's been helping me with my computer training."

For no discernable reason, Daniel's muscles contracted into battle-ready mode. "He never mentioned it."

"Probably because he knows you don't like me."

"What are you talking about?" Not like her? He wanted her more than he'd wanted any other woman.

Despite her total lack of encouragement in that area, he couldn't get rid of the desire that made his blood bubble like molten lava whenever she was around.

She rolled her eyes, her nose wrinkling. "You didn't exactly make a secret of it on the mission with Wolf and Lise."

"I never friggin once said I didn't like you." Could she really be this blind?

Her laugh was hollow, and her eyes went dark with something he didn't have a hope of defining.

The only thing he understood about women was their sexual response, and since Josie's was about as clear as an overcast day, he couldn't figure her out at all.

"You didn't have to. I mean, actions speak louder than words, don't they?"

Hell, he'd always thought they did, but since meeting her, he wasn't so sure. "I don't dislike you."

Her eyes went wide at his tone, but he wasn't used to having to explain himself. Most of the time he wouldn't have even bothered, but having her believe he didn't like her bothered him. For all her strength as a soldier, she was vulnerable.

"Maybe you don't dislike me, but you don't exactly *like* my company either. You made it pretty clear I was just in the way on the mission."

"You weren't in the way."

"That's not what you said the last night of the mission."

"I was in a bad mood." She'd been all over Hotwire after treating Daniel like the untouchable man on their cross-country drive together.

"Which seems to be your constant state of being when you're around me."

He opened his mouth to argue when he suddenly remembered they weren't alone. Tyler McCall sat on a straight-back wooden chair, an arrested expression on his weather-beaten, darkly tanned face. Daniel's lips snapped together, and he frowned, first at Tyler and then at Josie.

"We can discuss this later."

"Further dialogue on the blatantly obvious facts would be redundant."

"You sound like a schoolteacher sucking on a lemon." And a woman still very much convinced he did not like her.

The anger he'd learned to control fought to slip its leash as frustration ripped at his insides. It was as though she was being deliberately obtuse, only she was too natural to be putting on an act. *She really believed that crap.*

Did that mean she'd similarly misread his sexual signals?

He wanted her, and the truth was, an emotion as lukewarm as liking didn't begin to come into it. His feelings where she was concerned were much too hot for mere *liking*.

* * *

Josie kicked the covers off and flopped onto her back to stare at the dark ceiling above her.

Staying the night at the compound had been a bad idea. Nitro hadn't driven back down the mountain to his hotel until well after dinner, and her dad had insisted she stick around to discuss plans for the school with them. Even though she was no longer going to teach, he wanted her opinion on the new training program he'd been devising.

Usually, being asked for her opinion by her dad made Josie feel good. Tonight it had been an instrument of torture, keeping her cooped up in the same room with Nitro and his testosterone-laden body.

She wouldn't have been at the compound at all, but her dad had finally consented to her computerizing his files. She'd finished the week before and was done installing the new software. All she had to do was go through the easy entry procedure with him, and he would be good to go.

She supposed she'd have to show Nitro, too, since he was going to be her father's partner.

Her hands fisted at her sides while her body tingled the way it did every time she thought about him. Seeing him again had her hot and bothered and from past experience, she knew the feeling wouldn't be disappearing anytime soon.

He was just so sexy. Everything about him turned her on, and she wasn't used to feelings like this. From mahogany brown eyes that looked as though they held the secrets of the universe, to black glossy hair he wore just a little long, to a muscular but flexible body she desperately wanted to touch, he was the most appealing man she'd ever known, and she'd known a lot of men.

Her father's school had seen hundreds of pupils over the years, and she'd gotten to know pretty much all of them, ninety-eight percent of whom had been male. None of whom had impacted her like Nitro did.

Maybe if she'd been able to spend any bonding time with

the women who came through the school, she would now know what to do with the feelings Nitro elicited in her, but she hadn't known how to relate to the female soldiers. She had no more fit in among them than she had in the public school she'd tried out for a couple of months before returning to homeschool at her father's mercenary training compound.

She'd always felt like the rest of the world had a secret handshake she'd never been given, so she would forever be on the outside looking in. The only person in the world she was really close to was her dad, and he wasn't exactly sane by society's standards.

Josie didn't fit anywhere, and she wanted to change that. As much as she acted like one of the guys, she wasn't one, and meeting Nitro had brought that home to her in a way nothing else could have. She wanted him with a physical ache that was actually painful and didn't even know how to tell him so.

She'd thought he wanted her, too . . . until he started acting like he hated her.

She didn't know what she'd done to turn him against her, but it hurt. She'd spent so much time around men with nary a twinge of physical reaction that the wave of sexual desire that crashed into her upon meeting him had about sent her to her knees in shock. She'd never known anything like it, not before or since.

She'd tried dating a few times in the past months, but none of the men she'd gone out with had made her heart race or her hands itch to tear their clothes off. Her teeth gritted against the sexual desire tormenting her. If seeing him for such a short time this afternoon did this to her, what was going to happen when he was here every time she came to visit or upgrade the computer system?

She just could not believe Nitro was going into partnership with her dad.

Oh, sure, the two men had plenty in common. Both were

consummate soldiers. Both were so self-sufficient they didn't really need anyone else, least of all her. They were powerful, tough males with not an ounce of weakness in them. Still, it wasn't fair that her dad would pick as his partner the one man destined to torment her with what she couldn't have.

She knew her dad was disappointed she hadn't wanted to take a more active role in the training camp, just as he'd been disappointed when she'd opted for real missions over training others since reaching adulthood, but did he have to punish her by taking on Nitro as his partner?

She sighed, acknowledging she wasn't being fair to her dad.

He knew nothing of her feelings for Nitro. In fact, she'd told him she didn't like the man who made her throb in places she hadn't known existed. Ignorant or not, her dad's decision had her edgier than a deer scenting a bobcat.

With a groan of frustration, she climbed out of bed and into her fatigues. Maybe a walk would clear her head enough to sleep.

Forty-five minutes later, she had walked the entire perimeter of the camp and didn't feel any closer to sleep. She hadn't even had the satisfaction of moving undetected by her father's pupils because there weren't any.

It was the usual two-week hiatus between training groups, and the camp was deserted except for her and her dad. Even the part-time teachers that helped her dad teach stuff he wasn't so hot on, like computers and offensive driving, were gone. Not that most of them lived on site, but some stayed at the school during sessions.

Giving up on getting any sort of peace with the walk, she started jogging back. Exercise was supposed to be the panacea for all ills.

Suddenly, the ground shook, and a huge boom she recognized all too well rent the air. She fell to her knees, terrifying knowledge of just how devastating that magnitude of explosion could be slamming into her. Scrambling back to her feet, she saw orange flames licking toward the sky from the office section of the compound.

She started to sprint, her legs moving with fear-based adrenaline pumping through them. Where was her dad? He had to have heard the explosion, but she didn't see his big body silhouetted against the flames.

She bypassed the office and the bedroom all the students thought he slept in to the back of the building and the windowless room he actually used. The wall looked seamless, but she knew he had an exit, and it didn't take her any time at all to trigger the release on the hidden door.

It swung outward, and she saw her father's form sprawled across the bed outlined in the eerie light. The explosion had caused part of the wall to fall on him, and he was dangerously still. Heat blasted her as she ran toward the bed, the fire having reached the secret room through the decimated wall.

She didn't waste any time checking for a pulse, but started throwing debris off of him. When he was free, she dragged him out of the burning building, her muscles straining against his weight. They made it outside just as the wall collapsed with a whoosh of fire and a deafening crash. She kept moving until they were clear of it, relief flooding her as she saw his chest rise and fall with one choking breath after another.

Running to the jeep parked away from the office, her own lungs heaved against the smoke billowing around her, and she brought her arm to her face, breathing into the crook of her elbow. She sent prayers of gratitude skyward for the jeep's undamaged state as she drove to where her father lay.

Her own small Justy was a goner, having taken a direct hit of fire-heated timber when the office exploded.

It took more strength than she knew she had to get his unconscious weight into the passenger seat, but desperation sizzled through her muscles. With a flick of her wrist, she shoved the car into gear and started driving down the mountain as fast as she could without going off the track.

Her dad stored explosives underground, with each component carefully separated from the others, but she wasn't taking any chances on the initial explosion being followed by another. Her caution was justified as the ground rocked under the jeep, almost sending them sliding off the narrow track. She kept driving, the vehicle barely under control, her mind focused entirely on escape.

They were more than halfway down the mountain when she used the jeep's CB to call the explosion and possible forest fire in to the fire service. It had been a wet spring, and she had no doubt the water copters would have the fire under control before the forest surrounding the compound could be severely affected.

She hit the coastal highway at a speed beyond legal limits and just kept going, making a split-second decision to head toward the major metropolitan hospital to the east rather than the small community hospital ten minutes closer and to the west.

The instincts her dad had told her she would learn to live by were screaming at her that no carelessness on her father's part had caused that explosion tonight. If someone was trying to hurt her dad, they'd have a better shot at him in the small coastal town than the more anonymous metropolitan area surrounding Portland.

She drove without her lights until she hit the outskirts of civilization, glad for the three-quarter moon that lit the highway. Unless they were using night vision or radar, no one followed her. She made it to the nearest major hospital less than twenty minutes later, ignoring speed limits in the downtown district and pulling into the emergency parking lot with squealing tires and honking her horn.

Tyler McCall had not moved so much as a muscle during the entire trip. Emergency room personnel came rushing out, and her dad was on a stretcher headed into ER within minutes.

She spent the next half hour discretely securing the perimeter of her dad's environment while the doctors examined him. She was leaning against the wall, surreptitiously watching the emergency room entrance, when a doctor in a white coat and with an energetic demeanor approached her.

"Miss McCall?"

"Yes?"

"I'm Dr. Wells. I've been treating your father."

"And . . ."

"He has a nasty hit to the head, but he's regained consciousness."

Air escaped her lungs in a whoosh, and she sagged against the wall. "Can I see him?"

"Yes, but I think there's something you need to know."

"What?"

"He's experiencing a certain level of confusion, and I believe it's brought on because his memory has been compromised by the blow he received." His mouth tightened with exasperation. "Not that he will admit it."

That sounded like her dad, not to admit to weakness. It was a measure of the doctor's powers of observation that he'd noticed anomalies in her dad's behavior enough to make the diagnosis.

"He has amnesia?"

"Partial. He knows who he is, but avoided answering questions about where he had been or what he had been doing before the explosion."

"That doesn't mean he can't remember."

"I get that impression, but he wouldn't tell me what day it is either. He knows the year, but it's my guess there are some gaps in his memory, and without his cooperation, we have no way of determining what they are."

She almost wished the doctor good luck, but kept the facetious comment back. Her dad was stubborn and distrustful of authority. Apparently the doctor had already figured that out.

"Will his memory come back?"

"There's no way of knowing, but in most cases, unless there is significant damage, the brain learns to rewire itself, going around the affected area and retrieving knowledge. Without a previous MRI to compare his current condition to, it's hard to tell how widespread the impairment to brain tissue is. From what I *can* tell, it is limited to a small area in his left frontal lobe corresponding to a large external bump and gash."

Her dad wouldn't like knowing they'd been taking pictures of the inside of his head. He was funny about stuff like that, and they'd gotten away with it only because he'd been out cold, but it didn't bode well for his mood when she got to see him.

"Anything else?"

"He has some surface bruising, but no internal damage." She'd hedged when asked what had caused his injuries and could sense the doctor's curiosity now.

"I'd like to see him."

The doctor frowned, but nodded. "That might be best. Maybe you can convince him to cooperate in his treatment."

That brought a cynical twist to her lips. "I can try."

A nurse led her back to a curtained cubicle. Her dad was sitting up in bed, his eyes obviously unfocused, but scanning the room for any signs of danger nevertheless. The consummate soldier in crisis.

"Hi, Dad."

"Josie-girl."

She walked to stand beside the bed and laid her hand on his forearm. "How are you feeling?"

"I'll live."

"The doctor thinks you've got partial amnesia."

Her dad's pale green eyes narrowed. "Damn impudence."

She smiled, the first glimmer of humor sparking inside her since the ground shook beneath her feet. "Are you saying you don't?"

"I'm not sure."

"Do you know what day it is?"

"No . . ." He put his hand to his head, his eyes closing, sweat breaking out on his brow. "There are gaps."

"Don't worry about it. The doctor said it will probably all come back eventually."

"I suppose he thinks he knows because he used that fancy machine to look inside my brain."

So, he knew about that already. "He was just trying to assess the level of damage."

"If you say so." But clearly her dad didn't believe it.

She sighed. She supposed for a man who considered being asked for his middle name a gross invasion of privacy, and who had refused to go to a doctor in the decade since, an MRI would be over the top of his comfort level.

He opened his eyes and pinned her with a look he used for interrogation. "What happened?"

"You don't remember that either?"

"No, but if it was serious enough to land me in this white prison, I think I should."

"There was an explosion."

"Where?"

"The office and your mock room, but the fire was spreading fast when I pulled you out."

"You saved my life."

She shrugged.

His jaw clenched. "I can't remember what day of the week it is, and I sure as hell don't know why someone tried to blow me up."

She didn't bother denying the explosion had been planned. Her dad's instincts were better than hers, and hers were screaming the same thing. "Don't worry about it. I've got your back."

He nodded and then winced, bringing his hand to his head again. "Damn, this hurts."

"I'm sorry."

The next two hours were tense with Josie avoiding the

probing questions of the ER staff and a duty officer who had been called in to try his luck when they were unsuccessful. She told them her dad had had a fall.

They were bothered because that didn't explain the condition of her clothes or his. She refused to enlighten them, having learned a long time ago that no answer was a better form of evasion than adding lies on top of the initial one. Finally, a nurse came into say they would be moving her dad to a private room for observation.

After the nurse left, her dad said, "Call Nitro."

She supposed his new partner deserved to know their school had been blown to smithereens. "I will in the morning."

"Now, Josie-girl."

She frowned. Dawn was less than an hour away, and she could call Nitro an hour or so after that. "Why now?"

Confusion clouded her dad's face. "I don't know. Just do it."

He didn't like weakness, and he'd always been a bear when he was sick, so she didn't take issue with his general-in-command tone.

"Okay, but if you don't know why, then I don't see how you're going to tell him anything."

It sounded reasonable to her, but at his glare she gave in. Bending down, she kissed his cheek. "Fine. I'll go call him right now, but don't blame me if he doesn't like being woken up before the roosters."

"He's a soldier. He's used to it."

When Nitro answered the phone with an instantly alert voice five minutes later, she had to concede her dad was right.

"Nitro . . . It's Josie."

"What's up?"

She'd gone outside to an isolated phone and made sure no one was in hearing distance, but still she spoke in a low tone.

"There's been an explosion at the Mercenary Training Camp. When I left it looked like most of the compound was gone."

"Are you all right?" The words whipped out like bullets.

"I'm fine. I was out walking."

"What about Tyler?"

She couldn't help noticing he had asked about her first.

It made her feel tingly inside, and she wasn't sure what she was supposed to do with a feeling like that. "Dad was sleeping. He got hit by debris, and he's in ER right now. They'll be moving him to a private room shortly, and he wanted me to call you."

"What hospital?"

She told him the name and grimaced at Nitro's curse. "I wanted the anonymity of the city."

"Yeah, but it'll take me an hour and a half to get there."

"We're not going anywhere, not right now anyway."

"Tell your dad to stay put until I'm there, but here's my cell phone number just in case he doesn't listen."

She wrote down the number and rang off, her heart beating too fast for a simple telephone conversation with her dad's partner.

Chapter 2

Josie had to go to the waiting room while her father was moved. The holes in his memory had become more apparent the longer they'd talked, and she was glad she'd brought him to a larger hospital for treatment as well as anonymity. A nurse came to tell her that her dad had been moved, but had requested she wait to come to the room until he got cleaned up.

Josie took the time to talk to the doctor again, but the harried ER physician had little to add. So, she sat down and waited for a nurse to come and tell her she could go to her father's room. After thirty minutes, she was pretty certain she'd been forgotten, and she went to the nurses' station to inquire.

"He's in room 312. It's just around that corner," the young blond aid said as she waved her hand toward a corridor to her left.

Josie found her father's room, but the door was shut. Was he still indisposed? She knocked, but when no answer came a chill ran down her spine. She pushed the door open without knocking again and found an empty room. The bathroom door was closed. Her instincts were screaming at her that her father was not in there either. She pushed the door open to a dark cubicle and knew she was right.

Going over the room in minute detail, her instincts on high alert, Josie looked for sign of a struggle, but there wasn't one.

The I.V. shunt he'd been wearing was in the waste basket, and his clothes were missing from the plastic bag that still sat on the floor of the tiny closet. The blanket was folded neatly at the bottom of the bed, and a piece of paper was sticking out from under one corner.

She grabbed it, immediately recognizing her dad's handwriting. The note read, *Josie-girl. Read the journal in my private footlocker. Watch your back and don't worry about me. The Viet-Kong couldn't kill me and neither can these bastards.* He'd signed it, *Love Dad.*

She rushed out of the room, but knew before she talked to the nurse at the desk that no one had seen anything. Her dad was the best. He'd been a long range reconnaisance patrol in Vietnam and knew how to disappear too well. If she'd been expecting him to run, she might have been able to catch him, but she hadn't and therefore held out little chance of finding the smallest clue to his whereabouts.

It gave her no satisfaction to discover she was right.

Daniel overestimated the time it would take to get to the hospital by fifteen minutes. His cell phone rang as he pulled into a parking spot.

He flipped it open. "This is Daniel."

"Nitro, it's Josie. Dad's gone." She made a sound of annoyance. "I mean *he's disappeared*, not dead. How far away are you?"

"I'm in the parking lot by the main entrance."

"Oh." She paused. "Hold on and I'll be right there."

"Okay." He flipped the phone shut and got out of the car to wait for her.

She came jogging around the other side of the building looking as though she'd been fighting fires instead of escaping them.

She stopped in front of him, her moss green eyes red from lack of sleep. "It would probably be better if we got in the car to talk."

He nodded, expecting her to get in the car immediately, but she didn't. Instead, she stopped to stretch her arms above her head, small pops from her spine audible in the still morning air. "It's been a long night."

She wasn't wearing a bra.

"I can't believe I didn't guess Dad would run." She stretched again, this time bending over to touch the ground between her feet with her clasped hands.

She wasn't wearing panties either . . . unless she wore a thong. That possibility had sweat breaking out on his brow.

She straightened and put her arms behind her back, clasping her hands again. "You're awfully quiet this morning."

No. Definitely no bra. The tank top wasn't all that opaque either. That, or she had very dark nipples. He wouldn't mind finding out.

Her hands dropped to her sides, and small points formed behind the thin fabric. The longer he looked, the more prominent they became.

"Nitro?" Her voice sounded high and uncertain.

He lifted his gaze to her face again.

Her eyes had darkened, and her pink bow lips were parted on a breath that seemed to be suspended somewhere inside her.

Was she ready to admit to the attraction between them? If she was, she'd chosen damn awkward timing.

She crossed her arms over her small, pert breasts, pink tingeing her cheeks. "I . . . um . . . Dad . . ."

She *wasn't* going to admit it, and he wasn't sure if he was relieved or disappointed. They had to focus on the events of the night, but one day soon he was going to find out not only what color her still erect nipples were, but how sweet they tasted.

He stepped up to the SUV, watching with both amusement and irritation as she hurriedly moved back. She gave more confusing signals than a bug scrambler.

Opening the passenger door, he said, "Get in."

She climbed inside without a word, careful not to let their bodies make contact at any point, but that didn't stop her female scent from reaching out to touch him. Both sweet and spicy from her earlier exertions and fear, it overrode the lingering smell of smoke on her clothes.

He wanted to pull her to him and add another fragrance to the ones she was emitting . . . arousal.

Knowing it would make her uncomfortable, but not really caring, he slipped her seat belt across her body and clipped it into place. He didn't pull back immediately, but took a second to enjoy her proximity while her eyes rounded in confusion.

"What are you doing?"

He tilted his head, so their lips were mere centimeters apart. "Buckling you in."

"Oh." It came out a breath of sound.

He smiled. "Do you need anything else."

"Uh . . . no." But she didn't turn her head away.

She just waited.

His arms were as good as around her in this position, and it would be so easy to take her lips, to taste them.

He did, briefly. Softly. And she let him, hanging there, her lips attached to his, but not moving against his.

He pulled back, stepping away from the car. "I'm glad you're okay."

She nodded, mute, but her eyes were asking questions he didn't want to answer right then.

Soon he would, but not right now.

"Okay, what's going on?" he asked after sliding into the driver's seat.

She stared at him.

"Your dad, Josie."

She gasped, her cheeks turning cherry red, and then she burst into speech. "They moved Dad a little over an hour ago. He asked for some privacy to get cleaned up, and I gave it to him. He's wounded, confused, I thought weak. It never occurred to me he'd just disappear."

"Tyler has his own reasons for doing the things he does, and they aren't always comprehensible to others, but it's a safe bet he wasn't nearly as weak as he let on."

"You're right." She rubbed her eyes. "When no one came to get me after half an hour, I went looking on my own. His room was empty."

"Did anyone see anything?"

"No."

"Did he leave of his own volition?"

"Yes."

"You're sure?"

"Yes. He took the jeep and he left this." She handed him a note.

He read it. "Do you know where this footlocker is?"

"Dad keeps it in an underground storage unit that only he and I know about."

Of course. Some people might say Tyler McCall was on the paranoid side, but he was a damn good soldier and trainer of men. "Would it have survived the explosion?"

"I think so, but until we get up the mountain, we won't know."

"Are there any other leads to follow up on here?"

"No. He left nothing." She sounded dispirited.

"Don't blame yourself, Josie. Your dad is one of the best. He can take care of himself." Daniel started the car.

"But why would he leave?"

"I don't know. That's a mystery he may have to solve for us, but right now we've got other things to attend to." He pulled the big black SUV out of the hospital parking lot, noting with pleasure the dearth of cars on the road.

"Where are we going?"

"Back to the mountain."

She needed rest, but the longer they took to get back to the compound, the better chance whoever set the explosions would have to hide or destroy evidence, not to mention maybe finding the journal Tyler wanted his daughter to read.

"What caused the explosion?" he asked.

"I don't know. I haven't been back."

"I didn't think you had." But she had a damn uncanny ability when it came to identifying bombs. He wouldn't have been surprised if she'd known the type and volume of explosives used simply from the explosion itself.

She seemed to realize that and explained. "I was out walking when I felt the ground shake. By the time I made it to his room, half of the wall had fallen on him, and the place was in flames."

"Any chance it was an accident?"

"My gut says no."

He'd pretty much expected that answer, and he believed her. He trusted few people's instincts as much as his own, but she was one of them. Josie was a darn good soldier. He'd implied otherwise on their last mission, and maybe he owed her an apology.

From what she'd said before, she hadn't forgotten his frustration-induced words, but the apology would have to come later.

"Any ideas on who did it?" he asked.

"No, but I'm going to find out."

"I'm going to help."

"It's not your problem."

"It is. I'm half owner of the school now."

She sighed. "I'd forgotten. I'm sure Dad will understand if you want your investment back."

"I don't. I want to help you find out who tried to kill you and your dad and who blew up my new business venture."

"No one knew I was at the compound."

"I knew."

"You didn't set the bombs."

"Of course not."

"What I meant was, if no one knew I was there, then whoever did set the bombs weren't trying to harm me."

"Just Tyler."

"Right. We can't overlook the fact it happened during a hiatus between training camps."

"Meaning?"

"Whoever it was didn't want unnecessary deaths on their conscience."

"Or the chance of having witnesses."

"It could be antiwar protestors, but the fact Dad was so clearly targeted pretty much rules that out."

"You think they'd blow up some buildings, but stop at killing?"

"Yes."

"With a few exceptions, I think you're right."

"Since it happened when no one else was at camp, I also don't think it was targeted at the school in general."

"It's got a personal feel to it."

"Exactly."

"So, you think it's linked directly to your dad?"

"I do, which makes his disappearance all the more worrisome."

"Josie, if you can't find him, you can bet his enemies can't either."

"But how will I know?"

"You'll just have to trust."

It was early light by the time they reached the compound.

It had been a quiet drive. Nitro didn't talk much anyway, and Josie got tongue-tied around him. The kiss hadn't helped any. Why had he done it?

He'd said he was glad she wasn't hurt. Was it like a kiss of *relief?* Whatever his motives, he'd turned her inside out and hadn't even seemed to notice. He must be used to kissing lots of women, only that didn't ring true. Nitro was too private to sleep around indiscriminately, but even if he'd been with only one woman, and that scenario was more unlikely than the first one, he was ahead of her in experience.

However, despite that lack of experience and all that had happened in the last few hours, her first reaction to him—before he'd ever kissed her—had been violent physical need. Being next to him in the close confines of the SUV for over an hour had her senses on complete overload. It wasn't a good situation.

She was tired and likely to betray her feelings to a man who despised her.

She wished she could think of some way to get him to let her conduct the investigation alone, but he took his responsibilities seriously. And the minute her dad had become Nitro's partner, the Mercenary Training School and Tyler McCall had become two more things Nitro took responsibility for.

She climbed out of the car, the lack of sleep making itself known in the stiffness of her limbs. She wasn't tempted to stretch out the kinks, though, not after the way she'd reacted to Nitro watching her do it before. She could swear he had been looking at her chest, but there wasn't a whole lot there for him to see. At least there hadn't been until her nipples got hard.

She didn't want to know what he'd thought when he'd seen that, but his expression alone had burned through to the core of her.

Trying to forget the peculiar things Nitro made her feel, she turned toward the decimated compound.

The fire service had been and gone. She could see signs of their obviously successful efforts to put out the fire, but she was glad no one was there to question her. The FBI, and probably the ATF too, were probably already on their way, but she hoped she and Nitro would get out of there before the authorities arrived. There would come a reckoning, but she would avoid it as long as she could.

She started toward the wreckage, her senses on full alert. Of its own volition, her hand reached out to touch a piece of charred wood, and her mind went to that place it did when she focused on a bomb, trying to *feel* its composition.

Daniel watched Josie go into her woo-woo mode, and damned if it didn't turn him on.

Everything about her excited him, and it made him mad. He didn't like being out of control, and when he was around Josie McCall, his hard-won control was under a constant state of siege. Bent over, her sweet little bottom was outlined by the fatigues she wore, and she touched the burned debris with the sensual caress of a lover. He wanted that caress on his body.

Get your mind on the task at hand, boy-o. You don't have time to focus on that heart-shaped ass right now or the way she touches some burned-up piece of wood.

With a grimace of self-disgust, he obeyed his inner urgings to focus on the destroyed compound.

Whatever had been used, it had been effective. No walls were left standing, and the fire had destroyed pretty much everything before the fire service had been able to contain it. At least the woods surrounding the compound had not been affected. The fifty-foot expanse of dirt around the perimeter had made an effective fire barrier.

Tyler McCall was a man who prepared for every eventuality. Even someone trying to blow him up apparently. He'd been sleeping in a secret bedroom that students and faculty alike knew nothing about.

Daniel understood that kind of caution. All soldiers for hire did. Few men could be trusted in a world where money bought a soldier's allegiance. He'd been damn lucky to hook up with Wolf and Hotwire, but they were getting out of the business, setting up some kind of security consultant firm. He wasn't ready for that kind of *stability* yet. Maybe he never would be.

He picked his way across the wreckage to where partially

destroyed file cabinets indicated her dad's office had been. What had once been a computer was a melted mass of metal to one side, and the file cabinets he knew to be fire retardant had nevertheless been unable to completely withstand the temperatures of the blaze.

They were almost completely destroyed, too, but something interested him about them. The files, or whatever might have been left of them, were gone. No charred bits of paper or manila folders remained.

"It was a standard weapon of mass destruction augmented by cylinders of a highly volatile substance, probably petroleum based." Josie's voice came from right behind him.

He turned to face her, not even tempted to question her verdict. "Whoever did this was serious about getting rid of the compound as well as your father."

"Yes."

Maybe the bomb had been about the school after all, but Josie's instincts had said not, and even in the face of evidence to the contrary, his agreed.

"They've been back."

She stared at him, her expression not registering understanding. She had to be exhausted.

"Since the blast . . . They came and emptied out whatever was left of your dad's file cabinets."

Josie's moss green eyes widened, and she spun to look at where he pointed.

"But we didn't see anyone on the road."

"They could have hiked in."

"Then they would have left a trail hiking out."

"If they were moving too fast for caution, yes."

They found the trail and followed it, after Daniel saw that they were both armed with weapons he kept in his car at all times. The trail ended at a logging road, and fresh tracks indicated a four-wheel drive had been there recently. The width of the tires indicated a truck, but their tread was too common to get anything else from the tracks.

"Darn it." Josie sank to the ground, letting her head rest against her knees. "The tracks are too fresh for them to be very long gone, but we can't follow on foot with any hope of catching them."

He said something pithy and unpleasant.

She looked up at him. "That's one way of putting it, but I think you've got some verb confusion going on."

He was in no mood to appreciate her subtle humor. "If I'd gotten to the hospital sooner, or come by here first, I could have caught their sorry asses."

She shook her head.

"You doubt it?"

"I doubt your culpability in timing that they obviously took a lot of effort making sure was right."

"I'd like to see whatever it is they wanted from your dad's files." But that was about as likely as Tyler McCall showing up to allay Josie's fears.

"No problem."

"What do you mean?"

"I just finished computerizing dad's files. I've got a backup of the data on the hard drive in my apartment."

"I don't like computers much."

"Hotwire told me. Don't worry. I'll do all the interfacing with the computer." She yawned.

"You need to sleep before doing anything else."

"First, we've got to hike back. Then we have to see if Dad's journal survived. Then I can sleep."

When she stood up, she wobbled, but like the trouper she was, she started marching back toward the charred buildings.

He shook his head, caught up with her, then bent down and lifted her over his shoulder in a fireman's carry before she had time to figure out what he planned and stage a major protest. He started double-timing it back to the compound.

"What do you think you are doing?" Her words came out

funny, like hiccups, because her diaphragm was hitting his shoulder.

"You're too tired to hike back."

"I am not."

He didn't bother to argue, but she wasn't so sanguine.

"Listen here, Neanderthal man, I'm a trained soldier. A mile hike is nothing for me."

"You've been awake for twenty-four hours or more, inhaled smoke, saved your dad from a burning building and tracked perps at a running jog."

"So? I'm not a wimp."

"No, but you are a termagant."

"What's that?"

He smiled as he told her.

"I do not nag and I am not a shrew!"

"But you are overbearing on occasion."

"You can say that when you're the one carrying me against my will?" she asked furiously. "If anyone's a termagant here, it's you."

"Men can't be termagants."

"You use pretty big words for a mercenary," she grumbled.

"I like to read."

"I do, too, but the word I want to call you is one I learned listening to soldiers."

He laughed, something he rarely did . . . except when he was with Josie. How could she think he didn't like her? She made him smile, and that wasn't easy.

"Put me down, Nitro, or I'm going to get mean, and I don't want to because you're helping me."

"Call me Daniel." He didn't like being reminded of his past when he was with her.

"What?"

"Daniel. It's my name."

"Hotwire and Wolf call you Nitro."

"I want *you* to call me Daniel."

"*Daniel*, put me down or things are going to get ugly." The tone of her voice said she meant what she was saying.

They were more than halfway back to the compound, so he stopped and let her slide to her feet, his hands loosely guiding her at the hips. When she was solidly on terra firma again, he should have let go, but he didn't.

And she didn't move away immediately, but stood staring up at him like an accident victim. It was a look he'd gotten very familiar with on their last mission, but he still didn't know what it meant. She licked dry lips, and his body told him what he wanted it to mean. She was too close not to notice the change, and she jumped away from him like a scalded cat.

It wasn't the first time she'd responded that way to evidence of his desire, but his ability to deal with it rationally diminished the more he wanted her. "I can't help my reaction. If a woman is going to press herself against me like a succubus, I'm going to get hard."

"I didn't press myself against you like a succubus, whatever that is . . . I didn't press myself at all. You're the cretin who insisted on carrying me and then, and then . . ."

"And then?" he taunted.

"Letting me down *that way*." She glared at him, but her expression was wounded.

Damn it. She was right. His hard-on was his own damn fault, but his jaw locked on the words of apology he knew he needed to say.

She made a dismissive motion with her hand and spun away from him, setting off for the compound at a trot. He followed her the whole way back, letting her set the pace because of her fatigue, but anger must have given her strength because he had to jog to keep up with her.

When they arrived at the compound, he reached out and grabbed her shoulder.

She went stiff. "What?"

He wasn't angry with her. He was sexually frustrated, and it wasn't her fault except that she was the object of his lust, and he could hardly blame her for that. She didn't do anything on purpose to seduce his senses.

She didn't have to.

"I'm sorry." He could count on one hand the number of times he'd said those words in his life. The last one he could remember had been as he stood over his mother's grave.

Her shoulders slumped. "It's no big deal."

He turned her around to face him and got a sucker punch to his gut at the sight of shimmering green eyes.

"It's not your fault you set me off like a Roman candle."

"I . . . what?"

"Never mind. Just try to forget about what happened back there."

She nodded, about to turn away again when he remembered something.

"It's not because I don't like you. I like you too much, and *it's not your fault,*" he repeated.

"I—"

"Come on, show me where this footlocker is kept."

She let him direct her toward the burned building and then picked her way through the debris to an area on the far right. He didn't know what had been there, but judging from what was left of the building, he guessed it was Tyler's secret bedroom. She bent down and grabbed what looked like it might have been a metal plate and started digging the ashes out of an area. He looked around for something to help her with and found a helmet.

With both of them working, it didn't take very long to dig down to where the floor had been. Under it was a rectangular sheet of composite, the lightweight but extremely sturdy stuff airplane floors were made out of. He'd used it himself in both Wolf's and his homes' designs.

The composite had two handles, and as she lifted it, he realized it was a door to an underground room.

A cement stairway led downward in the dark. Josie stepped on the first tread, but he grabbed her before she could take another step.

Chapter 3

"You don't have a flashlight," Daniel said to her. "Wait and I'll get one from the SUV."

"Don't worry about it. There's a light at the bottom of the stairs. Dad's safety room has everything."

Everything turned out to be a supply of weapons sufficient to equip a small force, lights, food, a bed, two chairs, small table and the infamous footlocker.

"What, was he preparing for Armageddon?"

Josie just shrugged. "Something like that. Dad didn't trust the shirts in Washington to keep us out of war."

That sounded like Tyler.

"Grab the journal and let's go."

She lifted the lid on the footlocker and pulled out a sealskin bag big enough to hold several journals.

"They're in here. He didn't say which one he wanted me to read, but he's been keeping them as long as I can remember."

"Do you need anything else from here?"

She didn't answer, but took a minute choosing a selection of weapons, including a belt knife that had been clearly made for a woman. Tyler had said Josie wanted to leave the life of soldiering behind, but she had one final mission to carry out, and apparently, she intended being adequately armed for it.

"The rest should be safe if we bury the access again."

He figured she was right, and they did just that, taking time to leave the debris looking like all the rest.

They were halfway down the mountain when he said, "You might as well get some sleep. We have to drive to my hotel so I can get my stuff before I can take you to your apartment."

"You don't have to take me. I can rent a car and drive myself."

"Do you really think a small coastal town is going to have a car rental agency?"

"It's not that small." She bit her lip, obviously in thought. "I don't think."

"Look, I'm not leaving you to fend for yourself."

"I'm a big girl."

"Actually, you aren't. You're on the small size of average for a woman. It always puzzled me why you became a mercenary. You'd be at a major disadvantage during hand-to-hand combat."

"I didn't really have much choice, but as for proximity fighting, my dad taught me how to neutralize an adult male in one-on-one combat before I hit puberty."

"Did he teach you the distinct disadvantages you faced in a hostile environment after it?"

"Men are more vulnerable than women, particularly women as boyish in their build as I am."

"You aren't shaped like a boy, and I wasn't just talking about developing breasts."

"Rape isn't limited to women either."

She was right, but her size ensured she would always be more at risk for that kind of thing than he was. She'd probably call him a chauvinist if he said so, but he was glad she'd chosen to leave the soldier for hire world behind.

Josie woke up as the big SUV came to a halt and its engine went silent. They were parked in front of a motel.

"It could take a few minutes. Do you want to come up or stay here?"

She still felt groggy, and her mind had a difficult time translating his words. "What . . . Oh, I'll stay here."

Her eyes slid shut again to the sound of his car door closing. The snick of locks going into place indicated he'd pressed the lock button for her safety.

A blast of cold air woke her again when he opened the door. Summer did not always mean warm sunshine on the Oregon coast, particularly in the morning. A cold wind kept things chilly until close to noon most days.

He tossed a duffel bag and a weapons case behind his seat before getting in. "I think we should get some breakfast before going to your place."

She was so tired, the thought of food made her nauseous. "I'm not hungry."

He reached out and cupped her nape.

The feel of his fingers against her skin shocked her into stillness. Nitro rarely touched anyone . . . except her, and inexplicably, he seemed to touch her all the time. But beyond that was the sheer physical sensation the slightest connection between them caused. In her vulnerable, just-woke-up state, it paralyzed her.

His thumb brushed against the underside of her jaw. "You're pale."

"I need more sleep."

"No doubt, but you need to hydrate yourself, too. Especially after inhaling smoke."

Come to think of it, her throat was pretty raw. She'd been too stressed to take stock of her aches and pains before now, but suddenly each discomfort was all too grating.

"I want a shower and clean clothes."

His hand dropped away from her neck. "Hell, I should have thought of that before I checked out. You'll have to wait until we get to your apartment."

"House."

"What?"

"I live in a house, near the campus. I share it with a room-mate."

"You can't possibly need to share."

She knew what he meant. Mercenaries were paid well, and she'd been in the business since she was eighteen. "I own the house, but Claire was looking for a place, and I offered to let her move in with me."

"Why?" He sounded as if he could not imagine wanting a roommate, and probably he couldn't. Nitro was a loner despite his close friendship with Wolf and Hotwire.

"She's a computer geek who has a hard time communicating with anything not driven by binary code and electric impulses."

"Sounds like a lot of fun as a housemate."

"Actually, she is. We understand each other better than you might expect. Neither of us fits into the world around us, and that gives us a common ground. Besides, I like not being alone, having someone there when I get home from classes."

"Why did you decide to get out of the business?" He didn't sound condemning, or worried like her dad did when he talked to her about her decision to change her life.

Nitro just sounded curious.

"I woke up one day and realized being a soldier was my dad's vocation, not mine."

"So now you want to study computers?"

"Yes."

"And Hotwire is helping you?" There was something in Nitro's voice she was too tired to interpret.

"Yes. He's amazing with a keyboard."

"Being savvy with computers does not mean he knows what to do with a woman."

He sounded jealous. She must be really tired if her mind was playing those kinds of tricks on her.

"If you say so." She was the last person to comment on a man's abilities in that area.

She didn't quite catch the word that Nitro uttered in response. "What are you going to do once you're done with school?"

"Hotwire offered me a job with his and Wolf's new security consulting business."

"Is that what you want?"

"I don't know. I'm in an accelerated degree program, but I've still got several months before I have to decide where exactly I want to go with my new life."

Nitro pulled into a gas station and got out of the car, then disappeared into the convenience store attached to the station.

He came back carrying a small carton of milk and a muffin. "Here. I don't want you getting sick."

"What about you?"

He reached behind the seat and pulled a bottle of water from the small cooler on the floor. "This'll do for now."

She drank her milk and ate the muffin, which settled her stomach, and then fell asleep again.

Daniel woke Josie on the outskirts of Portland for directions to her house. She gave them, and he found himself in a quiet neighborhood west of the city center. He expected her to live closer to the PSU campus, but she had bought a house in a residential neighborhood obviously designed for families. There was a park right across the street from her modest white ranch-style house.

He grabbed his gear while she climbed out of the car and followed her to the front door. She unlocked it and pushed it open.

"Josette, what in the world happened to you?" The feminine shriek came from a bespectacled woman about Josie's height, but there the similarities ended.

Claire was soft and rounded, and where Josie's hair was a dark reddish brown, Claire's was the color of cooked carrots . . . or maybe a shade or two darker, but very red nevertheless. It sprang out from her head in curls she'd done nothing to tame. Her clothes looked as though she'd gotten them at a rummage sale. Worn and faded jeans, an oversized Portland State sweatshirt that had seen better days and tennis shoes that would have looked disreputable on a homeless person.

"There was a fire at the mercenary school."

Claire rushed forward and hugged Josie with one arm. "Are you okay? Can I get you anything? A cup of tea. I bought a new apricot blend. Maybe you want a glass of cold water."

"I'm fine. I just want a shower and bed."

"Right. Look, you take your shower, and I'll make you a cup of tea. You don't have to drink it if you don't want to."

From Josie's description, he'd assumed Claire would be quiet, but the woman was a chatterbox.

"I wouldn't mind some if you're making it," he said.

Claire and Josie both turned startled eyes on him as if they'd forgotten he was there. It was a new experience for him. He didn't court female attention, but he didn't seem to be able to avoid it either.

"Of course. My name is Claire." She let go of Josie's shoulder and stuck her hand out.

He shook it, impressed by her firm grip and steady brown gaze.

"Daniel Black Eagle."

Claire looked at Josie as if asking for an explanation.

"It's Nitro."

Claire's eyes widened, and she gasped. "Oh."

He frowned at Josie.

"He's dropping me off because my car was destroyed in the fire."

Claire's eyes filled with concerned dismay. "Oh, I'm sorry."

"It's all right. I'm alive and so is Dad. That's all that really matters."

"I'm not just dropping you off, Josette." He liked that name and figured if Claire could use it, so could he. "Until we find out whoever is responsible for the fire, you and me are going to be like Rodgers and Hammerstein. Always together."

She stared at him with nothing less than shock. "You can't stay here."

"Sure I can."

"I don't have a spare room."

"Your sofa looks comfortable." If a bit short, but it was longer than average.

The overstuffed couch looked a whole lot more amenable to sleep than a lot of *beds* he'd had over the years.

"That's not the point. You aren't staying here, Nitro."

"I asked you to call me Daniel."

She rolled her eyes, her frustration palpable. "*Daniel* . . . you cannot stay here."

"Then you are going with me."

"You're being ridiculous."

"I'm sorry you feel that way."

She groaned, and he couldn't help the smile that creased his lips.

She was damn cute when she was irritated.

"I'm a trained soldier. I don't need a bodyguard."

"Why can't he stay here?" Claire asked as if Josie hadn't spoken.

"You know why!"

"It would seem to me that would be the very reason to let him stay."

"It's a bad idea." Josie frowned darkly at him.

He hadn't understood anything the two women had just said except that Claire thought he should stay.

He turned toward her. "Someone tried to kill Josette's dad with the fire, and she could be at risk, too. I'm going to help her find the culprits."

Claire spun to face Josie again. "Someone tried to kill your dad? Where is he?"

He listened to Josie explain while he found a place in the hall closet for his duffel bag and weapons case.

Claire looked even more worried than she had when Josie arrived looking like a fire survivor, which she was. "You told me it was always better to have more than one soldier on a mission."

"So?"

"This investigation sounds like a mission to me. I think you should let Daniel stay and help you with it."

"He doesn't have to stay in my house to help me."

"Yes, I do." He was done discussing it. She could argue until she was hoarse with it, but he wasn't going anywhere. "Claire, you said something about tea."

"Of course. Josette, take your shower while I make your colleague some breakfast."

"He's not my colleague. I'm not a merc anymore."

"But you are going to work with him on a mission. That makes him your colleague." Claire's logic seemed to deflate Josie, who started down the hall.

"I'll take my shower. Why don't you *cook* Nitro some breakfast, Claire?"

"I think I'll spare him the pain and pour him a bowl of cereal."

"I'd rather you cooked," Josie threw back over her shoulder as she turned into a doorway to her left.

Claire just laughed and led Daniel into the kitchen where she pulled out a box of health-food-type cereal and a carton of organic milk from the fridge.

Handing him a bowl and spoon, she smiled wryly. "The last time I cooked, I set the kitchen on fire."

He looked around him. The maple cabinets appeared to be in perfect condition. "It didn't seem to do any lasting damage."

"No, but the fire department wasn't amused to be called out to put out a pan of flaming tofu dogs."

"You called them to put out the fire?"

"The neighbors did. I was working on something on the computer and didn't notice the smoke until the fire trucks arrived."

He could not fathom being that unaware of his surroundings and shook his head.

Josie came out of the shower a half an hour later looking clean, but pale with exhaustion. Claire cajoled her into eating some cereal and then bullied her into bed.

Daniel added his voice to the other woman's arguments, and Josie glared at him. "You're not staying here."

"Save it for after your nap."

"Grown women don't take naps."

"You're no good to me or your dad exhausted. Your brain isn't even working well enough to realize my staying makes the most sense."

That brought some more grumbling, but she turned smartly on her heel and stomped off, saying something about knowing when she wasn't wanted.

He could have argued that particular point by the simple expedient of standing up from the table and revealing evidence to the contrary, but he found himself smiling as he watched the cranky woman disappear around the corner to the hall.

"I'll look, but chances are he's not using plastic for anything and he's got an alternate identity set up somewhere."

Daniel knew Hotwire was right, and the chances of tracing Tyler McCall's whereabouts with the computer were slim, but they had to try. Because, frankly, unless Josie saw something in the journals he hadn't, they had no other leads for finding her dad.

He'd been reading them ever since she went to bed and Claire had left for her classes. He'd learned a lot, but none of it relevant to the explosion and fire at the compound. So he'd called his friend Hotwire for his input.

"His disappearing act doesn't make sense," Hotwire

added. "Why would he leave Josie to fend for herself if he knew the source of the threat and was hiding from it? Wouldn't he take her with him?"

"Maybe Josie isn't at risk."

"Someone willing to blow up his compound to kill him would be willing to use his daughter to get to him."

That's what worried Daniel. "It's not going to happen."

"You said he had Josie call you before he took a powder."

"Yes."

"Then he didn't leave her to fend for herself, did he? He knew you'd watch her back and better than he could in the state he was in."

"Maybe." But Hotwire was right. Tyler knew Daniel well enough to know he'd never abandon Josie to investigating the explosion on her own. Just as he had to have known Daniel would call his friends in to help.

"Besides, the guy's brain isn't exactly running on all six cylinders right now. For all we know, he's had a flashback and is living in some Vietnam jungle in his head."

"That's what worries me."

"You worried?"

"This is Josie's dad we're talking about here."

"And you don't want Josie hurt?"

"No."

"Now, that's very interestin'. I don't remember you ever being overly worried about a woman's feelings before." The deliberately accentuated southern drawl needled Daniel.

"Drop it."

Hotwire's incredulous laugh irritated Daniel to the point of cursing.

"Tch, tch, tch . . . You've got to clean up your mouth. You're staying in a woman's house now. Didn't your mama ever tell you it's not mannerly to swear in front of a lady?"

His mother had been cursed at on a regular basis . . . every time his dad drank. "No."

"Then take my advice. Clean up your mouth."

"Josie's a soldier, for crying out loud."

"Ex-soldier and her roommate is a sheltered little thing."

Claire hadn't seemed all that sheltered to him. She had a mind like a computer and even the personality of one at times, but she hadn't seemed particularly naïve.

"Why didn't you tell me Josie was getting out of the business?"

"Because you bit my head off every time I said her name over the past year."

"You're no shrinking violet."

"I'm also not stupid."

"You've been helping her with her computer studies."

"You make it sound like I've been breaking the Sixth Commandment instead of helping a friend change her life."

"So now you're *friends*."

"Josie and I have always been friends."

"Since when is friendship an automatic by-product of working with another merc?"

"It isn't."

"But you're friends with Josie."

"Unlike some people, I realized right off that not only is she a good soldier who can be counted on, but she's also a sweet woman worth knowing."

"What's that supposed to mean?"

"You haven't exactly gone out of your way to make friends with her."

"I don't go out of my way to be nice to anybody."

Hotwire laughed. "That's true, but I think your lack of enthusiasm for her company has hurt her feelings."

He'd come to the same conclusion, and it bothered him. "*I don't dislike her, damn it.*"

"Whoah . . . buddy, no need to go ballistic here."

"I don't go ballistic anymore."

"That's what I thought, but Josie brings out some pretty powerful feelings in you."

"Like hell." The only feelings he allowed himself to have

for women were sexual. He would never give a woman the power to tap the deeply buried root of his temper.

"Whatever you say, but I swear if you don't clean up your mouth while you're staying in Josie's house, I'm going to sic my mama on you. You'll straighten up, or she'll have your guts for garters."

"She raised you and let you live. She can't be all that bad."

"She's not, but she's hell on your conscience if you disappoint her."

"Mothers are like that." His certainly weighed on his and probably always would.

He would never forget the sight of her, bruised and motionless, in that narrow hospital bed. He would never allow himself to forget it had been his fault either.

"Josie said you offered her a job," Daniel said to banish the memories and change the subject.

"Yeah. She's a natural with computers. Wolf and I both think she'd be a real asset to the business."

"So your only interest in her is because of her computer skills?"

"I didn't say that."

Daniel's heart actually stopped in his chest. Women fell all over themselves getting to Hotwire. Josie wouldn't be any exception.

"You want her?"

Silence at the other end of the phone.

"Do you?"

"What difference does it make to you?"

"Just answer the question, damn it."

"Whew . . . Lise said she thought your bad temper covered something totally different, but Wolf and I thought she was sniffing the wrong scent."

"What are you talking about?"

"You want Josie."

"We aren't talking about me."

"Don't have to. It might have taken me a while to catch on, but I'm no backwoods Georgia farm boy."

The temptation to drop the conversation was huge, but Daniel had to know. "Is there anything between you and Josie?"

"Friendship."

He waited in silence, willing his friend to explain.

Hotwire laughed. "This is more fun than watching Wolf forget what he is saying when Lise walks into the room."

"*Hotwire.*"

"I don't want Josie."

The relief that went through Daniel was too overwhelming to dismiss. "Good."

"That doesn't mean she doesn't want me. I am, after all, a prime specimen of male flesh and have a certain amount of undeniable southern charm."

Daniel's reply was ugly and succinct.

Hotwire was still laughing when Daniel cut the connection.

Daniel relaxed against the overstuffed sofa back. Josie was still sleeping, and he'd decided to skim the earlier journals, hoping they held some clue because he'd found nothing in Tyler's most recent one. So far all he'd accomplished was to get a pretty good picture of Josie's childhood.

When she had said she'd had no choice but to become a soldier, he'd thought she meant her dad had pushed her into it, but it had been a lot more concrete than that. Her choice had been made when she wasn't even old enough to give up playing with dolls.

Tyler McCall had started training his daughter in combat at the tender age of six. The same year her mother died. Some would say the man's mind had finally snapped, and they might be right, but there was no denying he'd had his reasons for raising his daughter the way he did.

Tyler had seen things in Vietnam that would make any man leery of raising a child, particularly a daughter, in today's world.

A furious yell hit his eardrums and cut his musings mid-thought.

Chapter 4

Daniel met Josie halfway down her hallway, his blood pumping with combat-ready adrenaline, but he could see no threat.

Unless he counted the small, barefoot woman vibrating with rage, her green eyes shooting retribution fire at him. "I am not a demon!"

"I'm glad to hear it."

The growl that emanated from her throat would have done a grizzly bear proud. She was royally pissed, and apparently he was the reason.

Rather than being concerned about that salient fact, it was all he could do not to drag her body against his and kiss her until he didn't know his own name anymore. She turned him on in pretty much any mood. However, passionate anger was too close to passionate desire not to impact his hormones like a freight train running full steam ahead without a brake.

Not to mention her clothes, or lack thereof. If she normally slept in tiny T-shirts and short shorts like the pink ones she had on, he was going to expire from lust his first night in her place just thinking about it.

From the murderous expression on her pixielike face, he guessed she wasn't on the same wavelength as he was at all.

She smacked his shoulder with her open palm. Hard. "Nor did I attempt to seduce you!"

"Uh, Josie . . . Are you all right?" Maybe she had a little of her dad's paranoia. Or a bad dream?

"No, I am not all right." She was back to shouting again, but when she went to hit him a second time, he moved to restrain her and found himself on his back with her knee in his chest and her furious face above his. "I'm mad."

He didn't like her getting the better of him, and he reversed their positions, his hands clamping her wrists and his bigger body pinning hers to the hardwood floor. "I noticed, but why?"

Her body felt perfect under his—tone, but soft and warm, too.

"You called me a succubus!"

"I did n—" Then he remembered. "I said *clinging like a succubus.*" Not that the semantics appreciably changed the meaning and he'd clearly made a mistake letting his temper control his tongue, even briefly, but a man could try.

"I wasn't *clinging* at all," she snarled.

"No. You weren't."

She didn't look in the least mollified by his agreement.

"I apologized already," he reminded her.

She glared up at him, her body tense beneath his. "That was before I knew what succubus meant. A two-word apology and instructions to just forget about it don't cut it now."

She twisted unexpectedly under him, and he had to maneuver his hips between her legs to keep her flat. In her current frame of mind, there was no saying what she might do, and she was capable of doing a lot. But the new position was torture to his already excited body.

His pants and her shorts were no barrier to the heat of her pressing against the hardness of him. Making love to her would be like taking a trip to the sun.

She bucked, sending his temperature spiking. "Get off me, you cretin."

He had to keep this light. If he didn't, he was going to lose control, and that was an unacceptable alternative. "See, that's the second time you've called me that, and you don't see me having a temper tantrum because you've questioned my intelligence."

"Cretin also means vulgar, and calling me a demon intent on seducing you in your sleep falls in that category, or didn't you realize that?" she asked far too sweetly, her gaze still as sharp as his throwing knife.

"It's still a hurtful thing to call a person."

She laughed, the sound far from humorous, her expression one of angry mockery. "An exploding grenade under your pillow couldn't hurt you."

Maybe not, but a hundred and twenty pounds of female flesh under him was doing major damage to his nerve centers. His sex ached, and it was only going to get worse if he stayed where he was. A glutton for punishment, he didn't move.

"The point is, I didn't mean to hurt you."

She sighed, her body going limp all of a sudden, her expression turning sad. "I'm sure you didn't. You can't help the way you feel about me."

"That's true, but I'm trying. Doesn't that count for something?"

She shrugged as much as she could with her wrists still restrained. "You can let me up now. I won't take your head off."

He didn't want to. He wanted to make love right there on the hardwood floor, but what he wanted and what he got with Josie were rarely even in the same hemisphere.

Sucking in air, he rolled off her, then stood up and felt the pain of unsatisfied desire arc through him with debilitating force. Turning away from her, he bent at the waist, breathing heavily.

She touched his shoulder. "Are you okay?"

"I'll be fine. Just give me a sec." He hated her seeing his

physical vulnerability to her, but right now even his formidable mental control was no match for his body's urges.

He'd never been like this before. No matter how much he wanted sex, he'd never been unable to curb the desire and hide his reactions when the situation called for it.

"Did I hurt you?" She sounded bewildered.

How was he supposed to answer that? He hurt because of her, but she hadn't done anything harmful to him. "No."

"Then what's the matter?"

"Nothing you need to worry about." He breathed in deeply, willing his body to calm, forcing his mind not to dwell on the memory of what it felt like to have her under him.

Finally able to stand straight without feeling like he'd rip the seam on his fly, he turned back to face her.

Her eyes scanned him and stopped at the hard-on that had not completely gone away. "Does that happen every time you fight with a woman?"

Offended, he glared at her. "Of course not. I'd be a damn poor soldier if it did."

"But . . ."

"I told you. You set me off. Not all women. Just you."

"Set you off?"

Did she have to sound so clueless about sex? That in itself was another turn-on, and the way she was looking at him wasn't helping.

"My dick is only going to grow if you keep watching it like that." And then he was either going to go back to being bent over double, or he was going to bend over her.

"I'm not . . . I can't . . . You're wearing pants!"

He rolled his eyes. "And you don't know the log in my jeans isn't wadded-up cotton, right?"

She looked askance at him. "It's not, is it?"

"For crying out loud." He'd had enough. If he didn't get out of there, he was going to do something they would both regret.

*   *   *

Josie watched Daniel slam out the front door, her heart somewhere around her toes. What had just happened?

One minute, she'd been ready to kill him with her bare hands, and the next, he was telling her she'd turned him on. And then he'd gone. She eyed the closed door with a conflagration of emotions she couldn't begin to decipher, but chief among them was a certainty she wasn't ready for Daniel Black Eagle to walk out of her life.

Impulsively, she rushed after him. Swinging the door open, she saw him standing beside his big black SUV. He was leaning against it with one hand, his back to her.

"Are you leaving?"

"Yes." He didn't bother to face her.

"For good?" It's what she'd said she wanted, so why did she feel so rejected?

He spun around then, his stance dangerous. "I said I'd help you find the people who tried to kill your dad, and I will. I can control my sex drive enough to work with you. I'm not a needy adolescent, damn it."

"I didn't say you were." This conversation was getting bizarre, but then everything had been a little crazy since she went storming out of her bedroom to tell him what she thought of him for calling her a succubus.

"I'm going for a walk."

"Oh. The park is peaceful. There are ducks . . . in the pond on the other side."

"I'll be sure and look for them."

"Okay."

He sighed and rubbed his eyes with his thumb and forefinger. "Do you want to go with me?"

More than anything, but considering how he felt about her, she shouldn't inflict her company on him. "That's okay. I've got some stuff to do around here."

"Is it anything that can't wait?"

"No."

"Then come with me."

"Are you sure . . ."

He put his hand out. "Come on, Josette. I think we could both use the exercise to clear our heads, and I want to talk to you about what I read in your dad's journals."

"I . . . um . . ." She waved her hand down her body, indicating the pajamas she still wore. "I've got to get some clothes on."

He nodded, his expression unfathomable now. "I'll wait."

Daniel called himself names much worse than cretin as he waited for Josie to join him. Idiot and dumbass came to mind. What had he been thinking? His body needed a break from her temptation before his dick exploded from unrequited lust.

So, why had he invited her to join him? Was his brain even connected to his mouth?

The problem was that when he was around Josie, logic was not the overriding factor in his decision making.

It would have been logical to leave her behind, but he'd gone soft in the head when he looked at her. She'd appeared so forlorn standing there in the doorway, her bow lips turned down in a frown. How did a woman who was easily as tough as any soldier he knew contrive to look that way?

Especially after she'd made it clear she didn't want his company. But she'd looked as if his leaving somehow hurt her, and he'd been unable to leave it at that.

Idiot was right. She was the best-trained soldier he'd ever known. She didn't need him to take her for a walk to make her feel better. She didn't need him at all, but he couldn't seem to keep that straight in his mind.

When he was with Josie, he forgot she was a soldier. All he could see was the woman, a vulnerable woman he wanted to protect. Which had been the problem from the beginning.

The trip across country together should have been another routine, straightforward mission for him, but it hadn't been. He'd spent most of the time in the car in a state of painful arousal, fighting to keep his focus on the job of looking for a

tail instead of sneaking sidelong glances at the female mercenary. The nights together in small hotel rooms with one bed
in case Nemesis checked on their registry had been torture
plain and simple.

He'd taken a lot of cold showers and still woken up more
mornings than not wet and sticky in his BVDs . . . and pissed.
At himself and at the woman who seemed oblivious to what
the sight of her pajama-clad body did to him.

He'd had wet dreams about her, for crying out loud. He
hadn't dreamt like that since his voice had completed the
change from tenor to baritone.

At first, he'd thought Josie wanted him, too, and as much
as he had always believed sex on the job was irredeemably
stupid, he'd been desperate enough to make a pass. And been
shot down, the flames singeing his temper as well as his libido.

He should have got a clue from her behavior and not even
tried.

She jumped ten feet whenever he got within touching distance and avoided eye contact. When he'd kissed her, he
thought she was responding with the same helpless passion he
felt—until she pulled away and acted as if she thought it had
all been part of the cover of pretending to be Wolf and Lise.

He'd finally gotten the message. She wasn't interested, but
his body hadn't stopped wanting her. Hell, he even craved
her company. Like now. Taking Josie with him on the walk
was no hardship except to his aching sex.

He'd never craved the company of a woman outside of bed
before, but he'd been disappointed to learn Josie was sever-
ing her ties with the mercenary school. Because he'd been
looking forward to seeing her.

Dumbass was right.

Josie hesitated in the doorway, trying to get her heart and
breathing under control. It was always like this when she got

around Nitro, and the thought of him staying in her house during the mission scared the heck out of her.

One night her desire for him was going to break its leash, and she was going to end up trying to seduce him.

Which would be both hilarious and humiliating because she was worse than a virgin. She was a virgin who'd never even made it to second base with a date.

She took a deep breath and stepped outside, closing the door behind her.

Nitro had moved to the sidewalk and stood there waiting for her as if he had all the time in the world. He never looked out of place, and sometimes she envied his sense of unshakable confidence.

She wondered why he'd invited her to come along on his walk. She'd been sure he wanted to get away from her.

She moved to stand beside him. "I'm ready."

He nodded without looking down at her and started across the street. No holding his hand out to her this time. What would it be like to hold Nitro's hand? To walk with him and know she belonged by his side. Her mind boggled.

They crossed the street and stepped onto one of the paths surrounding the park, walking in companionable silence for once. She liked it and hesitated to so much as breathe funny to break the unusual rapport.

Nitro had no such reticence. "I read the last year of your dad's journal and skimmed some earlier entries."

"Already?" She'd been asleep only a few hours.

"He's a pretty sporadic writer, so it didn't take too long."

"Did you find anything?"

"No."

Disappointment weighted her insides. "Then why did he tell us to read them? You must have missed something."

"It's possible. He did tell *you* to read his journal, not me. Maybe there's something you'll recognize in his entries that I didn't."

That made sense. "There has to be."

"Maybe."

She frowned up at Nitro. "But he told me to read them."

His expression would have done one of his chieftain ancestors proud. "Maybe he wanted you to get something else out of them."

"Like what?"

"An explanation for the way he raised you."

Tension seeped into her until the muscles between her shoulder blades ached. "What do you mean?"

"You can't think it's standard parenting for a father to start training his little girl in combat before she's old enough to read."

"I started reading when I was five."

"And you were six when you handled your first automatic weapon."

"It was just Dad's way. He never let me be at risk."

"I know that, but it wasn't normal, Josette."

She didn't know why he insisted on calling her by her full name, but it felt intimate and increased the sense of connection she felt with him. Though she was sure that was not his intention.

"He was a good father to me, and he's not crazy."

"No, he isn't, but he is on the paranoid side."

"Don't criticize my dad. He has his ways just like anybody else. I thought you wanted to be his partner."

"I do, because I respect him, but no one is perfect, sweetheart."

Sweetheart? She flushed to the roots of her hair. "I didn't say he was."

"But he's not crazy either. Read the journals."

"I'd planned to."

"I mean the early ones."

"If they don't have a clue to finding the would-be killers, that would be invading his privacy." Something her father had a major issue with.

"He told you to read them, Josette, and I personally believe it had nothing to do with the compound getting blown to bits."

"That doesn't make any sense. Our personal relationship could be sorted out anytime."

"You've got to remember, your dad's memories and thoughts were confused. The most important issue in his life was bound to take precedence."

And Nitro was implying that issue was her. She chewed on her bottom lip in silence until they reached a fork in the path.

"Go to the left. The duck pond is this way."

He followed without comment.

"How much of my dad's journals did you read?"

"Enough."

Did Nitro think she was a real weirdo now? Very few people knew of her unique upbringing, but she'd always known it made her different. She was trying to change that, but maybe she never could.

She sighed, looking out over the pond now directly in her line of vision, so she didn't have to look at him.

"Josette, we need to talk."

"I thought we already were."

"I mean about us."

"Us?" she asked faintly.

"What happened in the hall can't happen again."

"I can't promise that." He was a pretty irritating guy at times and got to her like nobody else.

She wasn't sure she could always control her temper around him. It was strange, because before meeting Nitro, she'd never really thought she had a temper.

He said something nasty, and she flinched. She'd heard men swearing around her all her life, but nobody had Nitro's coldly controlled tone of voice.

"Sorry," he grumbled.

"For what?"

"Hotwire says I shouldn't curse around you since you aren't a soldier anymore."

"I don't understand. Why?"

"According to his mother, it isn't right to swear around a woman."

She'd heard that, but she still didn't get the distinction of *then* versus *now*. "I was a woman when I was a soldier." Heck, she was still a soldier . . . in all the ways that counted. Would that ever change?

"Too much of one."

"What?"

"Never mind."

"So, Hotwire told you to watch your mouth?"

"Yeah."

"When did you talk to him?"

"While you were napping."

"Oh. I would have liked to talk to him, too."

"There was no need." Nitro sounded awfully surly about it.

"I guess not. That's sweet how he told you not to swear around me." She smiled. She could just imagine how well the instruction had gone over with Nitro. "But don't worry about it. I don't expect you to change just for me."

"I can be as polite as the next guy."

She'd never noticed him wanting to. "Whatever you say."

"I can damn well stop swearing around you if I say I will."

She couldn't help it; she burst out laughing. "Yes, I'm sure you *damn well* can . . . ," she wheezed out between bouts of laughter.

Taking a sideways peek up at him, she saw burnished red along his cheekbones. It made her laugh all the harder. The prospect of Nitro blushing was just too much for her funny bone.

"If you can stop imitating a hyena, we can finish our discussion," he said with freezing cool.

After several deep breaths, she managed to stifle her mirth. "I don't know what else there is to say. You want me to promise something impossible."

"It would help if you'd wear looser clothes and more of them."

How was that going to help her temper? "My clothes aren't too tight."

"Your jeans outline your sexy little rear perfectly, and if you're wearing a bra under that shirt, I'll chew boot leather for dinner."

She gasped, shocked he'd noticed her lack of a bra. She hated wearing them, and because she was small she didn't have to. "I'm not that big. I don't wear one most of the time."

"I noticed." He sounded aggrieved.

"Oh." Her breasts tingled at the thought of him looking close enough to notice. She knew he was observant, but he had to have really focused in on her to discern that detail.

He stopped and glared down at her. "And it doesn't help."

"Help what? What exactly are we talking about here?"

"Me surviving another bout of close proximity to you on a mission."

"My lack of a bra is going to hurt you?"

"It already has."

"*What?* You don't look wounded to me."

"That's because you're not looking in the right place."

When her gaze dropped to where he was indicating, heat zoomed into her cheeks. She lifted her head to focus on his face again immediately, but the damage to her equilibrium had been done.

"I'm supposed to be walking off my sexual tension," he growled, "but instead all I can think is getting you alone somewhere and touching your breasts, tasting them until you almost come from the stimulation and then burying myself in you so deep, my dick will finally stop hurting."

She couldn't breathe. Couldn't speak. Couldn't believe what she was hearing. "You want me?"

"Don't sound so surprised. I'd say your effect on me is

pretty obvious. If not, just what did you think caused my hard-on?"

"You said . . ."

"That you turned me on."

Several things clicked into place. Things she probably should have taken into account already, but she was so ignorant of men. On top of her own ignorance was Nitro's confusing behavior. He acted angry with her half the time, not like a man who wanted her.

"You mean every time you get hard around me, I turn you on?"

His expression said that should be obvious even to her. "Yes."

"Oh."

"Are you saying you didn't know?"

"Men can get hard reading an ad for hot tubs in the Yellow Pages."

"I'm not one of them. Unless I was thinking of you in a hot tub."

Her jaw dropped, and her heart started galloping like the winning horse at the Kentucky Derby. Because he got hard around her a lot. He'd been that way on the mission with Wolf and Lise. She'd thought it was just his natural virility.

"I thought you were always like that."

"Hard?"

"Yes."

"Only around you."

That couldn't be true. "You're always mad at me."

"I'm always lusting after you. Can't you tell the difference?"

"No. I thought you didn't like me."

"I wanted you."

"Wolf doesn't act like he hates Lise."

"Lise is sleeping with him."

"Oh."

"Stop saying that."

"I don't know what else *to* say."

"I don't mean to act like I hate you," he said through gritted teeth.

She could be pardoned for questioning his sincerity. "Really? A man can want a woman without liking her."

"Yeah, he can, but I do like you."

She looked down at the ground, comparing the size of his big feet to her smaller ones. "You said not other women . . ."

"Yeah."

"You mean other women don't turn you on as frequently as I do?" She could barely believe she was asking this question.

"Other women don't turn me on at all right now."

Her head snapped up in total shock. "You're lying."

He spun to face her fully, his dark skin pulled taut across his cheekbones, the muscles in his jaw locked, his eyes almost black as they fixed on her with steady intensity. The silent regard was unnerving, but she didn't know what to say.

She could not conceive of such a thing being possible.

After several seconds of silence, he reached out and cupped her nape, his hands hot against her skin. "Have you ever known me to lie?"

"No."

"Exaggerate?"

"No."

"What does that tell you?"

The impossible. "You don't want other women."

"No." He didn't sound happy about it.

"You don't want to want me."

His brown gaze bored into her, and she could feel it inside as if he were touching her in places that had no name. "It's hell on a man's libido and ego, not to mention his mood, to want a woman to the exclusion of all others who doesn't want him."

"I do want you," she blurted out.

His gaze narrowed. "That's why you jump ten feet every time I touch you or come near enough to do it."

"I don't jump ten feet."

"But you do move away. Fast."

"That's because . . ."

"Because why?"

"You make me *feel* jumpy."

His face looked hewn from rock. "I scare you?"

"N-not exactly."

"What exactly?"

"I get all jittery when you get close, like I've had too much caffeine on an empty stomach. It makes me nervous."

"Nervous, or sexually excited?"

"I don't know."

"Don't you?"

She couldn't answer. It was as if his hands on her throat had drained her of the ability to speak.

"You're not jumping now."

She tried clearing her throat. "You're holding me."

"I held you once before."

She remembered. It had taken all her willpower to treat the embrace like the cover move it was. "That was just camouflage."

"Was it?"

Oh, man . . . What if it hadn't been? "I . . . I thought it was."

Chapter 5

Daniel stared down at Josie, trying to fathom the working of her mind and not getting very far. "Are you really that naïve?"

"I'm not naïve. I was raised around soldiers all my life. I heard things that would make most women cringe."

He was beginning to wonder if she had understood any of those things, though. "You thought I got an erection to make our cover more believable?"

"I thought you were always . . . I mean . . ."

She'd thought it was his *natural virility*.

While her belief was better for his ego than her rejection, it staggered him. "Have you known many men who walk around with a constant boner?"

"Of course not?"

"Any?" He had to ask.

"Well . . . no, but some men do get excited when I don't expect them to."

He could just bet. "But none of them acted on their excitement, so you assumed it had nothing to do with you, right?"

She focused on something beyond his right shoulder, her expression a study in pretending to be somewhere else. "This conversation is getting uncomfortable."

He'd spent hours in a state of *uncomfortable* arousal because of her; he didn't have a lot of sympathy for her mental discomfort right now. Besides, he thought maybe she needed to be set straight on some things for her own benefit as much as his.

"From the time you started developing, your dad threatened to maim the soldiers who came through his school if they touched you. Knowing your dad, I think the men took it more as a promise."

Her gaze jumped back to his face, her soft green eyes wide. "I didn't know that." She grimaced. "It sounds like something Dad would do, though. He was always pretty protective."

Probably a lot more protective than other fathers, considering the man's views of what it meant to raise a daughter who would not be at risk because of her femininity or size.

She pulled away and started walking again, her movements agitated. "By the time my dad thought I was old enough to date, I could beat any of the men I met in combat and knew more about weapons and explosives than they did, too."

"None of the soldiers wanted to date a woman who could neutralize him."

"No, and frankly, I wasn't interested in connecting with a soldier. I'm still not."

He ignored that. He could change her mind if she'd been honest about wanting him, but he thought it was interesting she had intimidated the soldiers as much as her father had. "You're not that big."

"You don't have to be big or even all that strong to maim someone if you know where to hit and how to do it."

That was true. There were blows that required a very light touch, but had a devastating effect on an aggressor. In order to use those techniques, a soldier had to be highly trained and disciplined. Tyler had made sure his daughter was the best.

"Dad taught me how to fight dirty, and I never hesitated to use that knowledge."

"Good. You've been in a lot of dangerous places."

"Yeah, I guess I have."

She didn't sound particularly bothered by that fact, and right now, it wasn't the uppermost thought in his mind either.

"You said you wanted me, too."

She stumbled, and he steadied her with his hand, then kept hold of her arm. She didn't try to pull away, and he figured that was a major step forward for them.

"Yes." She squared her shoulders as if she was preparing to face a major battle head-on. "I want you."

An irresistible smile curved his mouth. "I'm not intimidated by your prowess as a soldier or by your dad."

"You don't think much of my soldiering abilities."

"Not true."

"But you said—"

"A lot of stuff born of frustration, not fact."

"You said you never lie."

"I don't."

"Then—"

"I've always seen you as more woman than soldier, no matter how good you are."

She gasped, stopped, and turned to look up at him, her eyes glowing in a way that knocked the breath right out of his chest. "You did . . . You do?"

"Yes."

Then her face fell. "Is it because I dressed up to look like Lise?"

"No. When I first met you, you were wearing combat fatigues and a machine gun, remember?" And he'd gotten the first boner he'd ever experienced in a battle.

"How could I forget? Your team saved my commander's butt."

"Hotwire was right."

"About what?"

"Not swearing around you. You don't do it yourself."

"Mama told me ladies don't swear. It's one of the few things I remember about her. That and she was very soft." The wistful quality in Josie's tone made him frown.

"So are you."

She shook her head. "I'm hard. I don't know how to be any other way."

"Sometime I'll show you how wrong you are."

"I'm a virgin. I don't have any experience at all." She blurted it out as if it were something he couldn't possibly have figured out on his own.

Unlike her, he had no problem reading signs. "And you want orange blossoms and white roses to accompany the first time you make love?"

She shook her head, her expression resigned. "I'm not the type. That stuff is for the fairy-tale wedding, and I'm not anybody's version of a princess. I'm a soldier."

"You used to be a soldier. Now you're a student."

She shrugged. "Our circumstances don't always dictate what we are."

"Right. I met you in the middle of a battle and watched you fight better than most men, and I still saw you as an extremely desirable and feminine woman."

"You wanted me then?"

What did she think he'd been saying? "Yeah. It's become an obsession."

"They say to get rid of an obsession, you have to starve it."

He laughed, the sound harsh to his own ears. He didn't know what Josie would make of it.

"It doesn't work. We had our first mission together more than two years ago, and I still feel like an adolescent with my first major boner every time I'm around you. I can't even get rid of it by going to bed with another woman." He spelled it out in case she hadn't gotten it the first time.

"You tried?"

"I tried."

"It didn't work?"

"I told you, I don't want other women."

"You don't have to want a particular woman to have sex with her, do you?"

"Not always, no."

"But . . ."

"But in this case, that's not an option for me."

She licked her lips, her gaze probing him as if he was some kind of alien being.

He felt like it. The level of physical need he had for Josie wasn't something he was familiar with, and frankly, if he had been able to rid his body of the compulsion, he would have. The kind of reaction he had around Josie was a weakness, and he'd learned living with his parents just how destructive it could be to be that vulnerable to another person.

"Either I feed my obsession for you, or I keep sublimating my sex drive in work."

"Is that why you've gone on back-to-back missions since we worked with Wolf and Hotwire on Lise's mission?"

"Yes."

An undecipherable expression crossed her face, but the frown that followed it was anything but. "It's bad soldiering not to take leave between assignments."

He shrugged. He'd been trying to starve the obsession like she said. It hadn't worked.

The frown grew fiercer. "You're saying if I don't make love with you, you're going to keep up that kind of activity?"

"That's not your problem." But one way or another, he was going to convince this woman to share his bed.

"But you do want to have sex with me?"

"That's been well and truly established. The question is, will you let me?"

Oh, yeah. That had been real smooth. Ask a woman in the middle of a park path to have sex with him. And don't bother to dress it up at all. Just call it an obsession you want to feed. Right. That should do the trick.

Every virgin dreamt of having her first experience with a guy who offered sex and no finer emotions.

If he could have reached his own ass, he would have kicked it into next Tuesday. He couldn't have messed this up worse if he'd been trying.

She licked her lips again, her moss green eyes focused on his mouth. "I think I'd like you to kiss me again before I decide." She peeked up at him like a child admitting to getting into the cookie jar. "The first time I was so busy trying to keep it professional that I missed out on a lot of the finer points of what I was feeling."

He felt drunk, but he hadn't had a drop of alcohol since breaking up a bar in Lubbock, Texas, after one too many beers and insults to his heritage. "You want me to kiss you?"

"If you don't mind."

He didn't wait for her to change her mind, but pulled her body into immediate full-press contact. "Oh, I don't mind, Josette. Not at all."

Her expression turned wary at his predatory tone, but she didn't pull away.

Smiling at that reality, he lowered his mouth to cover hers, and everything inside him went still. She tasted like Christmas, his birthday, and a successful mission all rolled into one. Sweet and delicious, warm and soft, her mouth was everything he remembered it being and more.

He ate at her lips as if he'd been starving to death and she was the only food available. She made a sexy little noise and pressed her body into his while encouraging him to keep feasting with lips that molded to his in total surrender.

He'd never worried about being overly gentle before, but he didn't want to bruise Josie's lips; he wanted to savor them.

And he did, carefully controlling the desire raging through him, so every nuance of the kiss was designed to give her pleasure and a lot of it.

Josie couldn't believe the tenderness of Nitro's mouth moving against hers. She hadn't expected him to kiss her right then, not in full view of anyone going by the park. Even less had she anticipated the leashed force of his passion vibrating from his body to hers combined with a kiss so caring and gentle, she was ready to melt in a puddle of devastating emotion right there on the footpath.

Every nerve center in her body went on hyper alert, while her sense of time and space became hazy and indistinct. She rubbed her body against his, shocked at how tight and tingly her nipples grew. And things happened inside her, too, things that made her press her thighs together in shivery sensation.

His big hand moved down to cup her bottom, and she gasped from the pleasure of the unfamiliar contact. His tongue slid into her mouth, taking possession with unrelenting intimacy.

He tasted so intoxicating that if he were a bottle of wine, she would have been over the legal limit within seconds.

A growl sounded low in his throat as he explored every centimeter of her mouth, making it his.

She looped her arms around his neck, holding on tight and finally understanding why women kissed this way. They wouldn't be able to stand otherwise.

Her knees had turned to rubber, and her insides were melting with lavalike heat. He lifted her, and she let her legs spread without thought, wanting him to do something about the shivery stuff happening between her legs.

Oh, yes . . . just like that. The hard-on he'd been so preoccupied with earlier was rubbing against the apex of her thighs, pleasuring and tormenting her at the same time. She wanted, no *needed* more, but she couldn't make herself stop kissing him long enough to say so. She had to settle for making whimpering noises against his lips and trying to climb into his skin.

His other hand came up between them and cupped her small breast, rotating his palm over her tight nipple. Her tongue tangled with his, inviting him to higher levels of pleasure, and despite her lack of experience, he reacted to her efforts with extreme masculine enthusiasm.

The fact it was Nitro, the man she wanted and admired above all others, doing these things to her increased her sense of excitement and anticipation a hundredfold. For right now, his status as a soldier, his preoccupation with a life she wanted to leave behind, had no impact on her conscious mind.

He was giving her too much pleasure to think about anything else.

Pressing her rigid nipple between his thumb and forefinger, he tugged in a way that sent pleasure skyrocketing through her body. She locked her legs around his hips and pressed herself as intimately as possible against his erection.

And still it was not enough.

Tears seeped out of her eyes as her pleasure and frustration built in tandem.

His mouth broke from hers. "Josette? Josie, what's wrong?"

She looked up at him, too dazed to really focus. "Hmm?"

"Why are you crying?"

"I never cry."

His tongue traced the path of wetness up her cheek to the corner of her eye. "It sure tastes like tears to me."

"Do that again."

He tasted her other cheek in the same way, kissing her temple when he'd reached the source of her tears.

"I like that," she said with a sigh as she melted farther into him.

"But why are you crying?"

"How should I know? I've never done this before. You're the expert." She was getting annoyed by the interruption. Who cared why her tear ducts were engaging? "It's not because I'm sad, all right?"

She squeezed her thigh muscles, and his big body convulsed.

He frowned down at her. "Don't do that."

"Why not?" She liked it.

"I'm on the edge of taking you here and now."

"Taking me where?" Then it clicked what he meant. "Oh, that. Okay." She didn't care where they made love; she just wanted to feel his body completely naked against hers.

His bark of laughter surprised her. "We're in the middle of the park, Josette. I'm not into exhibitionism, and I'm pretty sure you aren't either."

She looked around her, her gaze focusing finally. A family of ducks waddled along the edge of the pond. Small children swung on the play equipment across the green expanse, and a jogger was on the path, headed their way.

"Oh, my gosh," she choked, unlocking her legs from behind him and vainly reaching for the ground with her feet. "Um, Daniel . . ."

"What?" He was looking predatory again.

"You need to let me down."

He did, and she took a quick step backward, needing distance from that Adonis-like body. But her muscles weren't cooperating, and she fell flat on her bottom.

He laughed again, and this time, it made her mad.

This was all his fault. He was the one with all the experience. He'd seduced her into total wantonness with his lips and body and had the nerve to laugh about it.

She swept out with her foot and brought him down to the ground with her. Rather than abating, his laughter just increased, the amusement in his brown eyes immobilizing her. She'd never seen Nitro like this.

He rolled toward her, and she had to maneuver quickly to avoid letting him pin her like he had in her hallway. She was on to his tricks now and willing to try a few of her own.

With a two-step execution he clearly had not anticipated, she had him facedown under her in a position most men would have found impossible to get out of. Anticipation thrilled through her at the prospect he wasn't one of them.

"Say uncle," she demanded.

"I don't think so."

He tried to reverse positions, and while she was able to avoid landing underneath him, she wasn't able to maintain her position of superiority either. She moved, and he counter-moved, never once letting her have the upper hand, but he didn't go in for the kill like he could have. They ended up rolling around in the grass, their laughter mixed as she engaged in her first ever noncombative tussle with a man.

Finally, she was laughing so hard, she just gave up and lay on her back in surrender. It was a totally new experience for her, but she didn't mind. She'd decided a nanosecond into the kiss that she wanted to try a lot of firsts with him.

He came over her, his mouth creased in that smile she so rarely saw. "I'm the better soldier. Admit it."

Now, that was taking it a step too far.

"No way."

"I'm on top."

"Only because you sucked all my strength from my body with that devil's kiss you plastered on my mouth."

"Are you saying I fight dirty?"

She felt her own lips curved in a goofy grin. "Yes."

"So do you; you said so. The fact you're still under me must mean I'm the better fighter."

"In your dreams." Then, reaching up, she did something she'd never done before—she tickled his ribs, and Nitro's body contorted as if she'd touched him with a live wire.

The tickling match that ensued could only have one outcome because she had absolutely no desire to hurt him. He ended up on top again, but this time he didn't give her a whole bunch of victory machismo. Instead he leaned down and kissed her again.

He kept his mouth closed and the kiss short, but by the time he raised his head, she was panting with something more than exertion.

"Are you going to let me make love to you, Josette, my small warrior?"

* * *

As they walked back into the house, Daniel was still reeling from Josie's yes. She hadn't stalled for time, or given him
a song and dance about not getting involved. She hadn't even
asked for any promises or declarations. She'd simply said,
"Yes."

A word he discovered he liked very much on her lips.

"Why don't you read through your dad's journals while I
call Wolf and check in with Hotwire?"

"But I thought . . ."

"If I make love to you right now, nothing else is going to
happen until tomorrow at the earliest. We've got too much to
do today to let that happen."

"You're right." She smiled shyly at him, looking about as
feminine as a woman could look. "But I wish we didn't."

"Me, too."

"I think I'll read in my bedroom. Less distraction."

"Good idea."

As soon as he heard her door close, he picked up the
phone and started making calls.

He began with a search in the Yellow Pages for a local
florist. He discovered that for enough money, they delivered
pretty much anywhere and anytime. The owner was also
kind enough to suggest a shop that might deliver another
item he wanted as well as a historic hotel in the city to deliver
it to. Reservations made, he put a call through to the hotel
concierge, who agreed to take care of the delicate matter of
having a box of condoms available in the nightstand drawer
beside the bed.

Once his preparations for the night ahead were completed,
he went into the kitchen and made a pitcher of brewed iced
tea. He put it and a glass on a tray for Josie and took it to
her.

She was lying on her stomach on her bed, her ankles
crossed and up in the air.

He put the tray on the small table beside the bed. "Drink something."

She looked up, her expression endearingly vague from reading her dad's most private thoughts. "You made me tea?"

She didn't have to sound so shocked.

Daniel might not be the cook Wolf was, but that didn't mean he couldn't take care of his woman. "I thought the caffeine might help. You didn't get all that much sleep even with your nap."

Her grin made his chest tighten. "Our exercise in the park did more for me than caffeine ever could."

"I'm glad to hear that. I wouldn't want you falling asleep on me tonight."

"That's *not* going to be a problem."

He was still smiling when he dialed Hotwire's private line, but he got off the phone more determined than ever to cement his claim on Josie that night.

Hotwire had insisted on flying out to help with the investigation. Knowing it would be best for Josie if he let his friend help, Daniel hadn't even tried to talk Hotwire out of coming, but he hadn't forgotten the fact that Josie had kept in touch with the other merc while keeping a wide berth around Daniel.

The doorbell rang as he dialed Wolf and Lise's number. He disconnected and, figuring Josie was still engrossed in the journals, got up to answer it.

When he opened the door, there was a state policeman standing on the small porch, his expression serious. "I'm Officer Ryan Johnson. Is Miss Josette McCall available please?"

Daniel's gaze flicked to the patrol car parked on the curb, then back to the officer.

"What's this about?"

"I'll have to speak to Miss McCall, if you don't mind, sir."

Daniel nodded. "I'll get her. Wait here."

He closed the door, locked it and went to Josie's room.

"You've got a visitor, honey."

She scrubbed at her cheeks and rolled over and came to her feet all in one graceful movement. "I do?"

She must have been "not crying" again. He only hoped the tears were good ones, not grief.

"It's a state patrolman."

Her pretty brow wrinkled. "I was expecting the Forest Service, but I hoped they'd take longer to find me than this. I suppose with Dad MIA, they want some answers."

"Don't give them any. There's no way they could know you were up there when the bombs went off, and you have no more idea where your dad is than they do."

She nodded and squared her shoulders. "You're right."

Josie followed Nitro to the door, glad she wasn't alone. She'd been trained to be a heck of a soldier, but she didn't lie worth beans.

He had to unlock the door before he opened it, and she looked at him askance. "You locked the officer out?"

"Of course. He's not exactly a long lost relative."

"You're as paranoid as my dad." She said it jokingly, but Nitro tensed.

He didn't say anything else, though, but pulled the door open, his body language anything but welcoming.

The state policeman waiting on her porch stood at attention, his face set in unreadable lines. "Miss McCall?"

"Yes. How can I help you, Officer?"

"Are you Josette McCall, daughter of Tyler McCall?"

"Yes."

He moved into the classic at-ease position, his feet eight inches apart, his hands clasped behind his back. "Miss McCall, we need some information if you have it."

Her stomach clenched in anticipation of fielding a bunch of questions. "Yes?"

"Can you verify the whereabouts of your father last night?"

"Why?"

"There's no easy way to say this, Miss McCall, but there's been an accident."

"Dad?" Josie could barely get the one word out.

"Apparently, he didn't make it, Miss McCall. I'm sorry."

Josie sagged, and Nitro grabbed her, pulling her against him. Her father had survived an explosion to die in a car accident, an accident he wouldn't have been in if he'd stayed with her instead of disappearing. And she'd let him walk away, not even suspecting his intention to bolt.

Bile rose in her throat, and she gagged it back down, her muscles painfully tight with tension.

"What happened?" Daniel asked.

Chapter 6

"There was an explosion at Mr. McCall's training camp. The subsequent fire destroyed the entire compound."

Nitro's hold on her tightened, and he spoke again. "No one else was hurt in the fire?"

"The school was on hiatus between sessions. McCall was supposedly staying there alone, but that was something we hoped Miss McCall could verify for us."

Josie finally found her voice. "But you said an *accident*."

"Yes. We believe the explosion was accidental. Mr. McCall was known to have explosive materials on hand at all times. It was part of his teaching curriculum. The subsequent fire burned uncontrolled until an anonymous female trucker called it in on her CB radio."

They'd assumed she was a trucker. That made sense. She hadn't identified herself and had called it in on the citizens band radio, which anywhere but Tillamook County, Oregon, would be operated almost exclusively by truckers.

"And you believe Dad died in the fire?"

"If you can verify he was at the compound last night, unfortunately I'd have to say yes, Miss McCall. No one could have survived in the fire that followed the explosion. Was your father staying at the compound last night?"

"Yes," she replied automatically.

He nodded, his expression not changing. "I'm sorry."

Nitro put his hand out to the patrolman. "Thank you for coming by. I'll take it from here."

The patrolman shook the offered hand. "You'll be staying with her, Mr. . . ?"

"Yes." Typically, Nitro didn't tell the officer his name. He and her dad really did have a lot in common.

"A shock like this can have unexpected side effects."

"She won't be alone."

"I have a roommate," Josie offered.

Taking in Daniel's proprietary hold on her, the officer nodded. "Can you be reached here if we have any further news or questions for you?"

"Yes." She gave the officer her number, which he wrote down on a small pad he kept in his breast pocket.

"Again, I'm sorry about your father, ma'am."

She bit back the urge to tell him the truth. "Thank you."

Nitro waited until the patrol car had pulled away from the curb before turning to her. "If your dad's enemies think he's dead, they won't be looking for him."

"You're right, but they're going to figure it out soon enough when they don't run across any bone fragments in the ashes. And it feels funny letting them think he's dead when he's really MIA."

"It would feel a lot less comfortable if it became a reality. The longer we can keep Tyler's circumstances from whoever is trying to kill him, the better. We don't know how muddled his thinking or strong his survival instincts are at the moment."

"I don't know. I think Dad could be out of his mind and in a fever and still act on the need to survive. It's been the driving force of his life for years."

"You read the early diaries."

"Yes." Her eyes burned with the same overwhelming sadness she'd felt in reading her dad's sporadic journal entries. "He witnessed so much brutality."

"And he was determined neither you nor your mother would be at risk like the women and children he'd seen hurt in Vietnam."

"Mom refused the combat training. They fought about it. He didn't want her to get pregnant. They fought about that, too."

"He wanted you, Josette."

"I know. He just didn't want to bring a child into a world capable of the brutal cruelty he had witnessed."

"He changed his mind about being a father."

"But he did everything in his power to raise me not to be vulnerable. He protected me the only way he thought he could."

"By training you to be a soldier."

"Yes. Mom wouldn't let him really train me while she was alive."

"He hated that."

"It made him feel helpless, like he'd felt in Vietnam."

"Yes."

"They had a strong marriage."

"Your dad may be paranoid, but he's not stupid."

"No. And he loved my mom."

"He loves you, too."

"I always knew that, but my life makes a lot more sense now." Her dad hadn't trained her to be a soldier because he'd somehow seen her as less feminine than other girls, or because he'd secretly wanted a son instead. He'd done it because he loved her more than his own comfort.

"You wanted me to read the journals. Thank you."

"So did your dad. He told you to read them, remember. You were his priority, even more than finding out who tried to kill him."

She'd always known her dad loved her, but after reading

the diaries, she realized she'd pretty much been the center of his world since the day her mom had died. She'd shared that spot with her mom before then.

"You were right about there not being a clue to who destroyed the compound." She bit her lip in thought, but the same reality she'd faced in her bedroom stared her in the face now. "Unless I'm missing something, I can't see any reason in those journals for someone to try to kill him."

"And burn down the school."

"Maybe that was incidental."

"I don't think so. Your dad could have been neutralized with a sniper bullet a lot easier and with less chance of discovery than setting the explosives and fire. Whoever did it wanted the compound destroyed as well."

"Then I guess the next place to start looking is the computerized files."

"After . . ."

"After what?"

"After you let me take you to heaven and then lay you gently back down on earth."

The words made her shiver from the tip of her head to her toes. They were incredibly beautiful as well as sensual. "You sure don't sound like a soldier right now."

"I was a Sioux before I was a soldier."

"You're Sioux?"

"Yes."

She reached out and touched his jaw with her fingertip. "You look like a warrior chief to me."

"I am not a chief."

"That's good because I'm not exactly an Indian princess."

"You are going to be my woman. That's all that matters."

"Will I?"

"What?"

"Be your woman?" She'd never considered the possibility he might feel possessive about her while he was trying to rid himself of his obsession for her.

"Do you want to go from me to another man?" he demanded sounding really irritated by the possibility.

What a ridiculous idea. "No, but I didn't know if you saw making love as a one-off deal."

"An obsession is not satisfied in one encounter."

"How many will satisfy you?" And once he was satisfied, would it be over? Would he walk away from her and go back to his solitary soldier ways?

"I do not know. Do you need a number?"

"No." She'd rather not know D-day. It would only give her something concrete to dread, and she didn't want anything marring the time she had with him. No matter how short or long it might be. "I don't need a number."

"How soon can you be ready to go?"

"Where are we going?"

He named a historic hotel downtown known for its romantic ambiance.

"Why are we going there?"

"I do not want there to be any distractions when we come together for the first time."

"You want to go to a hotel to make love for the first time?"

"Yes."

"But Claire—"

"You don't need the distraction of wondering if your roommate can hear the noises you make when I touch you."

She forgot what she was going to tell him about Claire for a second. "You think I'm going to make noise?"

"Oh, yeah."

She shivered deep inside again. "Enough noise that I'm going to be worried about Claire hearing in the other room?"

"Yes."

"Good noise or bad noise?" The first time was supposed to hurt.

He reached out and brushed his fingers across her lips, making them tingle. "Good."

That sounded promising. She licked her lips, tasting his subtle presence on them.

"So, how soon can you be ready to go?" he asked again.

Then she remembered what she was going to tell him about Claire. "We don't have to go anywhere."

"Are you having second thoughts?"

"No. The thing is, Claire works nights at a nursing home twice a week. This is one of them. She probably won't even come home between classes and going to work."

He shrugged as if that information made no difference. "A woman's first time should be special."

She felt her expression going all gooey, and she couldn't do a thing to hide it. "That's really sweet, Nitro."

"Daniel. I am not just another mercenary to you. After tonight, I will be your man." He sounded really serious about this, and she finally caught on to the fact that what she called him was of major importance to him.

"I can be ready to go in twenty minutes . . . Daniel."

He smiled his approval at her, and she got all warm and happy inside. "After we make love, I will tell you my true name."

"Your true name?"

"The one I was given by the Sioux."

"Then will you expect me to call you that?" she asked, thinking maybe this whole name thing could be taken a little too far.

"My name to you is Daniel."

"But you want me to know your true name." She was trying to understand and not getting very far.

"After we have shared our bodies, yes."

"Do all the women you've made love to know your true name?"

"Only two other living people know it, and neither of them are women."

Well, that was something. Maybe being an obsession was more important than a casual bed partner.

* * *

Later, Josie's heart fluttered in her chest as Daniel un-locked the door to their hotel room. Facing armed guerillas was not as intimidating as the unknown beyond that door.

She'd known soldiering her whole life, but the man/woman thing, seems it was all a complete mystery to her. Other women had started heavy petting when she'd been busy learning how to build and dismantle car bombs. The only orgasms she'd known had been of the self-made variety, and while they made pretty good battle tension relievers, they weren't anything to get excited about.

Not like the way she felt when Daniel kissed her.

Which was why she was here, ready to make love for the first time to a man who until that very morning, she'd been convinced didn't even like her.

He'd acted as though he liked her in the park. He'd played with her, and she had a feeling their tussling had been as new an experience for him as it had been for her, but the desire they felt was not.

He knew so much more about this than she did.

"My dad wouldn't have taken you on as a partner if you weren't a pretty good teacher, would he?"

Daniel turned his head to look at her, his hand on the doorknob. "What?"

"Your method of teaching isn't tossing someone into a river and seeing if they learn to swim before they drown, is it?" Her voice was high-pitched, and her breathing had turned ragged at the edges.

He winked, shocking her to her toenails. "Don't worry, Josette. I won't let you drown."

She swallowed and tried to believe him. He pushed the heavy, ornate wooden door open and indicated she should go in first, but her legs refused to cooperate.

His dark eyes narrowed. "Are you okay?"

"Yes, but I can't seem to get my feet to move."

"You're nervous."

What had been his first clue? The way she equated making love for the first time with death by drowning, or the deer-caught-in-the-headlights look she knew was in her eyes? "I shouldn't be. I'm not a child."

"But you are innocent."

"Only physically." She'd heard and seen things women married for forty years would never experience.

He shook his head, his mouth twitching at the corners. "Your heart and your mind are very innocent still, no matter what you think you know."

"Oh, really?"

"Yes."

That sparked another set of worries that kept her feet firmly glued to the floor outside their room. "Won't you be bored making love to me, seeing as how I don't know anything?"

"Josette, I could spend the entire night just looking at you and not get bored." His tone wasn't reassuring so much as bewildered.

Which was actually pretty comforting. Later, she would probably feel flattered and special, but right now, she just felt relief. At least something about this was new for him, too. "I take it you've never been that way with a woman?"

"No." And if the frown on his face meant anything, he didn't like it.

"It's a first for both of us." She couldn't help the satisfaction that laced her voice.

He let out an impatient breath. "It's not going to be anything if we don't get out of the hall."

She sighed and looked into the room. It was a suite. She could see the bedroom through the sumptuously decorated sitting room. It was like a room out of time, the colors and décor something from a bygone era.

"It's a pretty room," she said without moving.

"Not as pretty as the woman I'm bringing into it." Before

she knew it, the decision was being taken from her as he swept her up in his arms and carried her inside.

"This isn't our wedding night," she said breathlessly.

"I know that."

"But you just carried me over the threshold."

"It was the expedient thing to do."

Perhaps, but she liked the sensations zinging through her body as a result of being held securely in his strong arms. She looped her arms around his neck and buried her face in the warmth of his chest. He smelled so different than she did, but it was a good different. Masculine.

Maybe she wasn't as lacking in the feminine department as she thought she was. At least she now realized she smelled like a woman, not a man. She should have caught on to that sooner, as much time as she spent around male soldiers, but she couldn't ever remember actually smelling one before.

He carried her through the sitting room to the bedroom beyond, and her breath caught in her throat.

Did he want to make love right now, just like that?

Of course he did. She was his obsession. It wasn't the romance of the century or anything schmaltzy like that.

Then another scent, one very different from Daniel, invaded her senses. Roses.

She lifted her head from his chest and looked around them.

The room was filled with flowers—red roses, white roses, yellow roses and even lavender roses. They were everywhere. Swags of dried orange blossoms hung off the ornate head and footboard of the antique bed, too, but the thing that caught her attention and kept it was a white silk gown spread over the burgundy velvet bedspread.

"Daniel?"

He looked down at her, the hardened mercenary she knew him to be not quite hiding the man who cared enough to make this night special. "It's your first time. I want you to remember it for all the right reasons."

Tears filled her eyes, and she couldn't get a sound out past the big lump in her throat.

He let her down and stepped back, seemingly unconcerned by her display of emotion.

"I'm going to take a walk. I'll be back in a while. The bathroom is through there." He pointed to a door on the opposite side of the room. "Take your time getting ready. I'm not going to rush you tonight, in any way."

She was still shivering from the promise in that last comment when the outer door closed.

When Daniel came back to the room a half an hour later, the door to the bedroom was still shut.

How much longer would she be?

He'd promised not to rush her, but he wanted her with a hunger that left him feeling hollow and achy inside. Calling his need for her an obsession had been pure fact. If she had turned him down, he would have been on a collision course with spontaneous combustion.

The closed door mocked his promise of patience. He wanted to pound on it and demand to know how long it took to put on a nightgown, but he had just enough self-control left to keep him seated on the oversized Victorian sofa.

This was too important to mess up with impatience, even if it was born of desperation.

She'd waited twenty-six years to share her body with a man. After their talk in the park, he understood that better, but still found it difficult to believe a woman as sexy and beautiful as she was could have remained innocent so long.

If Daniel had been one of the soldiers going through Tyler McCall's training camp, Josie would have gotten educated about men and their desires a lot earlier. He would never have allowed the older man's threats-slash-promises to deter him from pursuing a woman he wanted as much as he wanted Josie.

The handle turned on the door to the bedroom, and he

surged up from the sofa. The door swung inward, and she came out, the sheer white silk gown clinging lovingly to her small curves.

His breath caught, and he had to clear his throat to talk. "You look beautiful."

"Thank you for the gown. It's the prettiest thing I've ever worn."

The exclusive boutique owner he had called earlier had followed his directions to a T. The nightgown was designed along the lines of a medieval dress. Its bell-shaped long sleeves floated gently around Josie's slender arms, and the skirt whispered against the smooth skin of her legs. The high waist tucked in just below her breasts, accentuating them.

He ached to taste the dark nipples peeking out at him from behind the sheer silk. He wanted to put his mouth right over each one, making the fabric wet and transparent and her nipples hard and tight.

Familiar sensations brought his sex to full attention as the images in his head grew increasingly erotic. "It'll look even prettier off of you."

Her mouth dropped open, and she stared at him as if she wasn't sure how to take what he'd said.

"The need to see your body without covering is driving me crazy, little warrior."

"Do you want me to take it off?" She looked as if she'd bolt into the bedroom and shut the door if he said yes.

He smiled a predator's smile, knowing his prey was within his reach, but shook his head. "Not yet."

He'd bought it for her to wear, no matter what his horny-ass mind was telling him. She deserved to feel special about her first time. Hell, she deserved declarations and promises, but all he could give her was pleasure. He didn't know how to love a woman, wasn't sure he could even learn. He'd had too many years training himself not to feel in order to survive.

Her hands fluttered around her head, where her chin-length hair had been brushed into a silky dark cloud. "I didn't know how to fix my hair to go with the dress."

"It looks fine to me."

She licked her lips. "You don't think I look silly like this?"

He couldn't believe she was asking him that when his dick was so hard from looking at her that he could drive nails with it. "No."

"You don't say much, do you?"

Did that bother her? "I talk more with you than I do other people."

"I suppose you do. Dad doesn't talk a lot either."

For some reason her classifying him with Tyler didn't sit well. "I'm not your father."

Her eyes darkened with unmistakable feminine arousal. "No, you aren't, and I'm glad."

Not half as glad as he was. He couldn't stand the distance between them anymore. He had to touch her. He moved toward her, relieved when she didn't back up or get all nervous. Some women had said he scared them in the bedroom. That he was too silent. Too intense. He didn't say things he didn't mean, which meant a lot of the time, he said nothing at all, but he doubted he was any more intense about sex than most men.

He reached out and cupped Josie's shoulders, liking the small hitch in her breathing at his touch. She felt delicate beneath his hands and incredibly feminine. His woman.

Letting his fingers smooth down her arms, he drew her closer until their bodies were practically touching.

"Are you still nervous?" he had to ask, but wishing he could keep his mouth shut because he didn't know what he would do if she said yes.

"No." She tipped her head back and met his eyes with hers, the message there one he didn't know how to decipher. "You went to a lot of trouble to make tonight special for me."

"It is special."

"I know. You're special, too."

"I'm just a man who wants you very badly."

"You ordered flowers to fill the bedroom. That meant a lot to me . . . *means* a lot to me."

"The flowers got rid of your nerves?"

"You could say that."

He didn't understand, but he was glad. "I want to kiss you now."

"Yes. Please."

Sliding his hands to her small waist, he lowered his head until their mouths were a breath from touching. "I am going to please you tonight."

"Will I please you?" she asked, but not sounding worried as she had earlier.

"Oh, yeah."

She lifted her mouth so their lips collided and flicked her tongue out to press at the seam of his mouth. He let her inside, reveling in her minor aggression. She'd brushed her teeth. He could taste the mint, but her own sweetness overpowered any other flavor within seconds of their tongues meshing.

He broke his mouth from hers, remembering something else he'd meant to do before making love. "Champagne."

She looked at him with glazed green eyes. "What?"

"I ordered champagne." It was chilling in a standing bucket beside the sofa.

"I'd rather taste you."

And just like that his good intentions went up in smoke. He slammed his mouth back on hers, taking the interior with all the grace of an invading army.

She didn't seem to mind, melting against him just like she'd done earlier, this time her hands rubbing over his chest in a tactile exploration designed to send him over the edge before he'd even made it out of the starting gate.

He didn't try to stop the touching, though. It felt too good. He'd fantasized a long time about having her small hands on him, and the reality was light years beyond the dreams.

She undid his shirt with more speed than finesse, and a button popped off. Neither of them cared as he allowed his hands free rein with her body, too. The gown was almost as smooth as her skin, and he ran his fingers over every curve, memorizing her like a sightless man. Her nipples were rigid beneath the fabric, and when he pinched them, she moaned and ripped his shirt in agitation.

Then her fingertips encountered the naked skin of his chest, and they both shuddered. He cupped her bottom, to pull her body into more intimate contact with his own, but her gown stopped him from getting as close as he wanted. Giving up one conquest for another, he broke the kiss and lifted her higher until her breasts were level with his mouth.

He closed his lips over one distended peak and proceeded to play with her with the tip of his hard tongue. It made her wild, and she squirmed against him, trying to close her legs around him and making small animal-like sounds. He moved to her other nipple, needing to possess every part of her body totally. This time when his mouth closed over her, she yelled. His name.

He liked it.

He pulled back, and she whimpered. "Don't stop, Daniel. Please."

"I'm not." But he wanted to see.

The silk had become transparent in the two wet spots over her stiff nipples. He could see every goose bump of pleasure through the now see-through silk that clung revealingly to her excited flesh.

"You're beautiful," he said in a guttural tone he had no hope of softening.

"I want you, Daniel. Now."

He brought her mouth back down to his level, needing to taste her again. She didn't wait for him to kiss her, but devoured his lips with her own, sucking on his tongue and moving her mouth against his ardently.

He felt pre-come wet his penis inside his pants and desperately wanted to be out of them. Taking a firm grip on her round little ass, he walked into the bedroom and headed for the big bed with one thought in his mind. Getting them both naked.

He ripped the blankets off the bed with one hand and tossed them on the floor. Then he put her on the big expanse of white sheet, coming down with her so their lips stayed connected.

Using one arm at a time, he tore his damaged shirt the rest of the way off and then went to work on the fly of his jeans. He shoved them off with his BVDs, glad he'd had the foresight earlier to take off his shoes and socks while he waited for her, or he wasn't sure he would have gotten his pants off before coming inside her now.

She arched up toward him, and the feel of her silk-clad mound rubbing against his erection brought a feral sound from deep in his throat.

If he didn't get inside her soon, he was going to come all over her pretty nightgown. He reared up off of her and started pushing the silk up her legs. She helped him, peeling it off over her head and tossing it to the side, no virginal reticence in evidence.

Then she looked at him and stopped breathing, an arrested expression on her face. "Wow."

Chapter 7

It occurred to him belatedly he should maybe have waited to let her see him naked until after he had excited her to the point of no return.

"Is it always that big?" Damned if she didn't sound intrigued by the prospect.

"Only when I'm excited."

She rolled her eyes, her lips twisting wryly. "I may be a virgin, but I'm not an idiot. I knew that. I meant, are you always this big when you're excited?"

"I've never measured it."

"Oh." Her face fell. "So, you don't know how big it is?"

"What the hell difference does it make?" And how could she manage to talk right now? All he wanted to do was get inside her and stay there until neither of them could walk afterward.

She zeroed in on his hard-on with her too innocent green eyes and licked her lips. "It doesn't make any difference at all. It's just I've read some stuff . . ."

What kind of stuff had she been reading where a man's penile dimensions mattered? "Reading isn't the same thing as doing," he growled, not liking the prospect she found reality less exciting than her reading material.

"I figured that out the first time you kissed me."

"Are you saying you'd never been kissed before?"

"No, but I never wanted a kiss to continue. I never wanted a man to let me taste his tongue."

His knees about buckled. "You acted like you didn't want that one to either."

"Yeah. What a wasted opportunity that was. I thought you were only doing it for our cover."

"I wasn't."

"I know." Then she looked at him through her black lashes, her lips glistening from her tongue's sweep over them. "Will you do it again not for cover?"

He couldn't believe she thought she had to ask.

"Lie down."

"Why?" she asked with a puzzled frown.

"I want to see all of you." Especially what was hidden by her tightly closed thighs.

"I want you to kiss me."

"Lie down first."

"You'll kiss me again if I do?"

"Yeah."

She let her torso fall back, and then reclined stiff on the bed like a sleeping nun. He couldn't help it. He smiled. She was such a mixture of innocence and passion.

And for tonight, she was all his.

He closed his fingers around both her ankles and pulled, but she resisted.

"I want to see."

Her breath grew choppy, and the pulse in her throat beat a wild tattoo under her skin, but she said, "Okay."

Her eyes wide, she let him separate her ankles and push her knees up until he could see the swollen, dark pink folds of her feminine sex.

Letting go of her ankles, he reached out and fluffed the soft, curling hair on her mound. "Pretty."

It was the same color as the hair on her head, right down

to the red highlights. He should have known those wouldn't have come from a bottle. Not with Josie.

"Uh . . . thank you?"

He laughed, something he'd never done in the bedroom. "You're welcome."

Dipping his fingertip into the dewy warmth of her, he felt his dick bob in response to her silky wetness. She was going to feel so good around him. He'd never touched anything so soft.

She moaned and tilted her pelvis up. "Touch me deeper, Daniel."

He loved the ring of his name on her lips. It sounded intimate, and it was. She was the first person to call him by that name in years.

"I'm going to touch you to the depths of your soul before I'm done tonight, sweetheart," he promised, pressing his finger in up to the first knuckle.

It was a tight fit. She was slick with wetness, but she was also swollen from desire and tight from never having made love. Penetration without pain was going to take some major effort on his part, but he didn't want to hurt her. A man should never hurt a woman.

He stretched her, pressing outward against her vaginal walls, trying to prepare her for his erect flesh.

She gave a voluptuous sigh and squirmed farther onto his finger. "I like this, Daniel."

Sweat broke out on his brow from the effort it took to go slow now that the moment had come. "Me, too."

He pushed farther inside until he felt a thin barrier and stopped, but he didn't pull back.

She flinched, her body going stiff. She didn't say anything, but she bit her lip.

"Does it hurt?"

"Only a little, but it's going to hurt more later, won't it?"

"Not if I can help it."

She closed her eyes, an expression he knew well coming over her features . . . that of a soldier facing unavoidable pain and prepared to carry on. "Maybe you should just do it."

"That's not the way it's going to happen, sweetheart."

She nodded, but remained rigid.

"Relax, Josette. I won't break your hymen yet."

She settled into the bed again, her eyes opening and her green gaze fixing on him in question. "Can you, with just your finger?"

"Yes."

"I didn't think you could. I mean, I've worn tampons for years and it's still there."

"They aren't as long or as hard as my finger, baby." As he spoke, he pulled out. Then he pressed his finger inside of her again, feeling the way she had to stretch to accommodate even that with a sense of desperation.

He wasn't worried about her body being able to take him—eventually—but he might just have a heart attack from excitement before he got inside her. Because it was going to take a *long* time to do this right.

His heart pounded, his breath sawing in and out, and thinking of multiplication tables did nothing to decrease his raging desire. Not when she was right there, naked in front of him. "I'm going to put a second finger inside you now. Okay?"

"Yes." The word ended on a long hiss of sound as he did just that, carefully sliding his middle and forefinger in together.

Once again, he stretched her, massaging her silken tissues until his fingers slid more easily in and out of her.

"I thought you were going to kiss me," she said, panting between each word, her hips moving betrayingly against his hand.

"I am."

"When?" she demanded, sounding meaner than he'd ever heard her, and he grinned.

"Now." And he did, but not where she was expecting him to.

Using his free hand, he separated her vulva so her clitoris was completely exposed to him and then pressed his open mouth over the engorged bud and kissed.

She cried out, arching off the bed, and grabbed his hair with both hands with all the strength of the warrior she was.

The pain of having his hair pulled gave him a primitive pleasure no woman could understand, and he laved her clitoris with his tongue, teasing her with the touch he knew was not quite enough to send her over. He kept it up until she was making mindless sounds that went straight to his sex.

Needing to experience more of her, he explored her entire vulva, getting drunk on her spicy sweetness and the incredible softness of her swollen lips. He pressed his tongue inside her along with his fingers, stretching her farther and getting more of the taste he craved like a child who'd had his first piece of candy. But he couldn't get enough.

He pulled his fingers out and tongued her as deeply as he could go, his whole body vibrating with the pleasure he got from tasting her.

She called out his name, her voice hollow and desperate. Trying to pull his mouth away, she yanked on his head, and when that didn't work, she tried pushing his shoulders with her feet, but he locked his hands on her hips and kept on.

He knew what she needed, and it wasn't for him to stop.

When she gave up pushing with her legs, he moved his mouth back to her now quivering clitoris and slid his fingers back inside her. He thrashed her violently excited nub with his tongue until her body went stiff with preclimax tension, and then he gently took her between his teeth and sucked.

She screamed, she bucked and she begged. For him to stop. For him to keep going. Until eventually his name was the only intelligible sound coming from her mouth as hot wetness gushed from her inner core. Her body shivered for a prolonged climax that kicked him right in the chest with an emotion he didn't understand.

She was amazing.

As the shivers receded, he gentled her with his mouth, but didn't let her come completely down again. He had been pressing his fingers against her inner barrier with a steadily increasing pressure, but now he withdrew.

Using his knowledge of the sensitivity of a woman's vaginal entrance, he caressed her while using his tongue on her sweetest spot to reignite the flame of need he'd so recently quenched.

His hard penis ached, as though someone had tied it in a knot and was pulling on it. He needed to come so bad, but he had something to do before they could make love completely.

This time she whimpered as her pleasure grew, repeating his name over and over again in a breathless voice, filled with drugged passion, and he had that kick-in-the-chest feeling again.

He started making love to her again with his fingers, pressing deeper with every thrust until she once again arched in utter abandon, her body tense as a bowstring ready to shoot.

He lifted his mouth so he could see her face and watch for discomfort before pushing through her barrier with less effort than a hot knife cut through butter. Her body jerked, but then she started riding his fingers, convulsing in another climax almost immediately, her face contorted with undeniable ecstasy.

He waited until she fell limply against the bed before kissing the top of her mound and then pulling his fingers from inside her and rolling to his feet.

"Where are you going?" Her voice was slurred and hoarse, her eyes filled with wonder at what she'd just experienced.

"To get something to clean you up. I'll be right back."

"S'okay." Her head fell to the side, her eyes sliding shut.

* * *

Josie didn't know how long Daniel had been gone. She was floating in a sort of waking dream, her body in a state of shock from the pleasure he'd given her. Then she felt a gentle warmth between her legs, and she forced her eyelids to open.

He was kneeling between her legs, a washcloth in his hand.

"What are you doing?" Was that croaky voice hers? She sounded like a refugee from a smokers' anonymous support group.

"Washing away the blood."

"Blood?" Was she supposed to bleed after climaxing?

He didn't seem bothered, so she didn't get all that worried, but she couldn't remember ever reading about anything like that before. Oh, man . . . What if she'd started her period? How gross would that be? Only, she wasn't even due for a couple of weeks.

"What blood?"

"I broke your hymen."

"You did?" He'd dispensed with the physical evidence of her virginity? Already?

"Didn't you feel it?" His dark eyes probed her, as if looking for the truth.

She smiled weakly. It was the best she could manage in her sensually exhausted state. "I don't remember. You made me insensate with pleasure. I didn't know it would be like that."

"It isn't always."

No. It wouldn't be, but she felt things for him that transcended the physical, and that was bound to make lovemaking with him more intense.

"So, I'm not a virgin anymore?"

"You're a virgin who isn't going to hurt the first time she makes love."

Finally, she understood what he'd been doing, and her heart contracted with feelings unlike anything she'd ever known. Her dad's idea of protection had been to teach her to protect herself. She'd never been cosseted, had never known a sense of feminine fragility with a man.

Daniel had given her both.

"Thank you."

He shrugged. "Men should not hurt women."

"But it isn't always possible to avoid it . . . the first time, I mean."

He moved his shoulders again, his expression unreadable.

She went up on one elbow to better see him and sucked in a breath of shock. Even her less than experienced eyes could see that his patience had come at a cost. His erection jutted out and up, purplish veins pulsing with blood standing out in angry relief against his smooth, dark skin.

"You hurt."

His mouth twisted. "Yeah."

"So you thought it was better to suffer pain yourself than let me feel it?"

"Always." He dried between her legs with a soft hand towel and then tossed it and the washcloth on the floor. "I'm going to make taking me pure pleasure for you." His head came up as he said it, his expression feral.

She shivered with anticipation.

Never dread. A man who controlled his own desire to such an extent simply so he would not put her through a natural part of making love the first time would never, ever hurt her in any way.

Physically, her mind amended, knowing that emotional pain was waiting for her down the road with this man. The chances of him wanting a permanent commitment were small. Even if he did, she could have him only at the expense of her dreams of living a more normal life and leaving the soldier existence behind.

She shoved all that to the back of her mind and put her hands out to him. "Make love to me, Daniel. Please."

He came over her, his mouth settling on hers with hungry need that turned her insides out and her already jellylike legs to water. Incredibly, he set about exciting her again, while her hands explored whatever she could reach of his body.

When she encountered his hardness, he groaned and pulled her hand away.

"Don't you like it?" she asked against his lips.

"If you touch me, I'll come."

"Yes." Oh, she liked that.

"I want to be inside you when that happens."

"Then get inside me, Daniel," she said between kisses. "Do it now."

His smile went clear to her toes. "Yes, ma'am."

He looped her knees over his forearms and pressed upward so she was fully open to him in a way she could never have imagined being comfortable with, but she liked it. A lot.

Nudging her opening with the blunt tip of his shaft, he asked, "Now?"

She arched up—"*Yes, now*"—and felt the beginning of his possession.

Then he reared backward, pulling out completely, a particularly vile four-letter word coming out of his mouth.

"What?" she asked in shock, her heart hammering against her ribs.

"I almost forgot the rubber."

"You mean we don't have one?" she asked, ready to blow something up or take an unforgivable chance if he said they didn't.

He lunged across the bed without answering and jerked the drawer open on the small night table. He grabbed something and then went up on his haunches, the evidence of his desire and his body leaning intimidatingly over her. With shaking hands that shocked her more than his withdrawal, he ripped open the package and then rolled the condom on.

"The suite came supplied with condoms?" she asked in disbelief as he came back over her.

"They do if you pay the concierge enough." Then his mouth locked with hers again, his tongue thrusting between her lips with exciting force, making it impossible to speak anymore.

Once again, he looped her legs over his arms and pushed them wide, but this time he didn't ask if she was ready. He had to know she was beyond ready. His broad head pressed inside her, and while she felt as though she was stretching beyond what her body should allow, she experienced no real pain.

He rocked against her, sending sensation arcing through her body with each deepened thrust until he was seated to the hilt and their pubic hair meshed.

She felt impaled and couldn't move, but she wanted him to.

"Are you all right?" he asked, his brow glistening with sweat, the effort it took to hold back reflected in the tense lines of his hard face, the rigid set of his shoulders.

"More than all right."

"Are you okay if I move?"

"Please . . ." She bit her lip, trying not to yell demands at him, but gave up when the movement he made was so small it was more torture than assuagement. She grabbed his head, her fingers curling into his dark, silky hair, and held on tight. "Move, Daniel. I want you to come inside me!"

Something seemed to break within him. Maybe it was his control. He began moving, pounding in and out of her with the power and speed of a jackhammer.

She loved every second of it and felt another stunning climax begin to build deep in her womb. Incredibly, he grew inside her. It should have been impossible, considering the condition he'd been in to begin with, but he got even harder, massaging her core in ways she couldn't fathom.

She clenched around him in involuntary spasms, on the edge of an explosion bigger than any bomb she'd ever built. He gave a deafening shout as his whole body went rigid in sexual ecstasy, and the explosion hit, rocking her foundation with its power.

She couldn't even scream, the pleasure was so great, and her mouth opened on a silent, prolonged cry as her body convulsed around him.

Afterward, he collapsed on top of her, his face turned away on the pillow.

His dark hair was wild and wet with sweat, and she kissed it, emotion tearing at her insides with too much beauty to be borne. "Thank you."

He mumbled something, but she couldn't understand what, and then didn't say anything else. She smiled, resting her face against his head. Her eyes drooped, and she felt herself slipping into sleep.

Daniel forced himself to disengage from Josie, so he could take care of the condom. Otherwise he probably would have stayed inside her all night long. And smothered her to death.

She was so tiny compared to him. She'd laugh in his face if he told her he thought she was fragile, but it was how he saw her, and that would probably never change. He'd seen her hold her own in combat, but that didn't seem to matter to the part of him that claimed her as his woman.

For now.

Not even a woman raised to be a soldier could stay in his life forever. He wasn't capable of that kind of permanent intimacy, but they had *now*. He was going to revel in the present, for once dismissing both his pain-filled, guilt-ridden past and the certain loneliness of the future.

Josie woke surrounded by heat and hard muscle. The room was dark, the heavy drapes on the window blocking everything but a crack of light from the streetlights outside. She could make out the murky shape of the dresser against the far wall, the one practically covered by a huge bouquet of roses. She could still smell the sweet fragrance of the flowers, but Daniel's scent was even more tantalizing.

The man-woman aroma of their lovemaking clung to him, enveloping her in an intimacy she'd never known. Josie snuggled in closer, becoming immediately aware of hard flesh pressing against her backside as a stifled groan sounded from Daniel's throat. She wiggled again, as intoxicated by his reaction to her as the memory of the way he made her feel.

He sucked in air as if she'd hit him, and a hard hand clamped on to her hip, stilling her movement. Did he think she was asleep?

She scooted out from under his hand and turned over to face him. Pressing her body against his, she welcomed the feel of his erection against her belly.

His big body shook, and he groaned again, this time a lot more loudly.

She looked up at him, unable to make out much more than the shape of his head in the darkness. "Hi."

"Hi." His voice sounded strangled.

"I couldn't help but notice you were awake."

"I've been awake for an hour."

She reached down between them and closed her fingers around the heated flesh of his arousal. "Like this?"

"Yes."

"Why didn't you wake me up?" She brushed up and down his length, amazed at how velvetlike and hot his skin was.

His hand clamped over her wrist. "Stop that."

"Why?" she asked again.

"You'll make me lose control."

After the way he'd made love to her earlier, putting her comfort ahead of his desire, she didn't think it would be possible. "Would I?"

"Yes."

"Good."

"No, it's not."

"I don't see why." She was no longer a virgin. She could handle him going a little wild. In fact, she looked forward to it. She shouldn't be the only one losing connection with reality when they made love.

"We can't make love right now."

"Did you only get one condom from the concierge?"

"No."

She leaned forward and inhaled against him before pressing an open-mouthed kiss to his smooth chest. He tasted spicy and all male. She couldn't help flicking her tongue out to explore more of his skin. His muscles were rock hard and so were the small nipples her lips found in the darkness. She circled one with her tongue and then bit it very gently.

He made the sound of a dying man faced with Heaven, but consigned to Hell. *"Stop."*

"I don't want to."

"If you don't, I'm going to end up buried deep inside you again."

"And this is supposed to be a bad thing?" She liked, no *loved*, having him deep inside her body, one with her in a way no other person could ever be.

"It will hurt."

"I don't think so."

"You made love for the first time tonight. You're bound to be sore."

"Why don't you feel me and find out?"

His entire body went rigid. "No."

"Don't be so Victorian about this. Women, even former virgins, are allowed to make love more than once in a night in this century."

"I don't want to hurt you."

"You won't. Touch me and you'll see how wet and ready for you I am." She reversed the hold he had on her wrist, looped her leg over his hip to open herself to him and pulled his hand into contact with the slick flesh at the apex of her thighs.

"Damn it . . ." But he turned his hand so his fingers could explore her.

"See?" she asked breathlessly, her body already quivering from his gentle ministration.

He slid one of his fingers inside her. "Does this hurt?" His guttural voice sent pleasure arcing through her as effectively as his touch.

"Pain is the last thing on my mind right now."

"Are you sure?"

She couldn't help being moved by his concern, but she didn't want it to prevent them from sharing something so incredible as often as possible for as long as they had together. "Positive."

She pushed on his shoulder. "Now . . . Can I touch you?"

He allowed her to press him to the mattress so he was flat on his back. "Yes."

"You won't tell me to stop again?"

"No."

"Can I touch you anywhere?"

"Touch me any way you want to, little warrior."

"I will."

She grinned in the darkness, anticipation fizzing in her blood like champagne as she straddled him. She should probably start off small, but she'd woken up aching for him, and patience had never been her strength when it came to waiting for something she really wanted. Without further thought, she pressed her swollen intimate flesh against his hardness.

He arched up against her. "Yes!"

Her smile faltered as intense pleasure radiated from the center of her femininity outward. Needing more, wanting to give him more, too, she rocked her pelvis so she slid up and down his length, groaning when the ridge of his head touched her clitoris. Man alive, how did women survive this much delight on a regular basis?

Her thighs quivered with it, and she stopped moving, not ready to orgasm yet.

The dark enhanced her sense of touch as her fingers learned the shape of his body that her eyes already knew. They encountered solid ridges of muscle on his stomach, the turgid small nipples her mouth had already tasted, and then went on to feel the sleek skin over bulging biceps of his arms and hard angles of bone in his face.

As she brushed over his lips, learning their contours in a different way, he opened his mouth and took her finger inside. His tongue did strange and wonderful things to it that made her breasts tingle and her woman's center clench with need.

She pressed down more firmly against his erection, but it didn't help.

She wanted to feel him inside her.

"Where are the condoms?"

"In the drawer."

She forced herself to scramble off of him and fumble for the bedside table. She opened the drawer in the dark and scrabbled around inside for a condom packet. Her efforts were hampered by the feel of his hand caressing her bottom. She stopped moving completely, forgetting for a second what she was doing.

"Did you find one?" His voice reached out in the dark to surround her like warm velvet.

"What? Uh . . . yes, here . . ." She grabbed the edge of one small packet and went back to him, climbing onto his thighs and straddling him again.

Her fingers slipped as she tried to open the foil square, and it fell onto his stomach. She brushed her hand across his stomach, looking for it. Finding it, she used her teeth to rip it open.

"Do you want me to do it?" he asked.

She shook her head, but then realized in the dark he couldn't see her. "No."

She pulled out the thin rubber, working out in her head how best to get it on him. It couldn't be that hard even if she'd never done it before. Reaching out, she found his hard-on with unerring accuracy. His fingers curved into her thighs as she gripped him one-handed.

It took some doing, but she got the condom rolled on, refusing his second offer of help when she'd fumbled at first getting it over the broad head of his penis.

Then she moved until the opening to her vagina was kissing the tip of his erection. "You know, there's something I've always wanted to do."

"What?" he asked in a strained voice.

"Go riding."

Chapter 8

Josie pushed down, closing over his straining head, and it took all his self-control not to surge upward and complete the union. This was her show, and he would let her run it . . . for now. She made a frustrated sound as she got him halfway inside, but couldn't seem to go any farther.

"Rock it, baby."

"Like you did earlier," she said, as though a lightbulb had gone on inside her brain.

She emulated his earlier movements like she'd been sexually active for years, taking more of him inside with every downward thrust. He thought the top of his head would come off with every slippery centimeter he went deeper into her hot little body. Her desire was so incredible. So intense.

She stopped moving and seemed to be trying to figure out how to achieve that last inch of penetration when his control slipped and he surged upward, completing their connection. Unable to stop himself, he kept surging upward, but she didn't seem to mind. She met his thrusts with her own, moaning each time he hit bottom. He squeezed her breasts, playing with her nipples, feeling them grow tauter with each small stimulation.

"Daniel!"

"What?"

"I . . . It's . . ."

"You're close, aren't you, sweetheart?" So was he.

"Yessss . . ." She rode him hard, her toned thigh muscles contracting around him in tense anticipation, but she didn't know how to take herself over the edge.

He reached down and separated her lips, exposing her clitoris to more direct stimulation, and then ground his pelvis against hers every time they surged together. She caught on right away, clamping her inner muscles around him and changing her tempo to one that kept their bodies locked while she moved against him rather than on him.

He felt her body tense further, and he pressed against her tailbone, keeping the friction steady, while he continued moving under her even as she started convulsing in climax. He grabbed the back of her head and brought her lips, open on a scream, to his. Her mouth was vulnerable to the possession of his tongue, and he thrust inside while he pleasured her body with his.

She shook with a second orgasm close on the first, and he came with her this time, his entire body exploding with more sensation than a nuclear blast.

She went limp, her body collapsing on top of his.

He kissed her long and lingeringly before tucking her head down onto his chest.

She rubbed her cheek against him like an affectionate kitten. "That was amazing."

"Mmmm."

"What does *mmmm* mean?"

"*Very* amazing."

She laughed. "That must be Sioux, huh?"

"No." But he smiled. He liked her teasing.

"I like this, Daniel."

"I do, too." He sighed, wishing he could stay where he was and knowing he couldn't. "But I've got to move, or we're going to decrease the effectiveness of this condom by about ninety percent."

"Would that be the end of the world?" She snuggled in closer. "Haven't you ever wondered what a little Daniel Black Eagle would look like?" she asked whimsically.

"No." He gently, but firmly pushed her off of him, his body rejecting her words as completely as his mind did, and rolled off the bed.

He knew exactly what his child would look like. Him. Just as he was the spitting image of his father. His father's blood wasn't a legacy he had any desire to pass down to the next generation.

He frowned down at her. "I'm not daddy material."

She turned onto her side and propped her head up on her hand. All he could see was the outline of her body, but he could feel her eyes locked on to him. "Why not?"

He wished he'd left a blanket on the bed, or a sheet or something she could use to cover up. Even with the cold chills skating along his nerve endings from her words, his body was reacting to the gentle curves revealed in the shadowy darkness.

"I don't want a family." He'd made that decision a long time ago and never changed his mind. "No wife. No kids. Not even a live-in lover to visit between assignments. I'm a mercenary, not a family man."

"You're a *mercenary trainer* now. There's a difference." She sat up, her posture not nearly as relaxed as before. "My dad has been a good father, and according to what I remember of his time with my mom, he was a darn good husband."

Tension clawed at Daniel's insides. Was she building fantasies in her head around him? She'd do better to wish for the moon, damn it.

"We had sex, Josie, incredible, mind-altering sex, and maybe because it was your first time, you're thinking there's more to it than there was, but I don't do long-term commitment."

He hated saying these things, had thought he wouldn't need to. She'd been a merc. She knew the lifestyle, and in a lot of ways, she knew him, but apparently, she didn't see him as clearly as he thought she did. The prospect of losing her because he couldn't promise her a future made him sick inside, but he could not have her under false pretenses.

"I'm sorry if I said or did something to make you think otherwise, but if you're looking for some kind of happily ever after with me, we need to call it quits right now."

"I don't believe in happily ever after, and I wasn't offering to have your baby, though I guess I made it sound that way."

The coward in him was glad she could not see his face, but he wished he could see hers. Was she hurt? Was she angry? He couldn't tell. From her tone, she could be either.

"Then why bring it up at all?"

"It was a joke, a lousy one apparently. I didn't expect you to take me seriously or make such a big deal out of it. And for the record, I may be pretty ignorant about what it takes to make a good relationship, but even I know better than to believe I can build a future with a commitment-phobic ex-mercenary who sees me as an obsession he wants to get rid of." She definitely sounded mad now.

"I'm sorry—"

"Don't apologize to me again, for goodness sake."

"I didn't mean to hurt you."

"Don't make assumptions you can't substantiate. I never said I was hurt."

True, and while she sounded angry, there were no tears in her voice. "I'm glad."

"I'm trying to change my life, Daniel. The last thing I need is a long-term commitment with a soldier. Once we find my dad and his would-be killers, I never want to set foot on another training compound or battlefield again."

He couldn't doubt the passionate conviction in her voice, but far from appeasing him as they should have, her words left a hollow place inside. They implied that once this mission was over, she never planned to see him again.

"Are you going to insist your dad come to Portland to visit if he wants to see you?"

"That's not your concern."

"It is if it means you aren't going to see me again."

She laughed, the sound harsh and lacking in any amusement. "Make up your mind, Daniel. You said you don't want long-term ties."

"I don't."

"Then how or where I see my dad after this fiasco is over is none of your darn business."

"So, you're saying you only want to be lovers while I'm helping you investigate the explosion at the compound?"

"That sounds about right. I doubt your sexual liaisons last much longer than that anyway."

She was right, but he felt shut out of her life already, and it frustrated him. He'd had no choice but to be honest with her, but he didn't have to like the consequences. "Do you want me to spend the rest of the night in the other room?"

"Are you saying you've sated your obsession already?"

"No." In fact, now that he knew what it felt like to come inside her, he craved it even more.

"Then why sleep on the couch?"

"You're angry."

"Believe it or not, I didn't go into this thinking you were going to marry me and give me babies."

Which didn't deny that she was angry with him. "I'm glad," he said again, thinking after he said it that maybe he could have been more tactful.

She huffed out a breath. "It's a good thing I didn't weave any romantic fantasies around you, isn't it? You'd have shot them to bits by now. You're great with your body, Daniel, but your relationship skills stink."

"At least you enjoyed the sex."

The words wounded Josie for his sake more than her own. She bit her lip as she listened with a heavy heart to Daniel's nearly silent tread across the room and into the bathroom. Her last comment had been uncalled for and untrue. He'd fulfilled every one of her romantic fantasies except one, and he'd never once implied he had any feelings for her not wrapped up in his sex drive. She had known he wasn't interested in marriage, or a future with her.

She didn't know why she'd said that about what his child would look like, except that her defenses had been obliterated by what she experienced when they made love. Postcoital bliss had sent her mind wandering down dangerous paths, and her idiotic comment had been the result.

She wished she hadn't said it. Wished even more that it had been truth rather than pride that had made her deny she wanted him to sleep elsewhere now. Her pride had refused to allow him to see how hurt she'd been by his blunt rejection. However, regardless of what she'd known before they made love, having him spell out his lack of any personal feelings for her beyond sexual desire *did* make her feel funny about sleeping wrapped in his arms.

Cuddling wasn't about sex. It was about caring and togetherness. Neither of which she shared with her lover.

She looped her arms around her drawn-up knees and waited for him to come back into the bedroom. The sound of running water was followed by the shower coming on, and she dropped her head against her knees to wait for him to finish.

She felt the bed dip under his weight before she realized he'd come out of the bathroom. She must have dozed, and he must have turned off the light before opening the door. Probably trying to be considerate and not wake her. He wasn't a total write-off, even if she wished she could convince herself otherwise.

He might not believe it, but one day Daniel Black Eagle would meet the right woman, get married and have kids. He had so much goodness in him, a gentle and playful side to his nature that she sensed only children would bring out in him fully. He'd probably marry someone like her mom had been, someone soft and ultrafeminine, who didn't know the difference between a pistol and a nuclear warhead.

She threw back the covers and scooted off the bed.

"Where are you going?"

"I want to take a shower, too. I feel sticky." She'd always thought it was the man's ejaculation that made a mess after sex, but she'd gotten so wet, she was slippery with it.

He didn't say anything, and she went into the bathroom. She didn't know why, but she locked the door before turning on the light. She avoided the mirror because she didn't want to see what a wreck she must look like after all that sweaty rolling around. Stepping into the old-fashioned claw-foot tub, she pulled the curtain around her and turned on the shower.

The hot water cascaded down out of the oversized shower head, and she began the task of washing Daniel's scent from her and the feel of his touch from her body. At least she tried, but no matter how much hot water she let pour over her, the sensation of his fingertips on her skin remained.

She finally gave up, hoping she'd taken long enough for him to fall asleep, and turned off the shower.

When Josie came back to bed, she got in on the side opposite Daniel and stayed there, keeping the expanse of the big mattress between them. After making love the first time, they'd gone to sleep wrapped in each other's arms. Now she seemed intent on keeping the distance of the great divide between them, both physically and emotionally.

Daniel hadn't expected anything different, not after hearing the quiet snick of the bathroom door lock before she took her shower, but he could try to bridge the chasm between them. He wasn't very good at that sort of thing. However, if it meant getting her back into his arms, he would do it.

"Come here, Josie."

"I'm too tired to have sex again tonight." Her voice was clipped with anger, not drowsy with fatigue.

Men and women were so different, and despite the way she'd been raised, Josie was Y chromosome all the way through. She was mad and didn't want to make love, but anger would never diminish his hunger for her. Hell, even if she really was too tired, he couldn't relate. He could be coming off a three-day assignment without sleep and summon up enough energy to make love to her.

However, despite the always there burn of desire, he hadn't been attempting to renew their passion. "I can hold you while you sleep."

"No." The one word held a wealth of repudiation.

"Why not?"

"I'm used to sleeping alone."

"You slept with me earlier," he ground out, frustrated by her emotional distancing masquerading as logic.

"That was then. This is now."

"Damn it, if you wanted me to sleep on the couch, why didn't you say so?" He got out of the bed with jerky movements, his muscles tight with the effort it took not to give vent to his temper.

"I have no problem with you sleeping in the bed."

He wasn't playing these man-woman games. He was no good at them. His responses weren't subtle enough. "I can't promise not to roll over and touch you. If I do, I'll probably wake up and want to make love. You don't want that to happen, so I'll see you in the morning."

He'd reached the door when her voice broke through the silence. "I don't mind if you want sex again, but I don't want to cuddle."

He spun around to face her and saw that she was now sitting up in the bed. "What?"

"We don't have that kind of relationship."

"What kind?"

"The caring kind."

"You don't care about me?" He didn't believe her. She was too vulnerable to him not to care at all. "*You think I don't care about you?*" he demanded before she'd answered the first question.

"You said you didn't."

He headed back to the bed. "Like hel—heck, I did."

"It's just physical."

Standing over her, he vibrated with outrage at her accusation. "If that were true, I could have gotten as big a high off my fist as I do your body, and lady, let me tell you, that's never gonna happen."

"You said—"

"That I wasn't looking for a forever. I didn't say anything about not caring about you in the present." Damn it, why did she have to make everything so complicated in her own mind?

"If you cared about me, wouldn't you want a future?" she asked, sounding more confused than condemning.

"I don't want a future with anyone."

"Are you saying you *do* care about me?"

"Of course I do."

"Oh. I care about you, too."

He'd never doubted it.

Before she could ask how much he cared or get into one of those emotional discussions at which he was so hopeless, he decided to take action.

She gasped when he pushed her back into the pillows and gave a half-hearted protest when he claimed her mouth, but an hour later, when she lay sated and curled into his body like the other half of his soul, he figured she wasn't thinking about how much he didn't care anymore.

One thought nagged at him as he tried to sleep.

If Josie thought wanting a future together was a sign of caring, did that mean that despite what she'd said, she'd hoped for one with him?

* * *

Daniel woke up with two thoughts uppermost in his mind. The first was that despite the fact Josie had allowed him to become her first lover, she didn't see herself as his woman.

Not only had she tried to sleep separate from him, even though she'd denied wanting him to leave the bed, but she had put a time limit on their relationship. Because they didn't have a long-term future, she didn't see herself as belonging to him in the present, and he wasn't sure how to change her mind.

The second thought that came close on the first was that Hotwire would be arriving in Portland today. A man Josie freely acknowledged as a friend and admired in ways she'd never expressed admiration for Daniel, Hotwire fit into the new life Josie was creating for herself.

Daniel didn't. He was a soldier, and she wanted a life free of them. She wanted a future, and he didn't have one to give her. She wanted to be normal, and he'd accepted long before he left home that he wasn't like other people.

That didn't stop him from wanting her to belong to him right now, and the need to cement what connection he did have with her before they left the hotel that morning rode him hard.

She'd slept cuddled into his body, her bottom snug against his groin, her head resting on one of his arms, his other arm looped over her waist. He savored the sensation of physical closeness for several minutes, pressing his hand against the warmth of her belly and rubbing his thigh against hers. Josie didn't stir. For a woman who had said she didn't want to be held, she slept remarkably well wrapped up against him.

He derived satisfaction from that even as he planned how best to wake her. Carefully pulling his arm out from under her head, he guided her onto her back. She sighed in her sleep and turned toward him, subconsciously seeking the heat of his body, but he gently pressed her to her back again, wanting her open to his touch.

Using the same skills he'd honed to almost superhuman precision to disarm a bomb, he lightly brushed the pads of his fingers along her curves. Tiny bumps of sensual pleasure rose to the surface of her silky smooth skin, but she didn't waken. He explored every inch of her tantalizing softness, stopping every time she moved toward wakefulness.

With gentle pressure, he pushed her legs apart, and she let them separate with another sleepy sigh, allowing his fingers access to the dew-kissed curls at the apex of her thighs. She moaned and mumbled his name as he investigated the level of her arousal. She hadn't showered after their last session of lovemaking, and she was still silky with her own rapidly renewing moisture. Her body was preparing itself for him, and his already stiff erection throbbed with the need to take her up on her subconscious offer.

He kissed each of her nipples in turn, tasting them with carefully controlled ardor because he wasn't quite ready for her to waken. The tender peaks beaded instantly, and her torso arched toward him in unconscious invitation. He accepted it, swirling his tongue around her aureole until she made a sound deep in her throat, telling him she was coming to wakefulness.

He kissed her sleep-softened lips, opening his mouth over hers, unable to resist the urge to taste her. Sweet, like warm candy, the first lick turned his craving for her into voracious hunger. Her mouth opened on a drowsy sound of pleasure, and suddenly she was kissing him back, her mouth every bit as ravenous as his. Her hand buried in his hair, she tugged him into a deeper kiss.

They made love with nothing held back, her body completely open to his, his body intent on giving her more pleasure than she would ever know again, and when they climaxed together, she cried out his name with emotion-filled intensity.

Josie finished dressing, her legs a little wobbly from her early morning lovemaking with Daniel. He'd woken her with a kiss and then proceeded to pleasure her until she was out of her mind with it. She'd thought she'd learned the last word on pleasure the night before, but he'd taught her they hadn't even scratched the surface.

Their shower together had been intimate and special, but not sexual—as if he was intent on proving to her that sex was not all they had between them. If that were true, then why had he taken such pains to point out how temporary their relationship, if you could call it a relationship, was?

There was so much she did not understand about Daniel Black Eagle, but that was nothing new. For heaven's sake, she'd just figured out the man didn't dislike her. How could she expect herself to understand the inner workings of his mind?

The breakfast he'd ordered the night before had arrived, and Daniel was letting the waiter in while she dressed.

It felt funny putting her typical khaki shorts and boring olive green T-shirt on after spending so many hours exploring her female sexuality. She wished she had a skirt to wear, or something slightly more feminine than her mostly androgynous clothing. Even a less militaristic color for her T-shirt would be an improvement.

Her gaze slid to the beautiful silk gown she'd folded up and put in her duffel bag. She reached out and touched it, awed by the luxurious softness of the silk. She doubted she would ever wear it again, but she'd never get rid of it either. It was too special.

Daniel had wanted her to feel that way last night, to feel like a sensual, *feminine* woman. She had, but the nightgown wasn't why. It was the way he treated her, the way he touched her as though she was the sexiest woman alive and could turn him on with a simple look. According to him, she could. She smiled to herself, but her expression soon slipped into a frown.

If he was so attracted to her, why wasn't he even remotely interested in a future together?

Obviously he expected to grow bored with her after a time. In fact, he planned on it. He saw her as an obsession he had to cure himself of, and by his own admission, he'd tried starving the obsession to get rid of it before going with the opposite approach of giving in to it. Did he expect the obsession to last even as long as their investigation?

She couldn't understand why he had insisted on her sleeping in his arms last night. She caught on fairly quickly that the issue had been as important to him as it had been to her, but what she didn't understand was why. If it were only sex, why care if they shared intimacy in sleep?

Maybe it was the sex again. He'd certainly availed himself of her willingness both last night and this morning, but she'd allowed him to because he'd said he cared about her.

Looking around the room, seeing the roses, smelling their sweet fragrance, she had to admit that he hadn't treated her like a substitute for his fist last night. Either he was a darn good actor, or she mattered to him. Her feelings mattered to him. He'd done everything but give her a ring to make last night the most exceptional one of her life.

It *had* to be about more than mere sex to him. If she were only an obsession, would he have tried so hard to make her first time making love one to remember for the rest of her life?

Then again, he was an honorable man. Maybe he saw his efforts as adequate exchange for what she was giving him . . . serious sexual release . . . and nothing more.

Chapter 9

Josie slid into the seat opposite Daniel, the smell of melting butter and waffles making her mouth water. He hadn't bothered to put a shirt on, and she found his naked torso a lot more interesting than the food, no matter how hungry she was.

"Stop that, Josette, or we won't make it out of the hotel room today."

Her gaze skittered to his face. His jaw was clenched, and his brown eyes were melting her with their heat.

"Doing what?" she asked innocently.

"Looking at me like you'd rather pour your syrup on my chest than on your waffle."

"Sounds sticky. I guess I'd have to lick it off then, huh?"

She watched in fascination as his male nipples hardened. "Yes."

Heat zoomed into her most sensitive body parts at the image, and she licked her lips, tasting him in her mind. "Would you let me do that?"

He made a choked sound, half laugh, half groan. "Another time, but not this morning. We have to get back to your house."

He was right. They had work to do, and Claire would be waiting for them. Josie had left a message for her at the nursing home, but things had been a little crazy, and she didn't want her roommate worrying unnecessarily. For a computer geek, Claire had a pretty strong maternal instinct.

"I suppose, but don't blame me if my mind wanders when you're not wearing all your clothes. You're a very sexy man fully dressed. Naked, you're a killer."

"To you."

"You can't tell me lots of women don't find you about the sexiest thing they've ever seen. You've got rock-hard muscles on a physique most men would kill for, the looks of an ancient warrior and eyes women get lost in." He'd certainly fueled her fantasies since she met him, but she had to admit, reality far exceeded her imagination.

He stared at her as if she was an alien species.

"What?" she demanded, frowning. "You aren't blind. You can see yourself in a mirror."

"My eyes aren't as kind as yours. When I look in the mirror, I don't see a man like the one you described."

"What do you see?"

"My father."

"You look a lot like your dad?"

"Yes." There was no pleasure in his voice at the comparison.

She'd never heard him mention his parents. "Do you see him very often?"

"Never."

"Is he still alive?"

"Yes."

Daniel's eyes burned with rage for a brief moment, but then it was gone. Nonetheless, it had been too poignant to mistake.

"You don't get along?" she fished.

"No."

"Does he still live on the res?" Hotwire had told her once that Daniel had been raised on a reservation, but not why he'd left it.

"No."

If he were anyone else, she'd be sure the short answers meant he didn't want to talk about it, but Daniel was laconic at the best of times. He was also blunt enough to tell her to mind her own business if she asked him something he didn't want to answer.

"Where is he?"

"In prison."

No wonder Daniel didn't like resembling his father.

"What about your mom?"

"She died before he went to prison."

"I'm sorry."

"I am, too. She was a gentle woman. Soft."

She stretched, pulling her T-shirt taut across her braless breasts, the nipples of which were still reacting to the image of licking syrup from his naked torso. "Unlike me."

Daniel's grim expression turned sexual in a heartbeat, just as she'd hoped it would. She remembered what he'd said about her softness yesterday and wanted to refocus his mind and take the look of grief out of his eyes.

"You feel soft enough to me."

She grinned, feeling soft in a place she couldn't afford to tell him about. Her heart. "I'm glad you think so."

"Hashkeh Naabah."

"What?"

"It's my true name among the Sioux."

"What does it mean?"

"Angry Warrior."

"Why?"

"I made no secret of the fact that as soon as I was old enough I would leave the reservation. The one way I knew I could do it was as a soldier, so I told everyone I was going to become one."

"Why angry?"

"I have a hel—heck of a temper."

She smiled at how he stopped himself from swearing. She

liked that he tried to around her. It was like an ongoing reminder he saw her as more woman than soldier. Not that she was a soldier anymore . . . at least that's what she kept telling herself. How well her attempt at transformation was working, she wasn't entirely sure.

After all, she'd armed herself just like the old days when she took Daniel into her dad's hidden underground room.

"I've never seen you lose your temper."

"That's because you didn't meet me until after I was assigned under Master Sergeant Cordell."

"He taught you to control your temper?"

"Yes. He knew about my dad and drilled self-control into me as an alternative to turning out like him."

"Your dad has a bad temper?"

"Yes."

She wondered if that was why he'd ended up in prison, but didn't want to hurt Daniel by asking. "Master Sergeant Cordell must be a pretty good trainer."

"He is. He's the one that nicknamed me Nitro. I hated it at the time. It was a constant reminder I was like my dad. He meant it to be. He pushed my temper every chance he got until I could control my anger in the most provoking circumstances he could imagine, and he had a pretty good imagination."

Josie read between the lines to the torment Daniel must have endured to learn his immovable self-control and shuddered. "I'm not sure I'd like this master sergeant."

"You will."

"You expect me to meet him?"

"I want you to."

"Why?"

"He's a friend."

"Where does he live?"

"He retired to Tillamook."

"Is that why you wanted to buy in to my dad's training school? So you could be near him more often?"

"That was one reason."

She knew the other already. Daniel wasn't ready to get out of the business, even though Wolf and Hotwire had been. He'd turned down their offer of partnership in the security consulting venture in order to go into soldier training with her dad.

Not wanting to dwell on his inability to move on from the paramilitary life, she said, "My mom used to call me Josie-bear."

One corner of his mouth tilted, and his brown eyes warmed. "Is that your secret name?"

She nodded gravely. "I don't bandy it about."

"I can see why."

"You think it's too kidish, or that it doesn't fit?" she asked archly, never having been flirtatious in her whole life. "Don't you find me huggable?"

"The name fits you perfectly, but you're safer not advertising how cuddly you are. Other men might get the wrong idea."

"You mean that they can cuddle me?"

"They can't." He was back to looking fierce.

"You're pretty possessive for a guy who sees me as nothing more than an obsession."

"You're *my* obsession." But he didn't deny that's all she was to him.

"For now," she taunted, unable to stifle the need to push him.

"For as long as you agree to share your body with mine."

"You mean our arrangement is exclusive?"

"Damn right it is."

"Watch it, *Nitro*, your temper is slipping." And wasn't it interesting she could impact it like she did, a mere obsession like her.

Her thoughts splintered as he stood up in a silent, feral rush. He came around the table with an unmistakable intent.

"I was just teasing you," she screeched as he pulled her out of her chair and swung her up over his shoulder. "*What are you doing?*"

"Feeding my obsession."

"Are you sure you're not just trying to assert your male dominance?" she asked breathlessly as she fell back on the bed where he tossed her.

"No man could dominate you, little warrior."

Maybe not, but her love for a man might make her submit to behavior she would normally crush beneath her size-seven combat boots. "I'm not a warrior. Not anymore."

"You're a warrior in here." He pressed his forefinger against her left breast. "It doesn't matter what you do with your life; underneath you'll always be who you are."

If someone else had said that, she would have felt despair, and a resurgence of her ongoing fear she would never have a normal life, but the way he said it made her feel as though being a warrior at heart was a good thing. His expression said that to him, she was anything but a freak, so she smiled and pulled his head down to hers.

Their lovemaking was elemental and fast and left her panting beneath Daniel in total shock at how quickly her body could find the ultimate pleasure in his.

"You're really good at this," she croaked.

"We're good together." He kissed her, hard and thoroughly, until she clung to him in renewed passion.

He pulled his lips away and looked down at her, his expression as fierce as any tribal chieftain. "Remember that. You wouldn't feel this way with another man." He kissed her again. "Only me."

She knew he was right, but was afraid it was because her emotions were a lot more involved than she could afford them to be rather than a simple sexual chemistry thing.

There was a city police car parked in front of the house when Daniel pulled his SUV into Josie's driveway.

"What in the world is going on?" Josie asked.

"Let's go find out."

Claire came out the front door as Daniel and Josie got out of the four-wheel drive. She looked even more disreputable than the first time he'd seen her, and her face was pinched with exhaustion.

She stopped in front of him and Josie, her expression bleak. "The house got broken into last night."

"What?" Josie asked. "When you were here?"

"No. It happened before I got home this morning."

Daniel put his arm around Josie's shoulders and hugged her into his side. "What did they take?"

"The usual . . . our computers, the television, my grandmother's l-locket . . ." Claire's face crumpled.

Josie pulled away from Daniel to wrap her friend in her arms. "Oh, honey . . . I'm sorry."

"I don't know what I'm going to do. My laptop is gone. I can't do my schoolwork. Yours is, too. I'm so sorry."

"Don't worry about it. We'll figure something out, and it's certainly not your fault."

Claire nodded. "The police don't think I'll ever see Grandma's locket again. It was the only thing I had of my family. It's like I don't exist anymore."

Daniel could hear the pain in her voice, but he didn't know how to comfort Josie's roommate and was frankly glad it wasn't his job.

Josie hugged Claire again. "Oh, sweetie . . ."

Daniel left Josie comforting Claire and went inside to talk to the police.

"It looks like a standard break-in and entry and burglary," the officer in charge said.

"Did the neighbors see anything?" Daniel asked.

"Not that we've been able to ascertain." The uniformed policeman referred to his pad. "The best we can do is narrow the break-in time to a six-hour window."

Daniel's instincts were screaming at him that this break-in had been anything but routine. It was linked to the explosion on the mountain; he could feel it. He'd wait to see if Josie drew the same conclusion before saying anything, though.

He went over the list of items missing with the police officer. "Your girlfriend will need to go through her things as well, so we can make sure the list is complete."

"I'll make sure Josie does that."

The officer nodded. "Well, there's not much more we can do here. I'll file my report and get back to you if we find anything out."

"Josie, are your CDs in their cabinet?"

Daniel looked up from the list he and Josie had been compiling of her missing property.

Claire stood in the doorway, her brows knit in a disturbed frown. No surprise there. According to Josie, her roommate was a long way from having the financial resources to replace her stolen computer equipment. Since her class load was weighted heavily toward computer studies, that was a major problem for her. He figured there had to be a way to help Claire without damaging her pride, but Josie would know best what it was.

They could talk about it later.

"I don't know," Josie said in reply to Claire's question, getting up from her swivel chair.

She crossed to the small corner entertainment unit in the spare bedroom she used as a study. Popping open a door on the lower cabinet, she revealed a large selection of CDs in their jewel cases. She looked up at Claire and asked, "Did you want to borrow one?"

"No, but the DVDs are in the entertainment center, too. And my portable CD player is still in the drawer beside my bed along with my music."

Josie smiled, her green eyes flickering with warmth. "I'm glad. I hate the fact they took as much as they did."

"I don't think you're getting the point your roommate is

trying to make," Daniel said, not happy to have confirming evidence the break-in hadn't been a run-of-the-mill burglary.

He felt certain it had been orchestrated by the people responsible for the attempt on Tyler's life. They had not balked at killing once. He could easily imagine what they would have done if either woman had been home last night. Josie could take care of herself, but even a seasoned soldier was at a disadvantage during a surprise attack, and her security measures were nonexistent.

Thinking about it made him ask, "Why don't you have a security system?"

"Because this is my house, not my fortress."

It was that *normal life* thing again. Her desire to leave her mercenary life behind was really starting to bite him in the ass. "Josette, normal people have security systems."

"Which are useless if the perpetrator has any kind of specialized knowledge." She closed the CD cabinet and came back over to her computer desk, where she'd been trying to identify what had been stolen.

"So go with something harder to circumvent."

"But then I wouldn't be living like a normal person, would I? I'd still be perpetrating the soldier mentality. Anyway, I don't see what my lack of a security system has to do with the thieves leaving my CDs behind."

"Whoever broke in last night is a lot more dangerous than a burglar looking for his next score."

Claire pushed her black plastic-rimmed glasses up on the bridge of her nose. "I think he's right, Josette. I read this article online a few months ago about petty theft and the used entertainment industry market. According to what I read, CDs and DVDs are popular items to steal because they're so easy to get rid of. You don't have to prove ownership, and a lot of used dealers will give cash on the dollar for them."

"If the perps who broke into your house were petty thieves, why take the television, which is easier to trace and more conspicuous to carry, but leave behind the CDs and DVDs?"

"Maybe they were in a hurry."

She wasn't being a smartass; she was being a good soldier and presenting another alternative, but she knew he was right.

"All of my CD-ROMs are gone," Claire said.

"Mine, too." Josie waved her hand toward her desk. "So are my disks, for that matter. They took pretty much everything related to my computer."

Claire frowned, her intelligent eyes sharp. "Diskettes aren't worth anything. Even new, they hardly cost anything. The only value they could have to a thief is the data stored on them, and you don't keep data that could be turned into income."

"You said you had copies of your dad's records on your computer," he reminded Josie.

"Yes."

"Did anyone else know about the computerization of his files?"

She shrugged, her mouth twisting wryly. "Probably quite a few. He complained about it a lot to the other trainers that worked for him."

"The school was destroyed along with all its files. Your computerized records were stolen along with anything that might conceivably have copies of them on it."

"You think someone tried to kill Dad because of what he had in his files?"

"Yes."

"But I've been through them. There's nothing there that could warrant that kind of reaction. Despite his personal paranoia, he doesn't keep track of behavior he deems suspicious."

"Your dad's records had to have something in them that someone didn't want him to have."

Claire sat down with a thump on the armchair in the corner and ran her fingers through her hair, making the wild tangle even messier. "Nitro's theory is scary, but it's the only one that makes sense of what has happened."

Daniel put the list he'd been holding down on the desk and curled his fingers into fists, using techniques he'd taught himself to control his inner rage. The whole situation was really starting to piss him off. First these miscreants blew up his and Tyler's merc school before Daniel had even had a chance to work out how he was going to turn wannabe mercenaries into soldiers. They tried to kill his business partner, and then they broke into Josie's home while he was elsewhere.

He didn't even want to think about the fact the woman whose body gave him so much pleasure would probably be dead if she hadn't been out taking a midnight stroll in the forest the night of the explosion.

"I have to agree with you two. Whoever broke in here took a lot of stuff to make it look like a regular burglary, but they dismissed too many things a real thief looking for easy cash would not have left behind." Josie's worried expression did nothing for Daniel's temper.

"Which means they aren't going to fence the stuff." From the despondent tone of Claire's voice, Daniel figured she was thinking of her grandmother's necklace. "They'll probably just throw it away."

Josie got up and went across the room to put an arm around Claire's shoulder. "I'm so sorry."

"You lost stuff, too."

"Not my mementos."

"At least we weren't home," Claire said, her voice stretching for a positive note.

Josie didn't say what Daniel was sure she was thinking, because he was thinking it, too. If Claire had been home, she wouldn't have had a chance against the perpetrators.

"I wish I'd been here," he said.

Claire's eyes widened, and she shook her head. "I don't think I could keep living someplace a person had died."

"I don't want to kill them," he said to Claire, wondering what the suddenly impassive expression on Josie's face meant. "I want to know who they are and why in the hel— blazes they tried to kill my business partner."

"I have every intention of figuring that out." Stubborn determination radiated off of Josie like the afterglow of a nuclear explosion.

"We've got pretty much nothing to go on." And he was a mercenary, not a trained detective.

Wolf was the tactician expert, and Hotwire knew more about searching out information than the ground staff for black ops, but Daniel knew best how to fight and win. If he couldn't identify his enemy, he couldn't fight.

Josie stood up, her pretty body enticing him, even though he knew making love should be the last thing on his mind right now.

"I wouldn't say that."

"You must see something I don't."

"We now know our enemies are worried about something Dad has in his records, worried enough to kill to make sure it stays buried."

"So?"

"All we've got to do is go through those records with a fine-tooth comb."

"We don't have them to go through, and from what you remember, there's nothing suspicious in them anyway."

"I wasn't looking for it when I computerized the files. And we do have a copy of the records."

"You have a backup?"

"Yes."

"But they took all your storage media."

"Not my jump drive. I keep it with me all the time."

"Everyone should. It's the most efficient form of backup," Claire said, sounding like a female version of Hotwire.

"What's a jump drive?"

"Hold on a sec, and I'll show you." Josie grabbed her hot pink backpack-style purse from the hardwood floor beside the door and dug in the outside pocket.

She pulled out a small silver object about the size of his finger. "This is my jump drive. It holds 256 megabytes. I keep my whole document directory on it all the time."

"And you've got the school's records on it?" He knew about bombs the size of pens that could blow up buildings, but the idea that a tiny thing like that held all the records stored in several filing cabinets made his head hurt.

"We don't have a computer to pull the drive up on," Claire said dejectedly from her chair.

"No problem." This was a logistics problem he could handle. "Hotwire should be here soon, and he always travels with his laptop, but is there any reason we can't just buy you two new computers?"

"Hotwire is coming?" Claire and Josie chorused at the same time, ignoring his suggestion to buy new laptops.

Claire looked dismayed by the prospect, but Josie looked overjoyed, and that did nothing for Daniel's temper. "Yes, he wants to help with the investigation," he bit out.

Josie smiled. "That's so sweet of him."

She hadn't thought Daniel was sweet when he'd offered to help. In fact, she'd tried to talk him out of it. His temper slipped one more notch.

Josie put the vegetarian lasagna in the oven and turned back to the counter to grate carrots for the salad she would serve with it.

"I didn't know you could bake the lasagna without boiling the noodles first," Claire said from the table, where she was spreading garlic butter on a loaf of French bread.

"It's a trick Wolf taught me." She sprinkled the grated carrots over the salad and then smiled at Claire, knowing anything she told the other woman had almost no chance of being used in practical application. "You increase the sauce a little bit and cover it for the first forty-five minutes of baking."

"So, Wolf is giving you cooking lessons while Hotwire teaches you how to be a computer geek?" Daniel leaned against the counter, so close to her that she could feel the heat of his body luring her.

Only he'd been acting as if he'd never had an obsession with her body, as though they hadn't spent the night before making love. He'd said he wished he'd been there when the thieves came, implying he regretted the night they'd spent together. She couldn't regret it, and knowing he did, even if his reasoning was more than justified, hurt.

"Wolf gave me a few tips, but labeling Hotwire as a mere computer geek is like calling an Olympic triathlete a Sunday jogger. Did you have a question about that?" she asked, nodding toward the list of missing items he was holding.

He'd come into the kitchen when she started making dinner and had been holding the list then, but so far, he hadn't said anything about it. He hadn't said anything at all until just now. He'd been standing there all broody and masculine, putting off male pheromones her body was reacting to despite his lack of overt encouragement.

Increased tension emanated off of him in indecipherable waves. What had him so uptight?

"Did you leave the journals off on purpose, or did you forget about them?" he asked.

Josie was puzzled by the question. She'd never said the journals had been taken. "They aren't missing."

Chapter 10

"What?" Daniel asked as if she'd said his fly was undone.

She frowned, thinking the answer should be obvious. "I hid them in the top of my closet before we left yesterday."

"Why?" Claire asked, and Josie realized her roommate might assume she'd been worried about Claire looking through her things.

"No particular reason. My dad drilled into me to always put important stuff out of sight when I'm going to be away." Hence his secret underground room.

It wasn't anything different than Daniel would probably have done himself, so why hadn't he expected her to do it?

"I wish I'd been that cautious with my grandmother's locket, but I always left it hanging from my mirror as sort of a talisman." Claire bit her lip and went back to buttering the bread, leaving some rather large clumps in one section while barely touching another.

"Don't beat yourself up," Daniel said. "It's not your fault you weren't raised by a slightly paranoid vet with a penchant for soldiering. Josette has a lot of her dad in her."

"I am not paranoid."

Daniel shrugged, and she wanted to slug him. "There's nothing wrong with being careful," she told him.

"It's more than that, and if you're honest, you'll admit it. You refuse to have a decent security system, but you practice defensive operative tactics at home."

"Are you trying to say you can take the soldier out of the battlefield, but you can't take the training out of the soldier?"

He didn't smile at her subtle joke like she'd hoped he would. "I'm just saying you've got a lot of your dad in you."

"I've never denied that, but I'm not a carbon copy of him."

His jaw set grimly. "We can't always control how much of our parents we have in us."

"Here." Claire laid a tinfoil-wrapped loaf of garlic bread on the counter, breaking Josie's eye contact with Daniel. "I've spread the butter, but I won't take responsibility for baking it."

Josie forced the expected laugh, moving so Claire could get by and put the butter back in the fridge. Her movement put her body into contact with Daniel, and he quickly stepped away, going into the living room without another word. She watched him go, feeling rejected.

Unwilling to focus on Daniel's confusing behavior when it just led her thoughts into a useless circle, Josie turned to Claire. "Even you can't get sidetracked and let the bread burn by a computer that isn't here."

Claire's smile faltered, and she sighed. "And isn't likely to be for a while either."

"Of course it will. My homeowners' insurance covers theft. I'll lend you the money to buy your new laptop until the claim is settled."

"You really don't think we'll get our things back?"

Josie sighed. "No. I don't. Even when we find the culprits, unless they're idiots or incredibly cocky, they'll have destroyed the evidence of the break-in rather than be caught with it."

Claire didn't reply, but closed the fridge and scooted around Josie to get out plates for the table.

"Set a place for Hotwire. I'm sure he'll be here in time for dinner."

"All right."

The front door slammed, and Josie's and Claire's eyes met.

"What's the matter with Nitro?" Claire asked.

"I wish I knew." She hoped it wasn't that he was preparing to end their newfound intimacy.

She didn't know what she would do if he expected her to go back to noncontact friendship. Act like the succubus he'd once called her and climb into his bed in the middle of the night with the intent to seduce probably. Wanting him and believing he did not want her but not really knowing what it would mean to have him had been almost bearable.

Wanting him but knowing the addictive and intense emotions she could feel when they were connected physically would be impossible for her to stand. Her sanity would never last staying in the same house with him but not touching.

Not after he'd shown her a kind of pleasure she hadn't even dreamed about, not to mention a closeness she had never known could exist between two people. When he touched her, they connected on a level far beyond the mere physical.

Didn't he feel it, too?

The doorbell rang as Josie was pulling her lasagna from the oven.

"I'll get it," Claire called from the living room.

Daniel would have told her to wait for him if he didn't know, with a certainty he could not have explained to someone else, who was on the other side of the door.

"It's your friend, Hotwire." Claire's voice had an odd quality Daniel was in no mood to wonder about at the moment.

He was too busy watching with grim acceptance as Josie quickly set the hot dish down on the counter and ran into the living room to greet the other man. Daniel followed her, arriving in time to see Hotwire wrap Josie up in a hug that required full-body contact.

It lasted several seconds, every one over the first unnecessary excess in Daniel's opinion.

Claire stood shyly to one side, and Daniel noticed right away that Hotwire didn't hug *her*.

"Thank you so much for coming." Josie smiled up at the blond man as if he'd found the cure for cancer or something.

"It's no trouble. You're a friend, Josie." He turned to Daniel. "Hey, Nitro. I tried to call you last night and early this morning on your cell phone, but I got voice mail. You didn't call back."

Daniel hadn't known his cell phone had almost no signal in the hotel room, so he hadn't heard it ring. He'd been relieved when he'd listened to the messages after realizing he'd missed two calls because they'd both been from Hotwire. His friend had only wanted to give an ETA for his arrival at PDX and to say he'd had no luck looking for Josie's dad via the Internet yet.

"I didn't check until early this afternoon." When he'd first become aware he'd missed the calls. "By then you were airborne."

"Why's that, I wonder?" Hotwire asked, his blue eyes too damn knowing.

"We had a break-in here last night. The whole day has just been crazy," Josie said, probably thinking she was explaining Daniel's uncharacteristic behavior.

Hotwire knew better, and his shrewd gaze met Daniel's. "I was real surprised you didn't answer last night. You usually sleep with your cell phone beside your bed. And there was no answer when I called Josie's phone either."

She sighed. "My cell phone was lost in the fire."

"I called here. Didn't any of you hear the phone ring?"

"I was working," Claire replied, her vague expression giving nothing away of Daniel and Josie's movements.

She was a discreet roommate, the best kind if you had to have one.

Josie turned an interesting shade of pink, and he waited to see if she would tell Hotwire the truth, but her lips stayed sealed while her moss green eyes assaulted him with mute appeal. Did she want him to explain, or to lie?

He'd never lied to either Wolf or Hotwire, and he wasn't going to start now. He put his arm around her waist in an unmistakable gesture of possession. "Josie and I weren't here last night."

She didn't pull away, but her body was tenser than that of a member of the NRA at an antiwar rally.

"Where were you?" Hotwire drawled, seemingly endlessly amused by the situation, if the twinkle in his pale eyes was anything to go by.

"We stayed at a hotel."

"For security reasons?"

"N—"

"Are you hungry?" Josie slotted in before Daniel could even get the word out. "Dinner's ready."

She stepped away from him and headed into the kitchen. "You know where everything is, Hotwire. Why don't you get freshened up while I put the food on the table?"

Josie had known as soon as she stepped away from Daniel that it had been the wrong thing to do. His expression had turned to stone, and he'd been more withdrawn than ever over dinner.

He hadn't even sat beside her at the table. There were six places at the table, and Claire had left one end and the chair to its right unset. Daniel had chosen to sit on the other side of Claire, leaving the chair to Josie's left for Hotwire.

He'd allowed the conversation to flow around him without making much contribution, leaving it to Claire and Josie to tell Hotwire about the break-in and their belief it had been the work of her father's would-be killers. Every time she tried to draw Daniel into the discussion, he answered monosyllabically, which was not out of the ordinary for him, but frustrated her nonetheless. She could just feel him smoldering, even if nothing showed on his face.

"You have no idea where your father is?" Hotwire asked her as he pushed his plate aside.

She directed her thoughts away from her lover and back to the discussion at hand.

"No." She stood up and started clearing the table so she could serve dessert. "I'm going to finish reading the journals just in case I'm missing something, though."

"We can start going through the computer files tonight."

She smiled at him, relieved they had a direction to go for their investigation. "That would be great."

She hated feeling helpless, and knowing her dad was somewhere out there, maybe even not remembering why he'd left the hospital, filled her with fear.

Daniel had risen when she did and silently began stacking plates. He put them in the dishwasher while she dished up four bowls of French vanilla ice cream and poured a berry compote she'd made earlier over them. Despite the smallness of her kitchen, she and Daniel did not bump once.

"Can I help with your investigation in any way?" Claire asked as Josie and Daniel each brought two bowls to the table and sat down.

"I'd love your help, but I don't want you missing classes on my account." Josie sighed, remorse eating at her insides. "I feel guilty enough that you lost so much just by having the bad luck to be my roommate."

"Don't say that," Claire replied, her eyes and voice filled with distress. "None of this is your fault."

"If I'd kept a better eye on Dad, he could help us identify his attackers a lot more easily and might even have known they'd want the computer files, too. We could have been here waiting for the thieves."

Hotwire reached out and squeezed her hand. "Not even you could keep your dad from bolting if that was what he wanted to do. He's too good a soldier, and if you'd been here, the perps wouldn't have tried last night, and you wouldn't be sure today that the bombing was linked to the school's files."

"Thanks." But she still felt badly.

She couldn't help it. Her dad was at risk, and she felt as though she'd let him down in some way.

"After what happened last night, I'd prefer to bunk on your floor out here rather than hit a hotel." Hotwire had already brought in his duffel bag.

Daniel could have told Josie she'd lost the argument before it began, but he let her go through the spiel about how Hotwire would be more comfortable in a bed and there was no need for him to stay at the house.

He gave Daniel a meaningful glance. "If Nitro can survive sleeping on the floor, so can I."

After the way Josie had acted earlier, Daniel figured that was exactly where he was going to end up sleeping. He didn't know if she was regretting giving herself to him, but she sure as hell didn't want Hotwire to know about it. As much as her denial of him irked Daniel, a woman had a right to choose who she took into her bed.

If she didn't want him there after last night, he didn't figure any male posturing on his part was going to accomplish anything more than embarrassing her and increasing his own temper. He had no intention of risking either outcome, so he remained silent.

"Daniel isn't sleeping on the floor." Josie bit her lip and then looked up at him. "At least I don't think he is."

Stunned by her *volte-face* from earlier, he tried to figure out if she was saying what he thought she was saying before he responded.

"Where's he sleeping?" Hotwire asked, his Georgia drawl

pronounced. "He's not kicking you out of your bed, is he, Josie?"

She swallowed and shook her head, her gaze not leaving Daniel. "No. He's sleeping with me."

Looking vulnerable and uncertain, her eyes asked him if she'd spoken the truth.

He reached out and cupped her nape, pulling her into him like he'd done earlier, but this time she relaxed against his side. She smiled up at him, her expression filled with relief, and he wondered if he would ever understand how the female mind worked.

He caressed her neck with his thumb. "Hotwire's not sharing our bed. It isn't big enough."

"I wasn't suggesting he should, but there's no reason for him to stay here when it means sleeping on the floor."

"I'm a lot shorter than you," Claire said from the hallway, looking at Hotwire. "I'll sleep on the couch, and you can have my bed. It's only a single, but it's longer than the sofa."

"My mama would string me up by my toes if I booted a lady out of her bed for my own comfort."

"But—"

"He's slept in much worse places, Claire. Don't worry about him." He looked down at Josie. "And don't try convincing him to leave. He's about as stubborn as a Missouri mule."

"So have I," Claire said earnestly. "I mean, slept in worse places. Really, sleeping out here would be no problem."

But just like Daniel had known he would, his friend refused to be budged, and after they did an external reconnaissance of the property and surrounding area, Hotwire got comfortable in a sleeping bag on the floor.

Josie's bedroom door opened, and a tattoo of anticipation started playing in her chest. She hadn't been entirely certain he would come, even after what he'd said. She'd hurt him when she hadn't openly acknowledged the closeness in their relationship, and she'd realized it too late to change any-thing.

She wasn't used to this kind of thing, and Daniel's blatant possessiveness in front of their friend had thrown her thoughts and reactions into a confusing morass before she'd finally got-ten herself straightened out sometime during dinner. She wanted to be his lover for as long as possible, and if that meant other people knowing about them, then she'd take out an ad in the *Oregonian*.

He came into the room, shutting the door behind him, and leaned back against it, looking dark and dangerous. "Do you want Hotwire?"

If he'd thought about it for an hour, he couldn't have found a more shocking question to ask her. Stunned into silence, she opened her lips, but couldn't make her mouth form an answer.

Finally, she asked, "What?" wondering if she'd misheard him. Hoping she had.

He stalked over to the bed, his expression giving no clue as to what was going on inside his head. *"Do you want him?"*

"No. How can you of all people ask me that?"

"You hugged him."

What was he talking about? "When?"

"When he got here."

"He's my friend. I was saying hi."

"You smiled like you were really glad to see him."

"I was."

Daniel's glare could have melted metal.

"Why is that a problem? You invited him here."

"I did not. He said he wanted to help, and I told him he could."

"What difference does it make?" This conversation was not how she'd anticipated spending their time alone together. "He's our friend. He's got skills neither of us has, and he wants to help. That's a good thing."

"You weren't glad to see me. When I told you I was going to help you, you argued with me, but as soon as you found out Hotwire wanted to take part in the mission, you got all happy."

And that really bothered Daniel, she realized belatedly. "You've been weird all day, ever since you told us Hotwire was coming. *Are you jealous?*"

As unlikely as she found the prospect, she couldn't think of another reason for Daniel's attitude.

"Do I have a reason to be?" he asked rather than denying it.

"You must know you don't." She'd been a virgin, for crying out loud. He had to realize she wanted him in a way she'd never wanted another man.

"All I know is you're glad to have him around, but you tried to get me to go away."

"It's different with him; it always has been." She'd never felt like all the oxygen had been sucked out of the room when Hotwire walked into it.

Daniel, on the other hand, had the impact of a fully armed tank engaged in battle on every one of her senses.

"Apparently."

"Daniel, until yesterday, I thought you didn't like me," she said with exasperation. "Hotwire's been my friend since the first mission we had together."

"I didn't dislike you dam—darn it. I wanted you, and I thought you didn't want me. My disposition suffered because of it, but I liked you—more than I wanted to."

"I know that now." Well, she'd known he wanted her, but she hadn't realized he really liked her. It was a nice thing to know about a man she planned to take into her body as soon as this strange discussion was over. "But before, I thought you couldn't stand the sight of me. You've got to see the difference between that and how it was with Hotwire. He didn't . . . I mean, doesn't threaten me."

Daniel swelled with outrage. "I've never threatened you."

"Not overtly, but the feelings I have for you threaten my peace of mind and my equilibrium. Thinking you didn't like me made it almost unbearable to be around you. You should understand that. You basically felt the same way about me because you thought I didn't want you. Our mutual discomfort just showed itself in different ways."

As she said the words, she realized how true they were, and a lot of the insecurity she felt about Daniel and his reactions to her dissipated.

However, he didn't reply, or get into the bed, or do anything to relieve the tension arcing between them.

She tossed around in her mind for something else to say, something that would decrease his insecurity like hers had just been. "Will it help if I promise to hug you every time I see you after an absence, too?"

"I'm your lover. Hotwire is only your friend. I want more than a hug."

"I'll kiss you, too, okay?"

"It's going to be distracting, but okay."

Were men always this illogical about relationships? "If you don't want to be distracted, all you have to do is say so," she replied, aggravated.

"I didn't say that." Then he short-circuited her ability to respond by peeling off his shirt and unbuttoning his pants. "I like being distracted by you."

"I'm glad." She was also glad they were done with a conversation she found nonsensical at best and totally incomprehensible at worst.

He unzipped his pants, revealing a bulge that showed their talking hadn't inhibited his sex drive at all. His almost black eyes spoke messages her inner woman could not misinterpret or ignore. "I'm sorry we couldn't stay at the hotel longer."

Her thighs clenched, and she let her gaze slide from him to her once unadorned bedroom. "I don't know. The ambiance in here is pretty nice."

He'd brought the flowers from the hotel back with them. At some point that day, he'd taken the time to put all of them but a bouquet he left on the dining room table in her bedroom. The roses had transformed her bare sleeping quarters into a secret garden. "Thank you for bringing the flowers."

He shrugged. "It seemed a shame to waste them."

"Yes." But she would have been too self-conscious to ask to keep them. Sentimentality had little place in the life of a soldier, and old habits were hard to break.

Daniel pushed his pants down his hips, along with his jockey shorts, and her thought process scrambled again. Smooth, dark skin over well-honed muscles made her breath catch in her throat, but even his magnificent physique was overshadowed by the sheer presence and male beauty of the hard flesh jutting out from his body.

"You're gorgeous."

"That's my line."

Her eyes reluctantly traveled up his body to his face at the humor in his voice. Despite the smile lingering at the edges of his lips, his look seared her.

She opened her mouth to speak, and nothing came out. She swallowed and tried again. "It's not a line."

"No. It's not." He stood, proud and unembarrassed by his nakedness. "Invite me into your bed, Josette."

"I thought I did that earlier," she said, her voice hoarse with the effect his nakedness was having on her.

He didn't reply, but stood there waiting in silence.

Apparently he wanted something more than tacit agreement, or a statement of intent. "Is an invitation so important?"

"Yes. This is your bed. Accepting my presence is not the same as welcoming it."

She wanted to know why the distinction was so important to him, but was not prepared to have another drawn-out discussion. She would ask him later.

Flipping back the covers, she revealed the almost there, sheer pink panties and short stretchy tank top she'd put on for bed. She didn't own sexy nightwear, other than the gown he had given her, but had started buying more feminine underwear some time ago . . . right about the time she met Daniel.

His dark brown gaze showed no disappointment in her lack of a proper negligee.

"Come to my bed, Daniel. I want you."

His nostrils flared, his jaw locking into granitelike firmness, and he came over her in a silent rush that left her tumbled back against the pillows.

"Do you want to feed your obsession some more?" she asked breathlessly.

He shook his head as though her words bothered him. "I want to make love with a very sexy woman, with *my woman.*"

She cupped his face and drew his head down until their lips were almost touching. "Make love with me, Daniel. Make me feel like a sexy woman, like your woman."

He made her feel like living fire. Taking what little clothes she wore off of her with a lot more urgency than he had shed his, his mouth devoured what his hands had uncovered, sending flames licking through her feminine core. As she arched under his lips and exploring hands, desire to consume him with the same blazing inferno inside her pierced her being.

She wanted him to feel everything she was experiencing, *everything!* The fundamental desire to be with a man created to be the other half of her. The agonizing emotion she had never expected to experience. The clawing need for completion that came from the sharing of spirit as well as flesh.

She needed him to feel it all.

Flipping out from under him, she pushed him onto his back, and he let her, his eyes black with need she would never again mistake for anger. She straddled him, shuddering when her labia kissed his erection. It was so profoundly intimate, she wanted to engrave the sensation on her mind for all of eternity.

His big body went rigid, and she smiled, loving this evidence of her effect on him. Licking her lips in needy anticipation, she gave in to the uncontrollable desire to lift her pelvis slightly, only to come back down and kiss his hard sex again with her highly lubricated flesh.

"Don't do that," he said harshly.

"What? This . . ." And she moved her pelvis once more.

He groaned and arched up to meet her hungry femininity. "Don't lick your lips."

Didn't he know that after saying that, she had no choice but to do it again?

"Why not?" she asked before slowly running her tongue along first her upper and then lower lip.

He watched her as if his gaze were welded to her mouth. "It makes me crazy."

She rocked so her swelling flesh caressed the entire length of his velvety hardness. "I like making you crazy." Then she bent forward and kissed him all over his smooth, rock-hard chest, nipping him below one nipple with her teeth.

"*Josette.*"

"I have absolutely no desire to do this to Hotwire."

"Good," he growled.

"This either." And she circled his nipple with her tongue until it was as hard as the rest of him and then sucked on it while he pulled in air like a man put on oxygen to survive.

After several seconds of the sensual torment, he grabbed her head and tugged her face up to his. She kissed him with hot, open-mouthed intensity that he returned with aggressive passion. His hands moved down her spine and over her backside until one finger slipped into the intimate crevice at the apex of her thighs.

She wriggled against the teasing finger, aching already for a more solid possession.

Moaning, she rubbed her clitoris against his sex in an effort to assuage the growing ache in her lower body. It wasn't enough, but heat pooled in her womb while her inner muscles clenched, telling her climax was imminent. She wasn't ready for the intimacy and touching to end. She wanted to come with him fully imbedded inside her, their flesh joined as deeply as possible. Only, she couldn't stop her body's movement, and she moved closer and closer to losing all control.

Whimpering, she tilted her pelvis and lifted her hips without thought until his hardness was poised at the entrance to where she most wanted him to be. Fingers like vises locked around her waist and stopped her from taking him fully inside.

Chapter 11

Her mouth broke from his, a protesting moan of anguish erupting from the very heart of her.

"Not yet, sweetheart."

She looked down at him, her vision blurred by passion, but even so, she could see the harsh cast to his features so at odds with the tenderness in his voice.

"Why not?"

He grabbed something from under the pillow, keeping her still with his other hand as she tried to move downward again. When she saw what he was holding, frustration for the need to delay roared through her.

"I'm going on the pill," she muttered from between gritted teeth.

His slashing smile touched her like a caress. "Fine, but tonight, we don't have any choice."

And no way did he want her getting pregnant. She scooted backward, making room for him to don the condom, but chilled by the reality of what it symbolized. The transitory nature of their relationship and Daniel's absolute certainty he did not want a child with her.

Of course safe sex wasn't all about pregnancy, but she knew deep in her soul that Daniel would never have made love with her if he was putting her at risk. Since she'd never been with anyone else, he couldn't be worried about what she might expose him to either. This was about keeping the intimacy between them physical and allowing no consequences to come from it.

No result but a heart she already felt cracking under the knowledge he would walk out of her life the same way he had walked into it. Alone.

Daniel held the dark blue foil packet up. "Do you want to put it on?"

Without meaning to, she physically recoiled from the question, her thoughts too close to the surface to ignore.

His brows drew together. "Josie, is something wrong?"

Did she really want to ruin what time she did have with him, entertaining ultradepressing musings about how much it was going to hurt when their relationship ended? No, of course not. That would be stupid.

And she wasn't dumb.

"Nothing's wrong," she said with what she hoped was reassuring brightness, and then she winked at him. "But I don't think it will fit."

His eyes narrowed and then glittered in understanding, and that incredible smile flashed again. "I didn't mean on you, little warrior."

She eyed his erection with blatant skepticism. "I didn't either."

He stared at her and then burst out laughing. She grinned in response and then remembering how successful the ploy had been in the park, tickled him. She loved the joyous sound coming from him. It made her feel special, because she knew that he hardly ever gave in to it with other people.

As it was, he laughed so hard she fell off of him. It took several seconds longer to get the condom on him than it should have, but by the time they did, they were both ready to finish what they'd started.

He flipped her onto her stomach, and she twisted to look at him. "I don't want a massage; I want you inside me."

"I will be."

He pulled her hips up and slid a pillow under them, making her realize he meant to enter her from the back. She shivered nervously as his fingers separated her slick folds. This was new and for some reason felt very different, as though she was more vulnerable to him than when they made love in other positions.

"Don't worry, you're going to like this," he whispered in her ear as he pressed into her from behind.

As he deepened his possession, she felt amazing inner sensations she hadn't experienced the night before. He touched a nerve center inside her that made her grind her bottom against him.

"It's so good," she moaned out, needing to give vent to the feelings of sweet torment.

"Oh, yeah . . ." He thrust deeply into her, and she realized he was nowhere near all the way inside.

By the time Daniel's pelvis was rubbing against her bottom, Josie was writhing under him like a woman possessed.

He kissed the back of her neck, her temple, her cheek. She felt completely surrounded by him, cherished and cocooned in his ardor. She turned her face toward him, and their lips met briefly, but she couldn't stay that way long. She didn't have the strength or muscle control . . . Pleasure had drained her, and she hadn't even climaxed yet.

Her head fell forward against her hands, and she gasped as each thrust caressed the nerve center deep inside her from an unfamiliar angle. Her body tensed until every muscle was taut, but she didn't go over the edge. Instead the feeling of an impending cataclysm subsided, and her muscles went involuntarily slack. The same sequence happened twice more, taking her to a peak that turned out to be a plateau. She was nearly sobbing with frustration as her body tautened once again, the feeling more intense than any of the times before.

"*Daniel,*" she cried out.

"What's the matter, baby?"

"I'm so close!"

"Yes." He thrust inside her, pulling her hips up toward him, and she thought she would die from the pleasure he gave her.

If she didn't implode first.

He kept thrusting, his hard penis caressing her insides intimately and with purpose, but the spring inside her only grew tighter and tighter.

"I want to come," she moaned against the bed, her hair wet with perspiration and her back slick with it.

"Okay, sweetheart."

What did he mean, *okay*? Did he think just by saying it, she would climax?

He slid his hand under her and cupped her mound—a statement of possession, but also an incredible source of delight. She pressed against his hand, instinctively seeking more. He slipped his forefinger and middle finger between her slick folds. Catching her clitoris between them, he rubbed up and down, squeezing his fingers together to increase the pressure and sensation on her sweetest spot.

She splintered apart, her sense of reality shattering as her entire body convulsed with unbelievable bliss. Grinding her bottom against him, she sought deeper penetration until no rational thought remained while wave after wave of sensation crashed through her.

Daniel rammed into her from behind, driving for fulfillment and holding her hips up when she would have collapsed onto the bed. Suddenly, he buried his face in a pillow she'd shoved to the side earlier, his body going taut, his hips forcefully pressed into hers.

The pillow muffled his hoarse shout of satisfaction, but she reveled in his uncontrolled reaction to her. He was rigid with orgasm for the longest time, his sex, big and oh so hard, inside her as he erupted in a series of convulsions that left them both limp and spent.

She was barely aware of him climbing off of her and leaving the bed and only registered in the periphery of her mind when he came back and pulled her into his arms for sleep.

Curled up on one end of the couch, Josie absently drank her coffee while reading one of her dad's journals. He had some odd thoughts, that was for sure, but everything he wrote made sense if you looked at life from the perspective of a man who had seen too much brutality to trust in the goodness of human nature.

She felt uncomfortable at times reading his most personal thoughts because his emotions ran more deeply than she had ever thought they did. But he'd been the one to tell her to read the journals in the first place. Well, he'd said journal in the singular, but how was she to know which one had the information he wanted her to glean out of his writings?

"Josie . . ."

She looked up to find Claire standing over her, dressed for exercise in a pair of Lycra shorts and an oversized T-shirt that had been washed so many times the athletic logo on the front was barely discernable. However, her running shoes were one of the best brands on the market and almost new.

"Going jogging?"

"Uh-huh." She pulled her hair up into a scrunchy, taming the wild curls in a slightly less wild ponytail. "I thought I'd ask if you wanted to come, but you look pretty engrossed. And come to think of it, Nitro would probably have a male mercenary's version of a hissy fit if you tried to go outside without him anyway."

Josie had to agree. "It's weird. I mean, he knows I can take care of myself, but he still acts like a mother hen about some stuff."

Claire smiled, tightening her ponytail. "Don't knock it. It's pretty great to have someone watching out for you."

"Even if it's a little confining?"

"So's a seat belt, but given the option of going through life without one, I'd vote for safety first."

Josie laughed, shaking her head at Claire's analogy. "I won't tell Daniel you think he's an oversized seat belt. I don't think he'd understand."

Claire's smile was rueful. "I appreciate that. Nitro is not a man I'd be comfortable offending."

"I'd say he's a pussycat under all that male bravado, but I'd be lying." The iron in Daniel's character ran bone deep, as if it had been forged early and tempered by life since.

"No kidding. Better you than me, is all I've got to say. Not only is the man as immovable as a stone wall, but he's got a possessive streak a mile wide, too. He looked ready to kill somebody every time you smiled at Hotwire last night."

"It wasn't that bad."

"Says you, but then you were busy looking at Hotwire and not your boyfriend."

"I wasn't flirting or anything." Even if she'd wanted to, which she hadn't, she didn't know how.

Claire headed for the door, talking over her shoulder as she went. "You're not the type to make eyes at one guy while being intimate with another, and Nitro will figure that out. Eventually. Until then, you might consider smiling less at Hotwire."

Claire might have a point. Daniel had reacted with unexpected insecurity toward Josie's friendship with Hotwire. It was probably one of those guy things she didn't get. She might have spent most of her life surrounded by men, but she didn't pretend to understand how they related to the women in their lives. It hadn't been part of their soldier training, and her father had never had a girlfriend around.

She didn't know how long she had been reading when the sound of slamming car doors caught her attention. Her mind more on what she'd been reading than what she was seeing, she looked out through the sheers covering the big picture window in her living room. It took a second for her unfocused brain to interpret what her eyes were telling her.

A news van and two cars were parked in front of her house. A woman had gotten out of the van, and the driver came around to open the back panel doors. The occupants of the cars got out, too. A couple of them had cameras. One was carrying a tape recorder with a microphone.

She scanned the scene, trying to make sense of it, and saw Claire approaching at a sprint, running in a direct line to the house across the grass. She didn't slow as she crossed the street either. One of the men from the cars tried to stop her, but she brushed him aside and ran straight to the door. Josie rushed to open it and let her in.

"Claire?"

"There are more of them." She bent over and panted, her hands on her thighs. "I was across the park, and I saw two more news vans headed this way." She sucked in air and tried to catch her breath. "I was listening to the radio while I was running. It's all over the news."

"What's all over the news?"

"The explosion at your dad's compound."

"For heaven's sake, why?"

"They're saying it was done by ecoterrorists. The FBI is involved as well as the State Police and National Forest Service." She straightened, still breathing hard, which showed how fast she'd been running because Claire was in good shape. "It's that Homeland Security Act thing. All the federal agencies are in an uproar, and the media is already speculating on who might be responsible for the destruction of the compound."

The doorbell rang. Josie and Claire both turned to stare at the door as if it would spontaneously combust any second.

"Ms. McCall? This is Alison Spencer from KYTO News. I'd like you to answer a few questions."

Claire sprang forward and pushed the door lock, then twisted the deadbolt into place with an audible click.

Someone started pounding on the window. Josie couldn't believe it, but several reporters were trying to peer in through the sheers, and one had a camera up to the window. The utter audacity of the action astounded her. The doorbell rang again, and Josie gave up shock for anger.

She headed to the door, ready to blast the reporters and throw a few people off of her property, when her tank top was grabbed from behind. She was pulled up like a dog on a short leash.

"Hold on, sweetheart."

Someone knocked on the door while the doorbell rang again.

She glared over her shoulder at Daniel. "Let me go. I'm going to tell them to get lost."

"You're not opening that door." His voice held the implacability of command.

He was not the officer in charge on this mission, and she was more than ready to set him straight. "I'm not?" she asked with interest and no small amount of fury.

"No."

"We don't know who all is out that door," Hotwire drawled in a more placating tone, but with no less firmness.

She turned her defiant stare on him. "A bunch of reporters who have no respect for my privacy, that's who."

"Maybe, and maybe one or two of them are involved with the guys who blew up your dad's compound."

Daniel hadn't let go of her shirt yet and actually started reeling her in. "Opening the door and letting you stomp outside in a rage is too risky." He pulled her around to face him. "We don't know if the enemy wants to get rid of you and whatever you might know permanently."

"Like they tried to with Dad?" she sneered. "We McCalls aren't that easy to kill."

His mouth quirked as if he enjoyed her feistiness. "I'm glad, Josette, but I'm not letting you risk it."

"*Letting?* You're not going to *let* me go outside? You're not going to *let* me risk it?" she asked, transferring her outrage at the rudeness of the reporters to his autocratic behavior. "Who signed the order papers to make you Major General?"

"Josie, he's right," Claire said for the second time in two days, earning a frown from Josie. "Even if ecoterrorists weren't involved, you can bet they'll be trying to get some media coverage out of this. You don't want to become one of their targets either. I read this article on the Internet and—"

"Ms. McCall, we know you're in there. You owe it to the public to answer a few questions," a strident voice shouted from outside, interrupting Claire midspate.

"Ms. McCall, can you confirm your father received threats from the Earth Liberation Front before his death?"

She felt the color leach from her face as an appalling thought assailed her. What if *they* had been looking at this whole thing from the wrong angle—she, Daniel, Hotwire and Claire? What if ecoterrorists *were* angry about her father's school in the middle of national forest lands, angry enough to do something about its existence?

They'd considered and dismissed the possibility the attack had been spurred by antiwar activists, but had not even given first thought to it being ELF sympathizers.

Privately held property was always at risk, and her dad had been forced to clear old growth timber to establish the compound before the timber controversy had become such a big deal. Only that had been so long ago.

"Josette, if it were ecoterrorists, why break in to your house and steal the school's records? It's possible the real culprits tipped off the press to throw up a smokescreen, but my gut tells me that the people trying to kill your dad aren't doing it because of his views on the environment."

She looked up at Daniel, feeling disoriented by how closely his thoughts ran parallel to hers. "Are you reading my mind?"

"Maybe I just know how you think." He massaged her shoulders, his eyes warm on her in a way that made her feel very special.

Which did not mean she was going to let him give her commands like a raw recruit, but it was possible he'd been right about not going outside just yet.

"It takes a soldier to know a soldier," Hotwire said, his voice laced with amusement.

"That's all well and good, but what are we going to do about the zoo in our front yard?" Claire asked acerbically.

Josie's mouth set with resolve. "We can call the police."

"Do you think that will do any good?" Claire asked. "There's the whole freedom of the press issue."

"It will get them out of my yard. If they want to stand yelling on the sidewalk, that's their business, but I don't have to listen to it through my front door."

Daniel leaned down and kissed her right on the lips, shocking her thoughts right out of her head. "Don't do anything yet. Let me and Hotwire go around from the back and scope out the scene. I want to see if any of the reporters are acting like maybe they aren't reporters."

"How would you tell?" Claire asked while Josie's brain was still adjusting to Daniel's public display of affection.

Daniel turned to her. "They messed up breaking in here by not taking the CDs and DVDs. Unless they make better reporters than fake thieves, they'll give themselves away somehow."

"I should go out, too," Josie said as her thoughts started stringing together in coherent patterns again. "I might recognize someone."

"No," Daniel said.

"It's too risky," added Hotwire.

"I don't intend to let anyone see me."

"Do you really want Claire left in here alone while we all go outside to recon?"

"Hotwire can stay inside."

"She's got a point, Nitro," Hotwire said. "If she stays out of sight, it wouldn't be a bad idea to find out if she recognizes any of the gaggle outside."

"I don't need a baby-sitter," Claire said, sounding as irritated as Josie by being managed.

Hotwire smiled charmingly. "Even if you weren't in here, someone would have to stay to make sure none of the reporters gained entry."

"I can handle that."

Hotwire's smile disappeared. "Not if the person gaining entry isn't really a reporter."

"He's right," Josie said, taking petty satisfaction in throwing the words back at her friend and then feeling instant remorse. "I mean—"

Claire's eyes filled with understanding humor. "Don't worry about it. I know what you mean, and you're *both* right." Then she sighed, looking out the window, and bit her lip, her expression turning worried. "I've got class in an hour and a half."

"I'll take you," Hotwire offered, "and I won't let any of that mob get at you on the way to the car."

Claire nodded, her curly ponytail bouncing and her relief palpable. "Thank you, that would be great." She turned to Josie. "If you don't need me to hold the fort, I think I'll take a shower and get ready for class."

Josie and Daniel's recon netted exactly nothing, and no adventurous reporter tried breaking in while they were outside. Which didn't mean they wouldn't make the attempt later, Daniel pointed out, taking the opportunity also to comment again that if Josie had a decent security system, there would be nothing to worry about.

She ignored the barb and made the call to the local police, who told her they could come by and get the reporters out of her yard, but there was no way of guaranteeing they would stay out once the officers left again. She got off the phone feeling frustrated, not only by that, but also the realization that Claire still didn't have a computer for her class work and her first class that day was an on-line lab.

Josie would be missing classes today, but there was nothing she could do about that. She had meant to do something about her roommate's lack of a computer first thing that morning, but had gotten caught up reading her dad's journals.

"Darn it."

Daniel watched as Josie's hands curled into fists at her sides and her pixie face creased with a fierce frown.

She'd made her phone call while looking out the window at the steadily increasing melee in her front yard. Eventually, the reporters would have to leave—out of boredom or the need to cover another story—but he was pretty sure they'd come back and keep hounding Josie. He didn't like it.

Maybe they needed to consider changing locations.

"Did the cops refuse to come out?" he asked.

"No. They'll come, but they said they can't promise any lasting results." She sounded resigned, which did not explain her tension. Sitting on the arm of the couch beside him, she ran her fingers through her chin-length brown hair. "Claire doesn't have a computer, and she needs one. Badly. I meant to take care of it this morning. She hasn't said anything, but she's got an on-line lab first thing."

"I brought two laptops with me," Hotwire said from his position by the window, as if it was the most natural thing in the world to travel with two computers when Daniel could never remember traveling with even one. "I'll give her one of them. They're both fully loaded with killer speed CPUs. They've even got GPS devices on them, not that yours did you any good."

"You mean the one in my car?" Josie asked. "It worked just fine before my car was destroyed by an arsonist's fire." The grim set to her mouth left Daniel with no doubt what she felt about losing her little car in the blast.

But Hotwire shook his head. "The one in your laptop."

"What are you talking about? I didn't use my laptop for GPS. Even if I hadn't had a unit in my car, that would have been too inconvenient while driving."

Hotwire came away from the window, his expression alert. "I meant the GPS unit inside your laptop. The one used to track its location if the computer gets stolen."

"Her laptop had a GPS?" Daniel asked. Then, "And why do *you* know about it, but she doesn't?"

"Hotwire helped me pick out my computer when I started taking classes at PSU."

"And the one we picked out had a GPS unit."

Josie twisted her body so she could look squarely at Hotwire. "I can't believe I didn't remember that. I'm not even sure I ever knew it, and I should have. It was my computer, for crying out loud."

"Like you're going to read the computer manual after you buy." Even he didn't do that, and Daniel was a lot less proficient with computers than Hotwire and Josie.

"Yes, but—"

"Are you saying we can track Josie's computer?" Daniel asked his friend, cutting in on her self-recriminations.

"If the GPS unit hasn't been destroyed, yes." Hotwire smiled then, his eyes cold with purpose. "If Josie didn't realize it was there, I doubt the thieves have either. It's a relatively new safety feature in mobile computer technology."

"So, how do we track it?"

"We call the manufacturer and report it as stolen. They do a satellite search which will result in a three-point coordinate location."

A three-point coordinate was pretty damn precise. "How long will it take?" Daniel asked.

"A few minutes."

"How accurate?"

"Within ten feet."

"It sounds too easy."

"It is." This from Josie. "The position can be as accurate as we want it to be, but there's no guarantee the laptop won't be moved before we can get to it."

"And if the location isn't at a known address, like out in the middle of the desert or something," Hotwire added, "we still have to track it."

Which was exactly what ended up being the case, although it couldn't be as easy as being in the middle of the desert and easily accessible by helicopter or plane. According to its GPS, the laptop was currently in an uninhabited area of the Rocky Mountains with no known public or private roads within fifteen miles of its location.

Before they could discuss what to do with that piece of information, Claire came out of her room, dressed and ready for class. Josie brought her up to speed, and then the phone rang. Looking over her shoulder, Daniel read *Oregon State Police* on the caller identification.

His gut clenched for no discernable reason, and he said, "I think you'd better take that call, sweetheart."

Josie held the ringing cordless unit in her hand, wishing she could just ignore its impatient summons.

How much should she share of what she knew? She didn't know why her father and his school had been targeted for destruction, and bringing in the authorities might harm him more than help him. On the other hand, maybe the authorities had information that would help her and the others find her dad's enemies before they found him.

The phone shrilled again, and she pushed the talk button before lifting it to her ear. "Josie McCall speaking."

"Ms. McCall, this is Detective Johnson with the State Police Arson and Explosives Division. I'm investigating a fire that occurred two nights ago on property owned by Tyler McCall in the Coastal Range. I would like to ask you a few questions, if I may."

"Yes, of course."

"Can you verify your father, Tyler McCall's, whereabouts on the night of July twelfth?"

Having already gone through this with Officer Devon, she

was more prepared to answer that question at least. "My dad was at his paramilitary training compound."

"Are you absolutely certain of that?"

"Yes."

"Did he call you from there, or in some other way confirm his presence on the mountain to you? Perhaps you were there with him at some point?"

"Why are you asking me this?"

"His entire compound burned to the ground, Ms. McCall."

"I'm aware of that."

"I see. Do you mind telling me how you learned of the fire, Ms. McCall?"

"It's hardly a state secret. It's all over the news," she said, hedging around the truth, and then added, "and one of your officers came by to tell me of my father's death yesterday."

"A *state* policeman came by your house to inform you of your father's death?"

"Yes." Surely that wasn't such a surprise, unless the departments didn't speak to each other—which, when she thought about it, wasn't all that farfetched of an idea.

"Do you have the officer's name?"

"Barry Devon."

"Thank you." He paused as if taking the time to write the name down. "Apparently the fire started with an explosion."

"Yes."

"Did the officer tell you that as well?"

"He did." She wondered why the detective was asking her about what his colleague had said. Why not simply ask the other officer? "He also said the Forest Service believed it was an *accidental* explosion. Is that still the case?"

"Can you hold on for a moment, Ms. McCall?"

Chapter 12

"Certainly."

She pressed the mute button on the phone and asked the others, "I'm on hold. How much do you think I should tell him?"

"If you don't tell them you were on the mountain with your dad, you could be charged with obstruction of justice," Claire said.

"Did you read that on the Internet, too?" Josie asked tongue-in-cheek. Her roommate had a brilliant mind filled with bits of knowledge about pretty much everything.

"Nope." She grinned. "I grew up watching Perry Mason."

"Her source might be suspect, but Claire's right," Hotwire said.

"But then I have to tell them Dad isn't dead."

"They're going to figure that out soon regardless, and once they do, it won't take them long to contact the closest emergency rooms and find record of you and your dad's visit, even if you gave an alias."

Hotwire was right. Not many women came into ER with a wounded man and smelling like smoke if they hadn't been in a fire. "Do I tell him about the break-in and the laptop locator?"

"If you do, they can tell you faster than anyone else what

or who might be located in that supposedly uninhabited area."

"If they're as open about sharing information as you're suggesting Josie be," Daniel added, sounding skeptical.

The detective came back on the line. "Ms. McCall?"

"I'm here," she said after turning off the mute function.

Claire waved, getting Josie's attention. "I have to go," she mouthed silently.

Josie nodded, indicating with her hand that Claire and Hotwire should take off.

"Are you positive it was a state policeman who came to speak to you?" the detective asked, bringing her attention back to the phone.

She had to think a second to refocus her train of thought, and even when she did, she couldn't figure out why he was asking her that. "He was wearing a uniform and driving a police cruiser, what else would he be?"

"I can't answer that, Ms. McCall, but he wasn't a state policeman. There is no officer by that name in the force, and no orders were given to inform you of a death we have yet to verify. Someone will be contacting you later for a description of the suspect."

"Suspect?"

"Impersonating an officer of the law is illegal."

"Yes, of course." But why had the man done it? She was fairly certain it was linked with everything else going on, but she couldn't see what the purpose would have been. Then the other half of the detective's comments clicked in her brain. "You don't think my father is dead?"

"There are no bone fragments in the debris."

"And if he had died in the fire, there would be?"

"Yes. It's a myth that everything is destroyed in a fire. There should be some indication of your father's remains in the debris if he were a victim of the explosion." He paused as if waiting for her to say something. When she didn't, he went on. "Either your father woke in time to get himself out or he set the explosion himself."

"Why would he do that?"

"According to our investigation, he does not have a completely stable temperament."

"My father is not crazy."

"Past students say that he subscribes to conspiracy theories."

"That's hardly unique in this country."

The detective actually chuckled. "True, but your father chose to act on his theories, living a lifestyle well outside the norm."

"Different does not equate to crazy, and my father would have no reason to blow up his own school. Training elite soldiers is his life."

"It's an avenue we have to explore, particularly since there is no evidence of his demise in the blast."

"I understand." And she did, but it wasn't a scenario she had anticipated. "Was there anything else, Detective?"

"There were three vehicles found at the sight that were damaged by the blast."

"Yes?"

"One of them was registered to you, Ms. McCall."

"Yes, my car was on the mountain that night."

"I asked you a question earlier that you neatly sidestepped, so I'll ask it again. Were you at your father's compound when the explosion occurred, Ms. McCall?"

"Are you accusing me of setting the blast now?"

"It is my understanding your specialty is explosives, is that right?"

"Yes, but I can assure you that I did not blow up my father's training compound."

Daniel went rigid beside her at her words. She met his eyes, hers asking him what she should say.

"Tell the truth," he mouthed.

She nodded. At this point, it was the only thing that would do.

"Ms. McCall." The detective was talking again. "We have to investigate every possibility when a crime like this is committed."

"So you are positive it was a crime?"

"It's highly likely, yes."

"Besides myself and my father, do you have any other suspects," she asked.

"No."

"What about the media's belief it was an ecoterrorist?"

"We do not know where they got that information, Ms. McCall. While every fire that threatens national forest must be investigated with that possibility in mind, there is no evidence to support that theory at this time."

"So, you've ruled it out?" Someone should have told the reporters milling around on her lawn.

"Not entirely, no."

Well, that was as clear as mud.

"We had hoped you might be able to shed some light on the subject."

"I'll try." And she told him everything that had happened from waking up and taking a walk in the dark, to identifying the whereabouts of her laptop.

She also gave him a detailed description of the phony officer, able to add the number on the patrol car because Daniel remembered it.

She hung up the phone and turned to Daniel. "He'll be here in an hour or so. He wants the backup copy of Dad's files."

"He accused you of setting the bomb?" Daniel asked, his expression unreadable, but his body language all about tightly controlled anger.

"Not exactly. Apparently Dad and I are the number one suspects; at least we were until I told him about the nature of yesterday's break-in and the GPS device on my laptop. He thought the current location was really interesting."

Daniel relaxed slightly. "I do, too." He rubbed his chin with his thumb and forefinger. "So, Officer Devon isn't an officer after all."

"Not according to the records division of the state police."

"He acted like a soldier, but a lot of police officers are former military, so that didn't strike me as anything out of the ordinary. I'd like to know how he got a hold of a state police car."

"So would the state police." She frowned, wishing they had more to go on. The longer her dad was MIA, the more chance something could happen to him. "The phony officer wasn't familiar at all."

Daniel shrugged. "You've spent a lot of time away from your dad's school in recent years. There are probably a lot of people he's come into contact with that you've never seen."

"His records included photos of each student. I scanned them all into the computer. I don't remember anyone looking like Officer Devon."

"You probably weren't paying close attention to them."

"That's true." She hadn't given any of the pictures more than a cursory glance.

"And although we know the school was as much a target as your dad, we can't assume we're looking for a former student."

"Besides instructors, potential and current students are about the only people my dad sees."

"That you know of."

"True. He mentions a lot of Vietnam buddies in his diaries. I don't remember meeting any of them, but apparently they kept in contact."

"That's not unusual."

"No, but a lot of them have died. It must have been hard for him, and he never told me."

"You and your dad are pretty close."

"Not as close as I thought, but our relationship is better than anything most of his buddies had with their families. Several who died didn't have anyone to mourn their passing but my dad. I wish he'd told me. I would have mourned with him."

"He was protecting you from the ugly side of life."

"I guess. Still, it's sad."

Daniel's eyes narrowed in thought. "What exactly did he write about these friends that died?"

"Just their names and where they were from, the fact he went to their funerals. No one could accuse my dad of being a flowery writer."

"Do you remember their names, or would you have to go back through and search for them again?"

She had a semiphotographic memory, which was how she reread books in her mind during a lot of long, dark, and of necessity, silent nights in the jungle or desert as a mercenary. "I remember them, why?"

"It's a lot easier to establish an alternate identity using that of a person who has died, but shares superficial life traits with you."

"You think Dad used the names of his former friends to establish aliases?"

"It makes sense."

She thought about it. "You're right. It does. For whatever reason, he believed he needed a bolt-hole and made sure he had it in the form of several established alternate identities."

"He hinted as much to me once."

"He trusted you a great deal to have done that."

Daniel shrugged. "He didn't tell me names."

"He didn't tell me either. He said it was safer for me that way."

"Was your dad intelligence during the war?"

"No. He was LLRP, but it was enough. A lot of the soldiers that came out of the field had a hard time acclimating to normal life. I've never understood what sparked this particular paranoia, but for the most part, it doesn't impact our relationship, and no way will he ever seek counseling to deal with it."

"It's going to make it dam—uh . . . difficult if not impossible to find him."

"If you're right about how he established his identities, we have a place to start at least." She began walking toward the study. "We can investigate each name for activity since their deaths, things like buying property, establishing residency, that kind of thing."

Daniel didn't say anything, but he followed her into the study.

He indicated a pile of print-out pages beside Hotwire's computer with his hand. "We've been going through the school's files looking for some kind of anomaly, and so far we haven't found one."

"When you don't know what you're looking for, it's almost impossible to find it," she said tongue-in-cheek.

He smiled. "That makes a convoluted kind of sense."

She grinned back. "Yeah, it does."

He sat down in a chair to the right of the computer desk, and she put herself in front of the monitor. She sent several search queries to databases she thought might have the information they were looking for.

When she was done, there was nothing to do but wait, so she said, "While my queries are being processed, why don't we go through the student pictures?"

"Good idea."

She moved her chair sideways a little. "Scoot over here, so you can see, too. We'll have a better chance of recognizing the fake officer if we're both looking."

He moved his chair beside hers, and as always, the closeness of his big body affected her breathing pattern. He laid his arm across the back of her chair, hemming her in, and she had to fight the urge to let her head rest back against him. They had a job to do, and snuggling wasn't it.

It took a few clicks of the mouse to bring up the image files related to her dad's school. She set the entire folder up to run as a slide show. The images began playing on the screen, each lasting three seconds, enough time to study bone structure as well as take in surface features that could change.

She grimaced as the third one flashed onto the screen. "There are a few hundred; this could take a while."

"I don't mind spending time with you." His fingers brushed her neck, and he leaned closer so that her shoulder was against his chest. "You smell good."

"I don't wear perfume."

"I know. I like it."

"The smell of unadorned woman?" she asked jokingly, but warm bubbles of happiness fizzed through her.

"Only one woman. You."

"I like the way you smell, too," she admitted.

"How do I smell?" he asked as another picture flashed briefly on the screen.

"Safe." She didn't know why she said it, but something about the very essence of this man gave her a sense of security in his presence.

It had been that way from the first, which was why she'd been so shocked by his hostile attitude toward her. Her instincts told her one thing while his actions had told her another. Or so she had believed. She now knew what she'd mistaken for dislike and anger had been him trying to rein in a passion that consumed them both completely when he let it go.

Regardless of the reasoning, she'd come to identify his unique scent with both security and sexual desire, not to mention happiness. She was beginning to wonder if that wasn't a pretty good definition of love.

"Safe?" he asked, his voice laced with shock and another emotion she couldn't quite define.

"Yes." She snuck a quick sideways look at him, but his attention was fixed firmly on the slide show. "When I'm with you, I feel as if you will never hurt me or allow anyone else to either. Which, when you think about it, is really funny. I mean, I've been keeping other people safe my entire adult life, and I've never been in a situation where I relied on someone else to fight for me."

He didn't say anything, and she took a deep breath, plunging on with an emotional recklessness she might regret later, but which felt utterly essential right now.

"I guess what I'm trying to say is that I trust you on a level I've never trusted anyone else except my dad, and all of my senses recognize it." It was hard admitting that, but she'd never been one to lie to get out of a tough situation, and his whimsical question had turned out to be just that.

His body shifted away from hers in what felt like a violent repudiation of her words. "I'm no white knight, Josie. Don't weave daydreams around me taking care of you because it's not going to happen."

"I didn't mean it like that." He made her sound like a parasite. "Didn't you hear what I said? I can take care of myself."

"Yes, you can. You don't need me watching over you. Remember that."

It was impossible to keep her focus on the computer screen. She jerked her gaze back to Daniel, who apparently was having no problem continuing to watch the slide show, his face impassive.

"If you are so intent on *not* watching over me, why did you refuse to allow me to go outside this morning? Why insist on helping me find my dad and investigate the bombing?"

His jaw looked hewn from granite. "I already explained that. I'm part of this mission because the school is half mine now and your dad is my business partner. Keeping you from taking unacceptable risks is part of succeeding with the mission."

"So, you're saying that I personally had absolutely no influence over your actions in the past three days?" she asked, unwilling to believe he could be as emotionally distant as he was implying.

"No."

Relief pulsed through her. She and Daniel were simply suffering another miscommunication, something she'd come to believe would always be a challenge for them. Their brains didn't work the same way. His thoughts were as alien to her as if he really were from Mars, like the popular book on male-female relationships said.

"The decision to take you to bed had nothing to do with the mission. It was entirely personal."

"But temporary," she heard herself saying.

"You said that was acceptable to you."

Had she, or had she agreed to the limitations he set for their intimacy because he hadn't given her any other choice? Did it matter? He hadn't changed his mind even if she had changed hers.

Having just convinced herself she'd misunderstood Daniel's earlier words, his confirmation that apart from sex, she had no personal interest for him felt like a double bull's-eye blow from a stun gun. The pain seared through her, leaving bruises that no one else could see, least of all him.

Her eyes flicked back to the computer screen, her brain screaming that she needed to focus on something besides her decimated emotions or she was going to break apart. And she saw him. Their state policeman *had* been one of her father's students.

She grabbed the mouse and clicked the back arrow three times, halting the slide show and taking them to the picture that had caught her attention.

"What are you doing?"

"I think I have an I.D. on our guy." Amazingly the words came out even and controlled, not giving away the wild torment inside her.

She'd used shaky evidence to convince herself that even though Daniel obviously didn't love her, he did care and even shakier reasoning to convince herself his caring was more than a temporary side effect of their sexual compatibility.

"I didn't see him." Daniel's voice sounded odd, but that was probably a trick of her hearing.

"He looked different." Her own voice was starting to wear around the edges, and she made a conscious effort to rein it in. "Dad takes the pictures of his trainees when they come to the camp, before he enforces his crew cut, no facial hair rule. This guy showed up with longer hair, sporting a mustache and a beard."

The picture was frozen on the computer screen, the man a dead ringer for Officer Devon if you took away the beard and buzz cut the hair.

"What's his name?"

"I'll tell you in just a sec." She checked the number on the file and cross-referenced it with client records. "Abner Jones. If that's not his real name, he's incredibly unimaginative when it comes to aliases."

"Your dad does background checks on his students before he admits them into the school."

"A determined person could fake his identification and past as effectively as Dad has set up his own aliases."

"Did Jones attend with anyone else?"

Josie checked. "His record isn't cross-referenced with any of the other soldiers in training during the same session, but their records are probably a good place to start for possible connections all the same."

"How will you do that?"

"Hotwire and I will compare their files and the information from their background checks for anything they might have in common. Dad's trainees are from all over the world;

even coming from the same state would be a pretty significant connection for two students to have."

She brought up the list of soldiers who had attended the training camp with Jones and printed it off along with the individual files for each name. Thank goodness her laser printer had been left behind by the thieves. It had probably been too unwieldy to take, being larger than the small television they'd lifted from the living room.

When the reports stopped printing, she handed them to Daniel without meeting his eyes. "Why don't you start going through these while I see what I can find on Dad's possible aliases? You'd probably be more comfortable spreading them out on the table in the dining room."

And she would be more comfortable with him out of the room. Her heart was still hemorrhaging, and she had to cauterize the wound, but she needed some time to herself to do it. It wasn't his fault she'd fallen in love when he'd only fallen in lust, but having him around while she came to terms with that truth was more than she could bear.

Daniel got up without a word, but stopped at the doorway. "You never asked what you smelled like to me."

"No. I didn't." What could he have said? Maybe that she smelled like sex, or stupidity.

She recognized the thought as a bitter one, but not necessarily an untrue one.

He waited as if expecting her to ask the question she had no intention of asking. "You smell like everything a woman could or should be."

With that he walked out, and Josie sat staring at an empty doorway in a state of incredulity.

Had she heard him correctly? Because if she had, none of what he'd said earlier made any sense, or did it? Maybe he'd only been talking about female perfection in a sexual sense. She smelled like everything a woman could or should be *in bed*.

She wasn't deluding herself into believing it could be anything else. Not this time.

Daniel made coffee and took a mug of it to a quiet, preoccupied Josie before sitting down at the dining room table as she'd suggested in order to go through the records.

It was hard going, though, trying to concentrate. He'd hurt her again, and that was the last damn thing he wanted to do. When she'd said he made her feel safe, he'd felt as if someone had taken a shredder to his insides. Of all the things she could rely on him for, things he'd do everything in his power to give her, safety was not one of them. He wasn't trustworthy with a woman's life.

His mother had learned that the hard way, teaching him an indelible lesson in the process.

But he hadn't told Josie that. He'd merely told her not to count on him, like she didn't matter to him, which was nowhere near the truth. He hadn't been honest with her, and she deserved better than that from him. In fact, he'd out and out lied to her when he implied she had nothing to do with his decision to find her father and the men who'd tried to kill Tyler.

Unlike Josie, who had told him she didn't lie very well, Daniel was an old hand at it. He'd started young, explaining away the occasional bruises on his small body to teachers as nothing more than the result of horseplay or clumsiness. He'd been so good at it, they'd never once suspected the man who had sired him made a habit of beating his beautiful wife and small son when he drank too much.

Daniel had kept right on lying when he faked his age to enter the army at the age of sixteen. He'd been the size of a man, but as undisciplined and untrained in the art of fighting as a small child.

That had changed, but his ability to overcome an aggressor hadn't helped his mom when she needed it. Daniel wasn't any good at protecting women . . . even the ones he loved. Not that he would allow himself to love Josie. To do so would be nothing better than emotional suicide. That was another lesson he would never forget that his mother had taught him.

However, that didn't mean he could leave her believing she meant nothing to him. Very few people knew the truth about his past, but Josie had earned the right to be one of them.

Chapter 13

Daniel didn't get a chance to talk to Josie alone for several hours.

First, the detective from the Arson and Explosives Division of the state police showed up ten minutes earlier than expected, and then Hotwire returned from dropping off Claire. He was carrying a box with a new laptop in it for Josie. She went into raptures, and Daniel and the detective both had to sit idly by while she quizzed Hotwire on what the computer could do.

Discussion eventually got back to the investigation. After Josie showed the picture of Jones to the detective, he unbent enough to tell them that a known white supremacist group had a paramilitary compound near the GPS coordinates for the laptop.

Unfortunately, FBI intelligence revealed there were only two ways into the compound: up a narrow path that could be traversed on foot or by a small, powerful ATV, or by helicopter. A clearing suitable for landing was located near the compound, but it would be impossible for the helicopter to land undetected.

"What about parachuting in?" Josie asked.

"It would have to be a long jump for the plane to be high enough not to be suspect," Daniel replied before the detective had a chance to. "And a drop from that altitude would make it difficult to land on target unless the clearing is fairly large."

The detective shook his head. "None of you are parachuting in anywhere, undetected or otherwise. This is an official federal investigation at this point, and while they are cooperating with state authorities, the FBI and National Forest Service aren't going to take kindly to a bunch of mercenaries stepping on their toes."

"I'm no longer a mercenary," Josie informed him.

"You're not FBI either. Stay out of it," was the detective's uncompromising response.

Josie's mouth set in a mutinous line Daniel had learned meant she was about to get stubborn. "These people tried to kill my father. I want to know why."

"You would do better using your resources trying to locate Mr. McCall than the assailants." The officer stared Josie down, which was quite a feat in Daniel's opinion. "If you interfere in a federal investigation, you could be facing charges."

"I have no intention of interfering," she said in a tone that would have shriveled most men.

The state police detective merely nodded. "I'm glad to hear that. Stay out of airplanes and we'll be just fine."

Glaring, she opened her mouth, and Daniel thought the time had come to interfere. "Why would this group target Tyler McCall?"

Detective Johnson met Daniel's eyes. "You recently bought in to the school, is that correct?"

"Yes."

"That could be the reason right there. This group is ideologically opposed to Caucasians going into business ventures, or any other legal tie, with non-Caucasians."

"That's ridiculous." Josie's moss green eyes shot derision at the detective.

She was still mad he'd told her to stay out of his investigation.

"I agree, ma'am. I was only giving you a possible reason for their aggression toward your father."

"But why target Dad out of all the businessmen in the U.S. who have non-Caucasian business partners?" She frowned in fierce thought. "That's too flimsy a connection. Besides, we know at least one of them was a student. It has to be something to do with the school itself."

"What type of training camp did he attend?" the detective asked.

Josie looked through the papers Daniel had left on the table and pulled one out, then handed it to the officer. "One that focused on high-level explosives and the more sophisticated forms of warfare. The particulars are here."

He took the paper and looked at it, his expression freezing into disapproval. "This is just the type of information we don't need domestic terrorists getting their hands on."

"Dad is very particular about what students he takes on. If their background checks link them to domestic or foreign terrorist groups even remotely, he refuses their applications."

The detective looked unimpressed. "You can fake a background. There's no way your dad can guarantee the character of the men and women he chooses to train."

Her gaze shot to Daniel's, and they shared a moment of perfect understanding, both remembering their discussion along a similar vein earlier. But then she turned back to the officer, deliberately breaking the link. "Neither can the army, but no one has proposed shutting its doors down."

Stone's lips quirked. "You have a point, but the fact is, your dad obviously did train some domestic terrorists, and I'm guessing they aren't wild about there being any record of them learning this stuff." He waved the paper at Josie.

"You think they blew up an entire compound, tried to kill my father and broke in to my house all just to stop other people from knowing what type of specialized knowledge and training they had?" Josie asked incredulously.

The detective shrugged, looking resigned and weary with

the knowledge he had of human nature. "We're talking about fanatics here. The kind of men who would blow up an elementary school if it was in the way of their agenda."

Josie was still reeling at the thought of her father unknowingly training domestic terrorists and being attacked because of it when Hotwire left to pick up Claire from her classes. The local police had gotten rid of the reporters, but the more stalwart had returned and were making a nuisance of themselves on the sidewalk.

They'd come into the yard again, but moved to the sidewalk after Daniel went outside and made his presence felt with silent, but palpable anger emanating from his every pore. He was back inside now, going over the records she'd printed earlier despite the detective's injunction to leave that part of the investigation to the authorities.

He'd taken her jump drive, but had no authority to require her to delete the records she'd already transferred to Hotwire's hard drive. Not that she'd mentioned them to him.

She was still trying to track down her father's possible aliases. It required meticulous research and reading through a lot of records that ended up having no information of use, but she'd read the phone book for every major county in the U.S. if it meant finding her dad.

Checking her e-mail, she opened up an automated reply from one of the databases she had sent a query to. It listed the purchase five years ago of a piece of property in the Nevada desert under the name of one of her father's Vietnam buddies, Andrew Taylor. The man had been dead for almost a decade. Excited at the breakthrough, she narrowed her search on that name to the area surrounding the property and came up with some other interesting pieces of information.

She wrote it all down, her heart lighter than it had been since her father walked out of his hospital room, his ability to remember still in question.

"I'm thirty-two."

She was so focused on what she was doing that the sound of Daniel's voice from behind her made her jump. She spun around in her task chair, her heartbeat accelerated. "What?"

He leaned against the doorjamb, his arms crossed, black hair framing his taciturn features. "I'm thirty-two."

"I'm twenty-six. Is there supposed to be something significant about that?"

"Everyone else thinks I'm thirty-four."

"Everyone?"

"Everyone but Master Sergeant Cordell."

"Why?"

"Because that's what I told them."

"Oh." Was she losing her mind, or was it him? Most people lied about being younger than they were, not older.

"I joined the army when I was sixteen, and I had to lie about my age to do it. I'm much better at prevaricating than you are. I've got a lot of practice."

She wasn't sure how she felt knowing that. "But your birth certificate . . ."

"Faked."

"I feel like you're trying to tell me something, but I don't know what it is."

Subtle tension seeped into his features. "I ran away from home when I was sixteen because when my dad lost his temper, he hit. Drinking made him more susceptible to anger, and he'd begun drinking more and more."

Daniel had said his mother was dead. Maybe his dad drank to forget her. Some men did. "Was your mom gone then?"

"No. She was the reason I left."

Josie felt her stomach twisting in a tight knot of apprehension. "How so?"

"They fought about me most of the time. She wanted me to go to school, to *make something of myself*. It made him furious. He accused her of thinking he was less of a man because he wasn't educated." Daniel pushed away from the door and came into the room, his tension more pronounced. "Thunder was raised on the reservation. He was an artist, following the old ways, but in order to live, he sold his work in a gallery that catered to tourists."

"Your mom had a problem with this?"

Daniel's face contorted for a second before all expression smoothed from it. "Not really, but she grew up off the reservation until she was sixteen. Her parents died in a sailing accident that year, and she went to live with my great-grandfather."

"Is that how she and your father met?"

"Yes. She never complained about her life with my father, but she wanted me to experience life beyond the reservation. She believed that a person's life should not be limited by their birth."

That was something Josie was trying to prove. Being born a soldier didn't make her a soldier. "Smart lady."

"Not smart enough to leave my father. He said she wanted me to deny my heritage and leave the reservation because our way of life wasn't good enough for her. When he drank, he did more than accuse."

"He beat her?"

"Sometimes he only yelled; sometimes he would yell until he totally lost his cool, and then he'd hit her. He had a violent temper, but I knew it was mostly my fault, that without me to fight about, he wouldn't get so mad at her."

Josie made a sound of distress, her heart constricting at Daniel's belief he was responsible for his dad's lack of self-control, or his mother's choice to tolerate it.

His eyes reflected pain she wished she could assuage. "The worst of it was that I never wanted my mom's dream for me. I wanted to be a soldier, had wanted it since I was a little kid. I wanted to know how to fight and how to win, how to stop my dad from hurting me and my mom."

"What happened?"

"After my first tour of duty, my mom begged me to get out of the army, to come home to the reservation and take care of my father. He was drinking more then and was finding it hard to keep a job."

"But you refused."

"I was a Ranger, and for the first time in my life, I was proud of what and who I was. I told my mom to leave him, that I would take care of her, but she refused. She loved him." He said the words with such scorn, and finally Josie understood where it came from.

His mother had used love as an excuse to stay in an abusive relationship that had destroyed her family and caused a separation with her son.

"A year after I signed on for my second tour, my dad lost his temper again and threw my mom against a wall. Her head hit at the wrong angle, and she was knocked out. She went into a coma. I flew home and sat beside her hospital bed for three days, but she died without ever coming out of it."

And he had been denied the opportunity to say goodbye, or tell his mom that he loved her. Josie's eyes stung with tears. "It wasn't your fault. Your mother chose to stay in a destructive relationship. *She knew the risks, and she stayed.*"

"If I'd gone home, I could have been there to stop him. I should have gotten out of the army and stayed with her. I should have taken care of her, but I'm no good at taking care of other people."

"Your mother didn't ask you to come home to protect her; she asked you to come home and take care of your drunk of a father," she said, taking a stab in the dark, "didn't she?"

"Yes."

"She wanted you to protect him, not her, and you couldn't have done that. You would have hurt him physically the next time he lost his temper and hit your mother. She would have kicked you out of the house and blamed you for not being patient enough." Josie didn't have a lot of experience with abuse victims, but Claire had taken her to a women's shelter once so she could teach a class in self-defense.

Most of the women there wanted new lives, but they had shared with her the kind of twisted thinking that had kept them in their victim roles.

Daniel moved toward her, his expression grim. "You're wrong. I was an adult then. I could have convinced her to leave him if I'd taken the time to go home, if I'd cared more about her safety than my pride."

"No. You're a good man, Daniel. You had to make a life for yourself away from your parents, or you would have ended up in the same ugly cycle they lived in."

"I'm not getting married, so that can't happen. I'll never hurt a woman like he hurt her."

So many things became clear to Josie. Daniel hadn't been rejecting her earlier. He'd been rejecting himself as someone who could make her feel safe. His mother hadn't been safe, and he thought that was his fault. He'd spent his adult life fighting other people's battles, saving people as part of a mercenary team that specialized in extractions, but he still believed he wasn't a protector.

It would be laughable if he didn't believe it.

Running his latest words through her mind again, she realized something else. He wasn't against a long-term commitment with her; he really did have an aversion to marriage.

"Are you seriously afraid you'd end up like your father?" The same man who had practically given himself a heart attack assuring her first time making love was special and as painless as possible.

"Everyone who's ever met the both of us says we're carbon copies, that we could be twins."

"On the outside maybe. Even if you got your to-die-for good looks from him, you've got something he didn't have where it counts." She stood up and reached for him, pressing her hand over his heart. "You aren't alike inside. You'd die for me before you would hurt me, no matter how angry you were. I know it."

Something sparked in his almost black eyes. It looked like hope, but then it was gone. "I don't believe in love and commitment, Josie."

"I know." And she understood, but that didn't change the way she felt. "It doesn't matter because I do believe in you. I still feel safe with you, Daniel."

"You shouldn't, damn it. Didn't you hear what I said? When the important moment comes, I could make the wrong choice. I could put myself first."

Both his parents had a lot to answer for in her mind, but Josie wasn't buying any of Daniel's fears. "I'm betting you won't." She didn't say *wouldn't* as if there was a possibility the occasion would not arise because she knew the time would come.

And either he was going to rip her heart out by its moorings and walk away, or overcome his fears to make a future with her. With this new insight, she believed that given enough time together, he'd do the latter. It would just take time for *him* to realize that fact.

In the meantime she wasn't going to dwell on her own unhappy truth: that in order to have a future with Daniel, she had to give up her dreams of leaving the soldiering life behind. She never had to be a mercenary again, but if she wanted to be with him, she would have to move back to the mountain and spend her time surrounded by soldiers in training.

Any children they had would be raised the way she'd been raised, maybe not as stringently, but soldiering would be the life they knew. They would be misfits in a world that had an uneasy alliance with its military. Perhaps she would have to give up her dream of being a mother at all.

She understood Daniel's mother's frustrations. She'd fought against her son being limited by his surroundings and paid a huge price for refusing to back down. According to

Josie's dad's diaries, the only thing her father and mother had fought about was his need to raise her with the ability to protect herself from any foe.

"What happened to your dad?"

"He went to prison for manslaughter. I was a witness for the prosecution. I wanted a murder charge." She could feel Daniel's pain reaching out to wrap itself around her and squeeze at her sore heart.

"They didn't take his pattern of abuse into consideration?" she asked.

"It was unsubstantiated. I'd been gone too long for my testimony in that regard to be taken into consideration, but there was no doubt that he was responsible for her death."

"But you weren't."

"We all have regrets to live with. I can't dismiss mine."

"Fine." She grabbed his shirt in both of her fists, needing him to hear what she was saying. "Regret not being able to help your mother, but don't blame yourself for her choices or your father's. They were both adults. She could have walked out any time, and you would have taken care of her. She didn't, and she paid a price for staying with a man who couldn't or wouldn't control his temper. None of that was your fault."

"Maybe he didn't know how," he said, ignoring her exonerating words. "It took me a long time to learn to control mine, and that was with a really good teacher."

"Does he get in a lot of fights in prison?"

"I don't know. I don't keep in touch."

She understood it, but wondered if that choice had taken another toll on Daniel. "Have you ever considered going to see him?"

"No."

"Has he ever tried to contact you?"

"No."

She couldn't tell if that bothered him or not. She couldn't imagine what it would be like to have one parent responsible for the death of the other. Love and family loyalty got irretrievably twisted and distorted in that scenario.

"Why did you tell me all this?"

"I hurt you."

"When you told me that I didn't count for anything but sex?"

His eyes flared, and his jaw locked, but she didn't give him a chance to say anything.

"Yes, you did hurt me. Are you trying to tell me that maybe *I* mean something to you and that despite your belief you aren't capable of watching over me and being trusted with my safety, you're doing it anyway because you care too much to turn away from me?"

She wasn't making guesses about anything with him anymore. She wanted his feelings spelled out. If he said no, it would hurt, but at least she wouldn't be deluding herself.

His hands locked on to her waist, and his body vibrated with tension. "I don't want you hurt."

She just looked at him, willing him to answer her question.

Something seemed to snap inside of him, and he gritted out, "Yes, damn it, yes. Are you satisfied?"

She reached up on tiptoes and pressed her lips oh so softly to his. "Thank you, Daniel. That means so much to me."

His arms locked around her, and the kiss they shared was both passionate and full of commitment. It was a confirmation of their value to each other, of feelings that went beyond sexual gratification, of a connection that reached into the spiritual. If only he would let himself see it.

"Uh, should we come back later?"

The sound of Hotwire's voice broke through the intimacy of the kiss, and Josie reluctantly allowed Daniel to pull away.

He turned with one arm still locked around her, effectively turning her, too. "If I say yes, will you go away?"

"Actually, I was going to suggest we all go away."

"What do you mean?" Claire asked, standing on the other side of Hotwire.

He smiled at her and then at Josie and Daniel. "Josie's a fantastic cook, no doubt about it, but maybe if we leave, go get some dinner, the straggler reporters will take off, too."

She liked Daniel's idea better, that everyone else leave and she and Daniel get some time alone, but didn't think they'd get away with it. "What if someone tries to break in again?"

"Already taken care of." Hotwire held up an independent motion detector device. "If it detects motion, it releases an odorless sleeping agent while alerting the remote unit of the compromised perimeter."

"That could be dangerous around pets." Claire was looking at the small device in Hotwire's hand with distinct wariness.

"You and Josie don't have any pets."

"True, but how sensitive is it? I mean, if I stay in my room, will it go off? What if I have to go to the bathroom?"

Hotwire looked bemused, and it was such an interesting, not to mention uncommon, expression on his face that Josie had to stifle a laugh.

"We're not going to have the units armed when you're home, Claire," he said.

"Oh." She didn't look appreciably relieved. "Okay." She turned to leave the room.

"Where are you going?" Hotwire's Georgian charm was obvious by its absence, but he didn't sound angry, just confused.

Claire looked back over her shoulder, her eyes saying she couldn't quite figure out why he was asking that. "To get a snack and then I'm going to study. Did you need something?"

"You're going to dinner with us."

"No, I'm not."

"Why do you think you aren't going?"

"I wasn't invited, and even if I had been, I've got studying to do."

"Your studying can wait until you've eaten. You admitted

in the car you'd had nothing since your almost nonexistent breakfast this morning."

Hotwire had quizzed Claire on what she'd eaten that day?

"Don't worry about me. I'm used to skipping a meal or two when I need to."

"Your brain can't function at optimum potential when you don't feed your body the fuel it needs."

Claire was still looking as though she didn't understand why Hotwire was asking her about something that had nothing to do with him. Josie was almost as bemused as Claire. Hotwire was all southern charm with women. Only he always kept a certain distance, but he was ignoring his self-imposed boundaries with Claire. From the look on Claire's face, he was ignoring hers, too.

"If you stay, the reporters will think there's still a chance of getting something worth printing and stick around," Daniel said.

The look of gratitude Hotwire sent him shocked Josie so much she didn't think to add her voice to Daniel's in convincing Claire to come to dinner.

But the other woman's face creased in a worried frown. "I hadn't thought about the reporters."

"But you did think about the bad guys coming back, didn't you?" Hotwire asked, almost as an accusation.

"Well, yes . . ."

Hotwire sighed. "Claire, I wouldn't leave you to face people who have already tried to kill once."

"*You* wouldn't?" she asked, her emphasis on *you* echoed in Josie's mind.

"None of us would," Daniel inserted before Hotwire had a chance to answer.

"Right," Josie finally had the wherewithal to say. "You need to come with us, honey."

Claire didn't need much convincing after that, but she did politely decline Hotwire's offer to help her with her studies. Josie wondered if Claire wasn't going to wind up with

Hotwire in her room going over program code, all the while not sure how he'd gotten there.

Josie told the others over dinner about the leads she'd uncovered on her dad's possible whereabouts. Both Hotwire and Daniel thought she was on to something, and Claire made a couple of suggestions on avenues Josie hadn't thought to research.

The motion sensor units did not go off during dinner, and the discussion progressed from Josie's dad's possible whereabouts to what to do if he really was in Nevada.

When they got back to the house, the front lawn was empty, as was the sidewalk, and no suspect cars or vans were parked along the street. Josie's relief was short-lived when a sedan pulled up just as they were getting out of Daniel's SUV.

A man jumped out of the passenger door, and a second later a powerful camera flash went off.

"Miss McCall, would you care to comment on the rumor that ELF was behind the explosion at your father's compound two nights ago."

She spun around at the sound of the reporter's strident voice. He was standing on the sidewalk, but that didn't keep his photographer from snapping more pictures of her and the others.

She marched up to the two men. "Just where exactly did you hear this rumor?" she demanded.

"Are you saying it's not true?" the reporter asked while the photographer took yet another picture.

She grabbed his wrist with a snakelike movement her father had taught her when she was fifteen. Pressing with two fingers on a vulnerable spot, she watched in satisfaction as the man lost his hold on the camera and it fell with a clunk to the pavement. She released him, and he scrambled backward, kicking his camera as he did so and causing further damage to the expensive piece of equipment.

"You should be more careful with your things," she said sweetly.

"You did that. You broke my wrist, you bitch." He was holding it cradled limply against his chest, but she knew feeling would return in less than a minute.

"No. I didn't."

"But if you call her another name, I will," Daniel said from beside her. "Pick up your camera and get back in the car."

"Hey, you can't tell me what to do. This is public property."

Daniel took a step toward the photographer. "Yes. It is. Which means I can stay out here as long as I want."

"You can't do anything to me. I'll call the cops."

Daniel's smile was chilling. "How long do you think it would take them to get here?"

"Are you threatening me?"

"No. A soldier learns early not to waste time or words warning his enemy of his intentions."

The photographer's nerve broke, and he grabbed his camera before heading back across the street to his car. "Come on, Dooley, it's not worth it. This story is old news already anyway."

"Stop being such a wuss," Dooley said.

The other man made a crude, but dismissive gesture with his hand and got back in the car.

"I told you, I have no comment, and that isn't going to change." Josie turned to go.

"There's something going on here, Miss McCall, and I'm going to figure out what it is."

"Be my guest," she said over her shoulder. "When you do, make sure you share your findings with the Forest Service."

"I find it very interesting that Daniel Black Eagle, the son of a known felon, buys in to an exclusive paramilitary training school and pretty soon that same school is blown to smithereens and burned to the ground."

Chapter 14

She barely stifled the urge to tell the reporter where to stuff it, knowing he wanted her to lose her cool.

"Even more interesting, the man is currently shacked up with his partner's daughter, and they are both explosives experts."

"What the hell are you getting at?" Daniel's voice was deadly, but not out of control.

She looked over at him, continuing toward the house. "Ignore him, Daniel. He's blowing smoke out of his behind, and pretty soon he's going to set himself on fire."

"Like you set fire to your father's compound? Is it true your father died in the fire, Ms. McCall? Do you think he died from smoke inhalation before the fire got to him? It puts a different complexion on the recent million-dollar life insurance policy your dad took out naming you as beneficiary, doesn't it?"

Two thumps sounded from behind her, and she spun around to see what was going on. Daniel was walking toward her, and the reporter lay unmoving, half on the sidewalk and half on the street.

"Daniel, what did you do?"

"He tripped. Over my foot."

She stared at the reporter and then looked toward the car

where the photographer was busy trying to fix his camera under the interior lights. From his lack of reaction, she had to assume he hadn't seen anything. He certainly hadn't gotten any pictures, not with his camera out of commission.

"You can't leave him lying half in the street."

"He accused you of killing your dad. He's lucky I didn't throw him in front of the next passing car."

The reporter groaned and started moving.

Daniel nodded toward him. "See. He'll be fine. Unfortunately."

"He knew an awful lot about you and me for that matter. Not to mention some insurance policy I'm darn positive my dad would never have taken out. He doesn't trust insurance companies."

"I know. I wouldn't buy in to the school until he agreed to insure the property."

"Why didn't Dooley mention *that* policy?" she asked as they walked into the house, and Daniel closed the door behind them. "It would support his whacky accusation you had something to do with the school's demise."

Hotwire and Claire were nowhere to be seen, but she could hear typing from the study, and Claire's bedroom door was shut.

"I don't know." Daniel pulled her around so she was looking up into his face. "Are you okay?"

"Other than knowing someone tried to kill my dad and apparently planned all along to lay the blame on me? Sure." She smiled to make a joke of her words, but it slipped at the seriousness of his expression.

"I don't like this one dam—darn bit. I don't think you're safe, Josette."

"I'm not a helpless little bubblehead, Daniel. If anybody comes after me, I'm more than ready to give them a taste of the temper I've been keeping under wraps for the past three days." And she meant it.

She would welcome a chance to meet her enemy face-to-face and take them apart with every trick her dad had taught her.

"They didn't meet your dad head-on. They tried to blow him up. If you hadn't been there, he would be dead."

"If I hadn't been there, the security system would have been set at a higher level for motion detection outside his room. I turned it off when I went for a walk."

"If they came prepared to blow up the compound, they came prepared to dismantle your dad's security features."

"I told myself the same thing, but that doesn't change the fact they didn't have to."

"And that doesn't alter the fact you saved your dad's life."

"Maybe you're right." Heaven knew she didn't believe in carrying false guilt around. Daniel had enough of that for both of them.

She moved into his arms until she was wrapped up against him, seeking his strength and warmth. "I know it's stupid, but, Daniel, I always thought he was indestructible. It never occurred to me that anybody could kill him. I guess I thought he was never going to die."

Burying her face against his chest, she couldn't say anything more past the lump of emotional revelation clogging her throat.

His hand rubbed up and down her back. "I know, sweetheart. There's nothing stupid about it. I used to think that my mom couldn't die either. I mean, she'd survived years of marriage to my dad; I couldn't conceive of him seriously hurting her. He needed her. Even I could see that, though I wouldn't call what he felt love."

"I'm sorry she died."

"I am, too, but I'm not going to make the mistake with you that I made with her."

She pulled back so she could see his face. There had been an odd quality in his voice. "What do you mean?"

"You're in danger right now."

"So?"

"I want you to go stay with Wolf and Lise until the enemy is contained."

"No."

"I'm not giving you a choice, Josette."

"Really? How do you plan to get me to Wolf's? Carry me there with my arms tied behind my back?"

"If I had picked my mother up and carried her out of the house, she wouldn't have been there for my dad to throw against a wall."

"She would have gone back to him, just like I'm going to Nevada to see if my dad is there, even if I have to walk down the side of Wolf's mountain and hitchhike cross-country. If you really want to make sure I'm safe, you're going to have to keep me with you."

"Josette—"

"Think about it, Daniel. I'm trained to protect myself and to neutralize the enemy. Please trust me to make the right decisions for my own safety."

"Do I have a choice?"

"No. You didn't have one with your mother either," she couldn't help saying.

He sighed, but didn't argue with her. No anger evident in his eyes at her mutiny, he brushed the hair away from her temple. "You're so perfect, such a special woman. I don't want you hurt."

Tears unrelated to her dad's dangerous brush with death filled her eyes. "I'm a former mercenary, Daniel, not a debutante."

"You're my woman." He nuzzled her face. "And so soft."

Her mind splintered away from their discussion as his gentle touch drew forth a reaction from her body that had nothing to do with making war. She turned her face toward his and met his lips halfway.

She opened her mouth, and their tongues collided in a mutual need to taste. Her hands slid of their own accord up his chest and around his neck as her body pressed into the hard length of his. His arms were already locked around her, but they tightened until she felt melded to him despite the clothes separating flesh hungry to touch naked flesh.

"This is becoming a habit." The humor in Hotwire's voice couldn't even dampen the need Josie felt to connect with Daniel.

She ignored the other man's presence and went up on her tiptoes to increase the pressure of her lips against his.

It was Daniel who drew away, holding her firmly separated from him when she tried to burrow back into his arms. He turned his head toward Hotwire. "This had better be good."

"I chased down the leads Josie uncovered and followed up on the suggestions Claire made at dinner. Someone is definitely using the deceased veteran's name to live under."

"Where?" Josie asked.

"You were right . . . Nevada. In a sparsely populated area south of Reno."

"That sounds like Dad."

"I made plane reservations for tomorrow, but we've got to do something about Claire. She needs to stay somewhere else for the duration."

"You're leaving tomorrow?" Claire came into the room and pushed her glasses up on her nose, looking at Josie with that vague look she got when she was concentrating on a new program.

"We think my dad's in Nevada. We have to check it out."

"And you need to stay somewhere else for a while," Hotwire added.

"Why?"

"The house has been compromised. You won't be safe staying here alone," Josie replied. "Will that be all right?"

Claire bit her lip and didn't meet Josie's eyes, but she nodded. "Sure. I'll get packed tonight and leave in the morning."

"Where are you going to stay?" Josie asked.

"Don't worry about it. There are plenty of places I can go."

Josie didn't like the vague answer. "Are you sure? You haven't had anyone over since you moved in, and the only time you go out is to visit the old people in the nursing home where you work, or volunteer at the shelters downtown. I don't want you staying in one of them while we're gone."

"That's not going to happen," Hotwire said, sounding meaner than Josie had ever heard him.

"We can rent her a hotel suite," Daniel suggested.

"No, thank you." Claire smiled at Josie. "That won't be necessary, believe me. I'll stay at the nursing home. They've got several empty beds right now, and the staff likes me."

She sounded surprised by the fact, but Josie wasn't. Claire was an angel to the old people, and the staff all loved her for it.

"You're going to live in a nursing home?" Hotwire demanded, not sounding appreciably more pleased by that idea than Claire sleeping in a shelter.

"I've stayed in worse places. Much worse if you want the truth. Staying with Essie or one of the other old ladies won't be a problem for me at all, and as long as you don't mind me borrowing your computer for a while longer, I can keep up with my classes."

"That's not a problem." He looked at Josie. "What about your classes?"

"I'm not carrying a full course load this summer like Claire is. I'll catch up later, and if I can't, finding my dad is more important than passing a couple of computer classes, but Claire shouldn't have to make that choice. None of this is her problem."

"Standing by my friends is not a problem," Claire said, her voice firm with purpose.

*   *   *

Hotwire insisted on seeing Claire settled into her new accommodations before informing Josie and Daniel he'd booked flights for only the two of them. "Someone should stay here in case the bad guys come back and try to break in again. Besides, I can use the time to investigate those fanatics in the Rockies that have possession of your laptop."

"You sure you can handle it?" Daniel asked.

"On my worst day."

"Then why did you make Claire leave?" Josie asked.

"She could be at risk if they did come back, and she'd be a distraction even if they didn't."

"I thought there was something going on there."

Hotwire frowned. *"Nothing's* going on."

"But you want her," Daniel said bluntly.

"Yes. I'm not going to have her, though. Did you know she's a pacifist *and* a vegetarian?" Hotwire asked, sounding as if he didn't know what to make of either of those facts.

"She's also a crack programmer and has design skills that are going to outshine Andy Grove's one day."

Hotwire just shook his head.

The pale yellow stucco house was listed as belonging to Andrew Taylor, but Daniel didn't doubt the dusty jeep in the driveway was registered to Tyler McCall.

"That's Dad's jeep," Josie confirmed as Daniel parked their rental car behind it and cut off the engine.

The Oregon license plate had been carefully smudged with dirt so as to be unreadable, but this close the distinctive image of Mt. Hood between the letters could be made out.

Hot, still air hit him, the minute Daniel opened his car door, compromising the air-conditioned interior. Nevada was no hotter than a lot of places he'd been, but its desert sun was strong and bright, shimmering on the sand like liquid air.

Josie came around the car, and they went together to the front door. There was no answer to their first knock, or their second.

She pushed the doorbell, and a muted chime sounded through the thick wooden door.

"Dad, it's me! Open up." At the continued lack of response, her brows knit in a frown. "Either he's not here, or he's pretending not to be."

With Tyler, either was possible. "Let's take a look around back."

"Watch for electronic eyes. Dad isn't going to have a safe house without some heavy-duty security features, and I don't want to deal with triggering one of his traps."

Daniel agreed and tread carefully as they made their way around to the back of the house. He almost missed the first eye hidden behind a scrub bush against one wall, but spotted the second soon after. He avoided them both. The back patio's weathered brick was devoid of outdoor furniture or any sign of life.

Josie made a sound of disgust as she looked around. "Well, that netted us nothing."

The sliding glass door to the interior was covered with a privacy curtain so they couldn't see into the house, and all the back windows had interior shutters, which were closed.

"We'll have to go inside," Daniel said, eyeing the subtle signs of Tyler's security system.

It took almost thirty minutes to disable it and break into the house. When they did, the sparsely furnished southwestern-style home was empty.

"Where could he have gone without the jeep? This house isn't exactly on a bus line."

"Maybe we should be asking who he went with."

Josie's features tightened. "Or more importantly, did he go of his own accord?"

"There's no reason to believe he didn't. There are no signs of a struggle, and we only discovered this place because you'd read the journals. What are the chances his enemies know about it, too?"

She smiled briefly. "Knowing my dad's penchant for privacy, very small, but where the heck is he?"

Daniel didn't bother answering the rhetorical question, but started searching through drawers in the kitchen. Josie joined him and when their search revealed nothing useful, they moved to the other rooms, looking in every conceivable place for an indication Tyler had even been there.

There was nothing. He'd made a clean sweep of the place before leaving.

Josie picked up the phone. "I'm going to try redial. It's the last thing I can think of."

"Good idea."

She pressed the button and listened. Her soft green eyes lit with satisfaction as the phone was picked up at the other end.

Then she said, "This is Andrew Taylor's secretary. I'm calling to confirm his return ticket to Reno." She waited, listening to the other person speaking. "No return ticket? But I'm supposed to pick him up at the airport. Perhaps you can find his ticket under his card number." She read off a credit card number Hotwire had identified as belonging to Andrew Taylor of Nevada. "Hmm . . . What flights are available for return tomorrow? . . . Yes, I see. Let me call him on his cell and ask which one he'd prefer. Thanks. Oh, is there any way we can link this ticket to his outbound, or are we going to have to pay one-way fares? . . . Thanks, that would be great."

She hung up the phone. "He flew to Missoula International Airport on an early morning flight, but he didn't book a return flight."

The location was too much of a coincidence, being the closest airport to the GPS location for her laptop. "He knows the group that blew up his school and tried to kill him."

"And where their headquarters are evidently. He's gone to face them alone. Why didn't he call us?"

He liked the way she subconsciously linked them together

as a unit, but he didn't agree her dad had gone off on a Lone Ranger mission. "More likely he's doing a recon."

"Alone," she said disgustedly. "What happens if he's caught gathering information?"

Daniel couldn't believe she'd asked that. "Josie, this is your dad we're talking about. He was LLRP in Nam and has been training other mercs ever since. He may be past his prime in age, but no one is going to see him unless he wants them to."

"So, do we follow him to Montana?"

"We'd be better off waiting for him to come back here."

"He didn't book a return flight."

"Not as Andrew Taylor, but it's possible he booked one under another alias as an extra level of security. It's the kind of thing your dad would do."

"Right. Let's call Hotwire and see if he can find out."

"Can't you look? You brought your new laptop with you." He wasn't as jealous of Hotwire since Josie had said she didn't want him and shown Daniel how much she did want him, even after he said tactless and sometimes stupid things.

However, it still bothered him that his friend's computer savvy gave him a role in Josie's life that excluded Daniel.

"Hotwire is a lot faster at this stuff than I am."

"Does he have the list of names you compiled from the journals?"

"Yes, and he's continuing to search on those names as well as Andrew Taylor. I hope he has better luck turning something up on the others than I did."

Josie made the call, and an hour later, Daniel's guess was proved right. A flight had been booked for the day after tomorrow from Missoula International to Reno under the name of Yancy Carpenter, another name off Josie's list.

"So, we just wait for him here?" she asked after hanging up the phone, clearly not thrilled with the idea.

"It's our best chance at crossing paths with him."

"We could fly to Missoula."

"And do what? We know the general area to look, but we have no way of knowing which direction your dad chose for his reconnaissance."

"So, we wait."

Daniel shrugged.

"What if he decides to fly back to Oregon instead?"

"Hotwire's at your house in case he goes there, and Tyler has my cell phone number memorized."

"If he remembers it."

"He remembered this place and enough to figure out who is trying to kill him. I doubt his memory is as impaired as you and the doctor thought."

Josie went to the sink and poured herself a glass of water from the tap filter. "You think he was faking me out?"

"Yes. Probably for your own protection."

She took a long drink and then licked her lips in a move guaranteed to spark libidinous thoughts. "Why? I could have helped him."

Daniel decided he could use his own glass of cooling water. "He may have raised you to be a soldier, but that doesn't mean he wants you risking your life for him."

"I've risked my life plenty of times."

That wasn't something Daniel needed to think about. "From what Tyler told me, he didn't like you going into the mercenary business. He wanted you to teach other soldiers how to fight."

She leaned back against the counter, her clingy pink tank top an invitation to sin. "He liked my move into computers even less."

Daniel did his best to drink his water and ignore the invitation. "He's worried you won't fit in, and he feels like it's his fault."

She shrugged, and her top lifted to expose a slim band of

silky skin above the waistband of her shorts. "He taught me how to be a soldier, but I'm learning how to be a woman now."

"I don't think you've got much to learn." He reached out and brushed his finger along the bare patch of skin. "You seem to come by it pretty naturally."

"Thanks." She smiled, as if his opinion really mattered.

After the way he'd screwed up with her more than once, that surprised him.

She looked around the small kitchen. "I guess we can stay here."

"No way. Did you see your dad's bed?" It was an extra-long twin, not a bed meant for two people to share, and Daniel planned to share Josie's bed every chance he got.

"If we leave, we might miss him."

"We can meet his flight and leave him a note here just in case. Until then, I say we check in to a decent hotel."

"Are you going to fill the room up with roses again?"

"Do you want me to?"

She shook her head, her eyes filled with soft green lights. "As long as you're in it, I don't care what else is there."

They found a room in a two-story Spanish-style hotel in a small town about fifteen miles from Tyler's safe house. Daniel checked them in to one of the hotel's two suites, available because the hotel was almost empty during the off season. Its courtyard boasted an outdoor pool and Jacuzzi.

Josie wanted to go swimming, and Daniel was more than willing to indulge her, but first they had to go shopping for swimsuits. Daniel insisted she try them on before buying.

First she came out of the dressing room wearing a dark blue one-piece with a white racing stripe down both sides.

Daniel shook his head. "I want to see more of you."

Josie could feel the blush crawl up from her toes as the sales clerk smirked, giving Daniel the once-over. *Her* expression said *she'd* be more than happy to try on two Band-Aids and a thong if that's what he wanted.

He didn't even spare her a glance, his hot, dark gaze fixed on Josie's figure under the demure swimsuit. "Please?"

"Okay."

Next, she tried a solid white bikini with a lift bra in the top that made her look as though she actually had a little bit of cleavage. The bottoms were styled like low-rider shorts, being slightly more modest than regular bikini bottoms. She liked the suit a lot and went out to Daniel with a smile on her face.

He made no effort to hide his obvious arousal at the sight of her, but shook his head. "Try on the green one."

He'd grabbed it off the rack, saying it was the same color as her eyes. It wasn't anything special, though, just a very basic string bikini. The small triangles that comprised the top did nothing to enhance her meager curves, and the bottoms made her feel almost naked in their briefness.

However, when she walked out of the dressing room, Daniel's approval was instantaneous. He looked ready to eat her like ice cream, and his hard-on was pressing against his jeans zipper in a definable ridge.

"It's perfect."

She looked down at herself. Okay, so the thin fabric of the top revealed her rapidly hardening nipples, and she could see that might be a turn-on for him, but did he realize how small the bottoms were? They barely covered her pubic hair and wouldn't have if she didn't wax her bikini line.

She did it for the same reason she bought sexy underpants, so she would feel more feminine under her clothes. It had hurt like Hades the first few times, but it worked. She got a major mental boost knowing she had a tidy triangle of curls adorning her most feminine place.

And now her secret little habit made it possible to wear a pair of bikini bottoms that had less fabric in them than a handkerchief.

Her gaze lifted to Daniel. "If you expect me to wear this, you have to buy a Speedo."

He shook his head, not looking even sort of repentant. "No can do." He pointed to the area below his waist with his whole hand. "You can see what being around you in a swim-suit does to me. A Speedo just won't cut it."

The sales clerk coughed and turned away, her expression priceless.

Josie was too busy trying not to blush, herself, to laugh, but she had to admit she could understand Daniel's dilemma. No way would a tiny pair of briefs hold his erection inside.

But, "The pool isn't heated."

"Ice cubes wouldn't help with you in that suit."

"Maybe I should get the blue one."

"*No.*"

She smiled, really liking the buzz his uncontrolled reaction to her gave her. "Okay, I'll buy the green one, but I get to pick out something for you to wear, too."

"Not a Speedo."

"Agreed." She smiled, wondering what he would think of the leather thong made to look like a loincloth she'd seen in an on-line catalogue once.

By the time they made it back to the hotel after shopping, they were both hungry for dinner and decided to eat before their swim. They didn't make it to the pool until a little after eight in the evening.

They were both used to getting a lot of physical exercise and started off swimming laps.

A hand on her ankle was the only warning Josie got before going under. She came up sputtering and glaring to be met by a grinning Daniel.

"You'll pay for that," she threatened.

He laughed at her, and no way was she going to let him get away with it.

Remembering his weakness, she attacked, tickling and trying to dunk him at the same time. She succeeded, only to get pulled under with him. She came up wrapped in his arms and with his lips locked against hers. They kissed and played and teased until she was so aroused from all the touching, she could barely stay afloat.

She anchored herself to his shoulders and wrapped her thighs around his hips, trapping the evidence of his excitement between them.

He grinned down at her, his hands gliding along her bare back and over her hips to cup her bottom in the water. "You surrender?"

She laid her head on his shoulder and sighed with contentment. "If this were really what surrendering was like, wars would end before they started."

Chapter 15

"You feel good to me, too, sweetheart."

She loved it when he called her that, and she rewarded him with a kiss against his neck.

"You ready to go back to the room?"

Darkness had fallen while they played in the pool, and no one else had come out to disturb their solitude. Summer wasn't exactly high season in the Nevada desert. It was too hot, but she didn't mind the heat, and she liked the fact the hotel wasn't booked to capacity.

"I'd rather go in the Jacuzzi. Is that okay?"

"Will you make the delay worth it?" he asked with a mock leer.

This teasing Daniel was someone she could spend the rest of her life with.

She tipped her head back and fluttered her eyelashes at him, surprised at how naturally some things came to a woman. "Don't you think I can?"

The kiss he gave her answered that question and any other she might have on her desirability.

"I'm counting on it," he said when he lifted his head.

"Good."

He started walking through the water to the pool steps,

and she let him carry her, but when they reached the first step, she tried to unwrap her legs.

His hold on her bottom tightened. "No. Let me carry you to the spa."

She looked around and didn't see anyone, not sure that it would matter if she did. "All right." She wasn't sure her legs would hold her up anyway.

His resilience amazed her.

It was incredibly erotic being carried in such an intimate position across the pool deck. Her imagination drummed up some pretty interesting scenarios in the same position, but without any swimsuits to hinder them. He stopped at the whirlpool controls to turn on the jets before stepping into the now bubbling hot water with her.

Her body tensed in involuntary reaction to the shock of the high temperature after the colder water of the pool. "It's *hot.*"

"You'll get used to it pretty fast." Then he dipped down, immersing them both up to their necks. "This is the quickest way."

She gasped and tried to shoot up out of the almost unbearably hot water, but he held her tight. "Relax, it will get better soon."

He was right. Within a second or two, it felt too good for her to want to get out. "It feels wonderful."

"I know something that feels even better." He unwrapped her legs from around him and changed his hold on her to one at her waist.

Lifting her through the water, he placed her on the cement seat running the circumference of the spa. A jet of water shot against her lower back, massaging her with a steady stream of water pressure.

Her eyes closed, and she reveled in the delicious sensation. "Umm . . . That *is* nice."

"I know." He sat down beside her and started kneading

her shoulders with strong fingers. "I designed my house with a multiperson hot tub in the master bath."

Tension drained out of her as a sense of utter peace pervaded her being. "No luxury like this for your guests?"

"I'd share with you, but there's another, much bigger one in the backyard." His fingers moved up her neck. "It's fed by an artificial waterfall pumped up from a natural spring."

"Wolf's house has a hot spring under it," she remembered out loud.

"I know. I incorporated it into his house's design, too, but his is heated. I have to heat the water for mine. Summers are hot, and the rest of the year isn't much cooler, so I leave it set at a low temperature most of the time." He guided her into a position leaning with her back against his chest. "You can stay in it longer that way."

"It sounds wonderful." She let her head fall back onto his shoulder. "I'd like to see your house someday."

"I'd like that, too."

"I can't believe you designed it and Wolf's house, too. His is amazing. I've never seen anything as beautiful as the jungle room downstairs."

"Thank you."

"How did you learn to design like that?"

He shrugged, causing her shoulders to lift and fall in unison with his. "When I first joined the Rangers, everything was so intense, I realized I needed something to do between assignments that wasn't related to warfare. Architecture and design interested me, so I started reading about it."

"You've done a lot more than read to have designed Wolf's house the way you did."

"I played around with plans, designing things on a small scale, and then I met this old guy who was a retired architect. He would look over my plans and tell me what was wrong with them until I learned the fundamentals. Then he suggested I start using computer simulation programs for design. It's the one thing I like doing on the computer."

"He sounds like a neat man."

"He was. He died the year I designed Wolf's house, but he liked my plans." The sense of accomplishment in Daniel's voice was unmistakable.

"Have you ever thought about becoming an architect?"

"I'm a soldier." He said it as if it was an incontrovertible fact.

"But if you weren't one, would you have pursued architecture and design as a career?"

"Maybe, but it doesn't matter now."

"No, I don't suppose it does." Except that he was obviously not open to a different way of life.

Just like her dad.

"Where's your house?"

"New Mexico."

"Isn't that a long way from the merc school?"

"I can go home between training sessions the same way I stay there between assignments now, but I might build again on the Oregon coast. I haven't decided yet."

"What part of New Mexico is your house in right now?"

"About an hour from Roswell." He slipped his arm around her waist and spread his fingers out over her naked stomach.

She sucked in a breath. "You mean the Area 51 Roswell?"

"I don't think there's another one."

"Are you interested in UFOs?" Her interest in their conversation was rapidly dwindling as his fingers brushed up and down on her wet skin.

"Not really, but I like the sparse population of the New Mexico desert. You can drive miles without seeing any signs of civilization but the road you're taking. It reminds me a little of where I grew up, but the winters aren't cold like they are in South Dakota. To be honest, I like that as much as not having a lot of neighbors to disturb me."

She rubbed her head against his shoulder, loving how solid he was. "Do you ever want to go back?"

"To the reservation?"

"Yes."

"I visit once a year."

That shocked her, and she jerked around to look at him, dislodging his hand so it settled on her hip. "You do?"

"Yes, but my close family is gone, so it's more of a pilgrimage." He'd been looking up at the sky, but transferred his somber gaze to her. "My grandfather's art is displayed in one of the small museums. I like to go and see it, to remember my dad's temper isn't the only legacy I have from that side of the family."

"You learned to control your temper, so I'd say it's not much of a legacy anyway."

"Maybe you're right."

She scanned his sculpted features, wondering what his dad looked like if everyone said the two of them could pass for twins. He must be a very beautiful man, on the surface anyway. "Do you remember any good times with your parents?"

He was silent for a long time, and she thought he was going to refuse to answer, but then he nodded. "They got along great when he wasn't drinking and she wasn't trying to talk me into going to college and him into paying for it. He used to teach me how to carve with his hands over mine. I still do it sometimes; it's good for my manual dexterity."

A huge bubble of emotion welled up in Josie and spilled over, warming her from the inside out. Daniel had made choice after choice to keep the best of his past and dismiss the rest of it. If only he could see how far he had come from being anything like his lost father.

Daniel sighed. "She loved his art, and he acted like he loved her."

"But he didn't love her enough to stop drinking."

"No." He shook his head. "Looking back now, I realize they could have had a great marriage, but his violent rages stopped that. There were times he went to kiss her that I could tell she was just tolerating him. She never denied him, but he had to know she didn't want him. I vowed I'd never do that to a woman, would never touch her unless she welcomed my touch."

That's where he'd gotten the need to be welcomed, not just accepted into her bed.

"Your mom must have believed it would get better."

"Maybe in the beginning, but by the time I was in school, the pattern had been set. He drank every weekend and lost his temper almost as often. The older I got, the more frequently he drank during the week as well. She always made excuses for him, but the truth was, he didn't care about anyone else enough to stop, and she didn't think enough of herself to leave him."

"That must have hurt you a lot."

"Yes."

She liked that he didn't try to deny it.

"Dad may have strange ideas about how to raise a daughter, but he always loved me. He would never have hurt me. I know it doesn't change anything, but I'm sorry your dad hurt you."

"I'm sorrier he hurt my mom, but it couldn't have been easy training to be a soldier when you were so little."

"He was a lot easier on me than he was his soldiers . . . until I got older, and then he expected me to be better than all of them."

"You are."

"I tried. I thought my dad's love depended on me being the best soldier I could be. I didn't realize he loved me for being me until a couple of years ago."

"What happened then?"

"I got shot on assignment and almost died. I was in a hospital in the Middle East for ten weeks." Remembering that time made her shiver despite the hot water bubbling around her. "He cancelled his spring training session and flew out to be with me. He sat beside my hospital bed that first night and cried, telling me how much he loved me and begging me not to die. I'd never seen him cry before. I couldn't talk much, but I tried to tell him I would be okay. He never left my room until the danger zone was past."

"He realized that what he'd raised you to be put you at risk in just the way he'd been trying to protect you from all your life."

"You're pretty smart. I think that's exactly how he felt."

"I read enough of his journals to realize how he would have reacted to you almost dying. It would have hit me the same way."

"You and my father have a lot in common."

"Not so much. He succeeded in protecting you."

"He didn't think so when I got shot. He kept saying he was sorry, and I couldn't understand why. Now I do. But one thing became very clear: He didn't love me because I was a superior soldier. He loved me because I was his daughter."

"Is that when you decided to get out of the business?"

"When I realized I didn't have to be a soldier for my dad to love me, I asked myself if I wanted to spend the rest of my life being one. The answer was no."

"You'd rather work with computers?"

"In some capacity, yes. I'm not like Claire and Hotwire, though. I'd be content to work in a job that used my computer skills, but didn't focus on them."

"So, you don't know if you'll take the job Wolf and Hotwire offered you with their security business?"

"No, I don't. There's a whole wide world out there, and I don't know where I want to live in it or what I want to be. It's pretty strange realizing at the age of twenty-six I can be anything I want."

"All I ever wanted was to be a Special Forces soldier. I chose the Rangers because the army was the easiest military organization to join."

"Why did you get out?"

"After my mom died, I couldn't stay in it."

"Because she asked you to leave the army and come home to take care of your dad and you refused? You felt guilty having your dream when your mom was dead."

"Yes."

She understood, but she thought it was such a waste. "You're an incredible soldier, Daniel."

"There's a lot more freedom being a merc than there was in the Rangers."

"Yes, but I think you would have been happy if you'd stayed."

He pulled her back against him, tucking her head into his shoulder again, but didn't respond. The silence lasted a long time, and she let her gaze drift lazily across the now star laden sky.

"My dad is up for parole this year." His voice after such an extended silence surprised her, but no more than the words.

"I thought you didn't keep track of him."

"I don't, but Sergeant Major does. He's gone to visit Thunder in prison."

"Does he encourage you to go, too?"

"No. He says that kind of thing is something a man can only do if his soul leads him to it."

Daniel's sergeant major was a wise man.

"Do you want to talk to your dad again?"

"I want to ask if the drinking was worth killing her."

Josie knew with the same instincts that had saved her life more than once that Daniel wanted to ask a whole lot more than that, but she said nothing. If he ever did decide he wanted to see his father, she hoped Daniel would let her be there for him because no matter how hard he sounded, his heart wasn't as invulnerable as he wanted to believe.

"Has he told the sergeant major he wants to see you?"

"If he has, Master Sergeant Cordell didn't pass it on, but he wouldn't."

"No matter what you decide, you're a good man, Daniel."

"You're good *for me*, Josette."

"Thanks."

In her mind, they had spent enough time talking about deep subjects. Daniel needed his thoughts directed to something more pleasant, and she had a pretty good idea how to do that.

Slipping her hand up his thigh, she brushed it quite deliberately against his sex. His body went instantly rigid, and she could hear the increased pounding of his heart against her head.

She smiled and relaxed against him as if she hadn't a care in the world, while at the same time guiding her hand beneath his waistband. "Keep your eyes on the stars, Daniel."

Anyone looking at them from outside would think she was just resting against him while they both unwound in the spa. Her hand slid inexorably downward until her fingers tangled with the light, curling patch of hair above his penis.

His hand latched on to her wrist, stopping her from moving lower. "What are you doing?"

"Can't you tell?"

"We're in a public place, Josette, or hadn't you noticed?"

"What I noticed is that the bubbles make it impossible to see what is happening under the water."

"You don't think my raw shout of ecstasy will give you away?"

She laughed softly, wiggling her fingers against him even if she couldn't reach her main target. "That's a long way off. If you keep your face expressionless, no one will know what I'm doing. You're good at controlling your temper, Daniel. Do you think you can control your passion?"

"You make it hard," he growled.

She grinned at the double entendre. "Don't you like it?"

"Yes . . . ," he hissed, and his grip slackened.

She immediately went in search of and found his penis. She began stroking up and down his length. "Just relax and let me pleasure you."

"You are pure pleasure, sweetheart, but I'm not sure this isn't torture." He groaned as she squeezed his quickly growing member, and his head fell back against the stone edge of the spa.

She snuck a peek at him and smiled. His eyes were closed, and his face was impassive, but there was a line of stress around his mouth. Arrows of pleasure shot through her core at the evidence of how strongly she affected him. She turned her head away, her eyes fixed on the stars overhead.

It felt deliciously naughty to have her hand inside his swim trunks and touching him intimately while anyone looking on would think she was doing no more than contemplate the night sky. With a sense of wanton delight, she slid her palm over the head of his penis. Wetness more slick and silky than the water told her he was closer to coming than she could have imagined, and she felt a corresponding moisture between her legs.

She played with the silky wetness, rubbing it over his head with her palm and then caressing his length in turn until his legs were jerking with the effort to stay still. She felt close to orgasm herself, and he hadn't even touched her. She stroked him, enjoying the sounds of pleasure and need he was making and letting her mind run wild with images of him inside her.

Suddenly he erupted from the water, lifting her from the pool with him.

She squeaked out a shocked, "Daniel," but he ignored her surprised protest and carried her at double time to their room, the expression on his face one that would live with her for a long time.

He was a feral warrior claiming his mate, and she exulted in being that woman.

Daniel carried Josie into their room, his body on a collision course with a desire he could no longer control. Her little green bikini had started a chain reaction in him that was set to explode with nuclear proportions any second.

Stepping over the threshold, he kicked the door shut with enough force to leave it reverberating on its hinges.

"Daniel?" Josie's eyes were fixed on him with a mixture of breathless passion and trepidation.

"I want you," he growled down at her and then took possession of her mouth with all the hunger crashing through him.

He ate at her lips, tasting the sweet warmth that she reserved for him alone. His tongue pressed into the seam of her lips, and she gave him entrance, letting him taste her, tasting him, sucking on his tongue as though she couldn't get enough of his mouth against hers.

The need to bury himself inside her expanded with each slide of her tongue against his and the swollen responsiveness of her lips until it was too big to contain. He dropped her to her feet, but couldn't stop kissing her long enough to do something about the storm raging through him.

Finally, with a monumental effort of will, he broke the kiss and stepped back.

Damn, that little nothing of a swimsuit was going to give him a heart attack. The water had turned the green fabric dark, but it clung to her obviously aroused nipples and swollen curves in a way designed to send him over the edge of reason. If he wasn't already there. His gaze shot down to where two small bows held the secrets of her femininity hidden behind a shimmering wet bit of fabric.

He wanted to get rid of that barrier.

"Take it off," he ordered, his tone so guttural it was a wonder it didn't scare her.

He forced himself to look at her face and make sure, but she didn't look frightened at all, just dazed. Her eyes were dilated with passion, and her lips pouted an invitation to be taken again.

She licked them. "What?"

"Take off your swimsuit." He'd managed a marginal improvement in his tone, but not enough to make his words sound like anything but a demand.

"Is that an order, sir?"

"Yes."

"Then I'd better obey. I don't want to be court-martialed." The words were teasing, but her voice was filled with desire.

He waited for her to comply, too far gone to help her without ruining the suit.

She reached around behind her and undid the bottom string holding her top in place. It fell down her sides, pulling the material away at the edges, but not revealing what he most needed to see.

"The other one, too."

She reached up and untied the bow at her neck, pulling the top farther up until the underswell of her breasts showed, but nothing else. Her eyes glowed feminine challenge at him as she peeled the top away to reveal dark red nipples, puckered and swollen. She cupped her own breasts and rotated her palms over her turgid peaks until he thought he would explode in his trunks from watching her.

Her head tipped back, her mouth parting and her breathing rupturing. "This feels good, Daniel, but not nearly as good as it does when you touch me."

"Then let me touch you."

He started forward, but she put her hand up. "Not yet."

He stopped, every muscle in his body vibrating with tension at the stress of holding back.

"I'm not finished." Her hands dropped to her sides, and she tugged at the ends of the bows on either side of her hips.

Sweat broke out on his brow, and his fingers curled into tight fists with the effort it took not to reach out and touch her.

With teasing slowness, she unraveled the ties, but the wet suit stayed attached to her body.

"Pull it off." He kept his hands locked at his sides, needing to watch her unveil herself for him on a primitive level he couldn't begin to understand. *"Please."*

Using them to tug the bottoms away from her skin, she spread her legs, and the green scrap of material fell to the floor, leaving her gloriously naked.

The burnished brown curls at the juncture of her thighs glistened with moisture that could be from the spa or her own excitement. The scent emanating off of her said she was very aroused, and he needed to taste that wetness to tell.

He fell to his knees in front of her and pressed her lips apart with his fingers. More glistening moisture beckoned as well as her clitoris, deep red with arousal. He put his mouth on her, and she screamed his name, her fingers locking tightly in his hair.

Swirling his tongue around her swollen bud, he reveled in the way she thrust her hips toward him, silently demanding more. He wanted to give it to her and changed the angle of his mouth so he could taste her very essence.

So sweet. He could eat her like this into eternity.

With a desperate rhythm, she pleasured herself on his tongue, but her panting pleas told him, she couldn't find the ultimate satisfaction without his cooperation.

He wanted to be inside her when it happened and surged to his feet. She swayed, and he reached out to steady her, ready to pull her to him and make love.

But she stepped back. "Wait right here."

"Where are you going?"

"I'm still wet."

"That's not a problem."

"I mean my body," she croaked on a laugh that should have been impossible considering how excited they both were.

She spun on her heel and disappeared into the bathroom. She reappeared scant seconds later holding a fluffy bath towel. She used it to dry herself off, touching herself in places he was dying to taste again, and then moved forward until she stood directly in front of him.

"I want to dry you off, too."

"Okay." His voice cracked like an adolescent's, and he didn't even care. "But hurry."

She started by taking his trunks off, carefully pulling the wet nylon over his throbbing hard-on and then pushing it down his thighs until he was as naked as she was.

"Step out of them," she instructed, and he did, wondering how long he could let her be in charge.

If he'd thought the way she dried herself off was erotic foreplay, it was nothing compared to the way she used the towel to soak up excess moisture from his skin while exciting him to a painful level of arousal.

"I need you," he whispered thickly as he lifted her against him.

"I need you, too, Daniel. Always."

He couldn't concentrate on the significance of that word, but he relished the knowledge she was as much his as he was hers. The ongoing obsession was a shared one.

She locked her legs around him like she'd done in the pool. This time there was no barrier of swimsuits to get in their way, and his sex pushed up inside of her. She pressed downward, so slick with her own excitement that he achieved penetration in one smooth advance.

Wrapping her arms around his head, she kissed him with voracious passion he more than matched. Using his hands on her hips, he moved her up and down on him, gyrating his pelvis with each thrust, and she came without warning on his fourth surge upward.

She convulsed around him, her body locked to his with complete and utter abandon. He couldn't stop thrusting, and she made a guttural noise low in her throat, tearing her lips from his.

"Daniel, it's too much!"

He just shook his head, unable to verbalize, but she wasn't

trying to get out of his arms, so he didn't stop. Suddenly, she buried her face in his neck, and her body shook in a second orgasm. She bit him, and he reveled in the small violence, feeling his own orgasm build at the base of his shaft.

He wanted to drive for fulfillment with everything in him. Moving until he could press her against the wall, he started thrusting inside her with the power and depth he needed.

"I'm going to come!"

Chapter 16

Josie shook her head frantically, her hair sweeping against his chest. *"Stop, Daniel."*

Was she crazy? *"I can't."*

"You have to." She grabbed his head by the hair and pulled. "You're not wearing a condom."

For the first time since he became sexually active, he seriously considered finishing without it, but that wouldn't be fair to Josie.

He barely had the strength to make it to the bed, but he did, and he laid her down before scrambling for a condom. He put it on with shaking fingers, his body strung so tight, he was a hairsbreadth from snapping.

He came back over her, looking down into her beautiful face. "You know the damage could already have been done?"

"My period is due any day. You're safe." There was something in her voice he didn't like, but he forgot about it as she pulled his body into hers once again.

He wanted to come so bad he could taste it, but he needed her to be with him, not merely accepting his body into hers as reciprocation for the pleasure he'd given her. He leaned down and took a ripe raspberry nipple into his mouth and started sucking.

Her fingers dug into his shoulders. "I love it when you

take me in your mouth," she panted, her willingness to go on the journey of pleasure with him once again lacing every syllable.

He didn't reply, but kept stimulating her with his teeth and tongue, moving to her other nipple as she started to writhe under him again. She whimpered and arched toward him as his hand moved between their bodies to find her already swollen sweet spot and touch it in the way he'd learned brought her the most pleasure.

She thrust upward, and they moved together, both seeking the ultimate pleasure in each other's bodies.

Rational thought disintegrated as sensation overtook him, and pressure built until he knew his explosion was imminent.

"Come with me," he demanded.

"*Yes.*" She went stiff, her whole body arching wildy against him, and they came together with cataclysmic force.

The next two days were idyllic. Josie and Daniel played in the pool, talked about their pasts and made love.

On the third morning at the hotel, Josie woke up to cramps, and she turned over in the bed, moaning as pain shot through her lower back and abdomen.

She'd never understood how she could be so incapacitated by something women the world over experienced on a monthly basis, but debilitating pain and exhaustion accompanied her period pretty much every month. Thank God for ibuprofen. It had saved a mission from total meltdown failure more than once.

She crawled out of bed, knowing if she didn't take care of things right that minute, she would regret it. A long, hot shower left her feeling only marginally better. She needed pain reliever, and she needed it two hours ago.

She rummaged through her bag and found the pads she'd packed in case of such an occurrence, but no ibuprofen. The curse that erupted from her throat would have shocked

Daniel if he'd been awake to hear it. How could she have forgotten something so important?

She had her Glock, extra ammunition and a terrain map of Nevada, but no small white bottle of pain reliever.

Moving gingerly, she dressed in a long T-shirt and pair of bikini-style briefs. She couldn't stand anything around her waist just yet, but considering her pain and the absence of anything to deal with it, she would have no choice.

Daniel woke up as she was pulling the T-shirt on. He smiled at her, looking all too sexy and more masculine than any other man she'd ever known. "Come back to bed, sweetheart. We don't have anything we have to do today but be together."

She would put paid to that attitude of togetherness soon enough. "I started."

He looked blankly at her.

"My period."

His expression cleared. "I guess we really were safe last night."

"Yes." She turned away and grabbed up a pair of shorts.

She might as well bite the bullet and get them on. She couldn't go into town dressed in Daniel's T-shirt.

"What are you doing?"

"Getting dressed."

"Why?"

"I need pain reliever. I can't go shopping dressed in a T-shirt. There are ordinances for that sort of thing."

He was off the bed in a heartbeat and taking her shorts out of her hands. "Lie down. I'll get it. If you're in pain, you shouldn't be driving. What kind do you need? Do you need anything else?"

She stared at him, shocked by the quick succession of words out of his mouth. It wasn't that Daniel never talked to her, but he sounded panicked, and that wasn't like him. In fact, she could never actually remember a time when he had used that particular tone in her hearing.

His face creased in a frown of concern. "I really think you should lie down, Josette."

"I'm having my period, not infected with a deadly disease."

"You said you were in pain."

She winced as her womb knotted in another cramp. "Yes."

"I'll take care of you."

And that was what he did, literally putting her back into bed and tucking the blankets around her. He asked if the air conditioner was set too high, then if it was too low, and when she said it was just fine, his relief was blatant. Then he made her a cup of tea, sweetened it and insisted she drink it before he left to pick up her ibuprofen.

He came back an hour later with a grocery bag filled with chocolate of every kind and a single bottle of the pain reliever.

"They didn't have any of the special woman's stuff in the local grocery store, so I had to drive into the next town and go to their pharmacy."

"I could have taken something else."

"But it wouldn't have been as effective."

He was right. "What is the chocolate for?"

He looked sheepish. "My mom used to crave it once a month. I thought you might want some, too, but I didn't know what kind you liked, so there's a little of everything."

She felt a smile creasing her face despite the pain in her lower back. "I like pretty much all of it. Thanks. For everything."

He brought her a glass of juice from the minibar fridge and watched her drink it and take the pain meds. "Do you want me to order some breakfast?"

"No. Actually, I'm tired. I'd rather just sleep."

Daniel nodded, looking a little haggard himself. They'd had a long night of making love, and it was still very early. She looked at the digital clock on the nightstand. No wonder

Daniel had needed to drive to another town to get her meds. The local pharmacy probably wasn't even open yet.

"Sleep as long as you need." He picked up her now empty glass and turned to go.

"Daniel."

He turned back to face her. "Do you need something else, sweetheart?"

"You look tired, too. Do you want to catch another couple of hours of sleep?"

"I can sleep on the couch in the main room."

"It's a king-size bed, Daniel. If you don't want to cuddle, there's still plenty of room for both of us to sleep in it."

"I might touch you in my sleep. It could hurt."

She couldn't believe he was so worried about her. "I'm fine. Really. In a half an hour, I'll be feeling a lot better, and I'd rather you slept in here if you want to."

"But if I touch you . . ."

"I like sleeping with your arms around me."

"Are you sure?"

Man, he would be a total case if he ever did get a woman pregnant. He'd probably want to sleep on the couch the whole nine months.

"Yes."

He stripped down to his skivvies and then climbed into the bed beside her. He pulled her into his arms, careful to cuddle her without putting any pressure on her abdomen.

She slipped back into a blessedly pain free sleep.

Daniel curled Josie close to his body, the need to make everything right in her world overriding every other impulse at the moment. He couldn't believe how much it bothered him to see her in pain. He'd witnessed atrocities he would die never sharing with anyone else, but the sight of Josie's pale face that morning had been enough to give him the shakes.

And she'd thought he was going to let her go out and buy her own pain reliever. Was she insane, or just too damn independent for her own good?

Her sanity might not be in question, but he was beginning to think his was. How would he come to terms with the fact that he'd been disappointed to learn her period had started? A part of his brain he had not given daylight in years had played with the idea of having a baby with his former-soldier lover. Learning it was absolutely not a possibility made him face the fact he might have actually wanted it to be.

Josie snapped Daniel's cell phone shut, frustration making her stomach cramp. "Detective Stone says they aren't doing anything to move in on the enemy despite the fact we know exactly where my stolen laptop is."

"Why not?" Daniel looked up from where he sat at the suite's small table oiling his weapon.

"The FBI is afraid of another Waco situation." She rubbed her stomach, but it didn't help dispel the tension tightening her insides. "All their intelligence indicates the compound is heavily armed, but that wives and children live there along with the self-appointed whites-only militia. An attempt to go in could result in a bloodbath. The situation is under consideration by the FBI and the rest of the coalition involved in the investigation."

"Tyler isn't going to stand around waiting for the shirts in Washington to get their heads out of their as—butts before he acts."

"That's what I'm afraid of. The nutcases in that group hiding in the Rockies tried to kill him and did destroy his home. Dad's going to be planning revenge."

"The question is, do we try to help him or stop him?"

"We may not have a choice. Stopping my dad when he's in full-throttle battle mode is like putting a hand brake on a rampaging elephant." She plopped down on the edge of the bed and sighed, exhausted by the prospect of even trying.

Daniel looked as dangerous as she knew him to be. "Where

did those idiots ever get the idea they could learn what he had to teach them and then dispose of him?"

"And blame me for it." She was still mad about that. Being accused of attempted patricide was not her idea of a good time. "The authorities were already buying in to me as the culprit. If my house hadn't been broken in to, I would still be under investigation."

He gave her one of those looks he was so good at, the ones that made her feel shivery on the inside even when she was pretty sure he hadn't meant to. "There's no reason to believe you aren't."

"They let me leave the state."

"You didn't tell them you were going, and I made darn sure we weren't tailed to the airport."

She'd thought he'd been watching for the media, or the terrorists. It hadn't occurred to her he had been just as intent on eluding the police. "Detective Stone didn't tell me not to go anywhere, and he told me to concentrate on finding Dad."

"He said to stay off airplanes."

"He was talking about parachuting from them into the compound."

"Maybe." Daniel finished with his weapon and laid it on the hand towel he'd spread out on the table.

She shook her head, not convinced she was still under suspicion. Her dad and Daniel both tended to be overly cautious about some things. "I still think the enemy made a mistake breaking in to my house."

"That wasn't their only one."

That was true, the extremists had made a lot of mistakes when she stopped to think about it. "Stupidity or arrogance, do you think?"

"Both." Daniel didn't sound very interested either way. "They're not going to get the best of Tyler or us."

"I hope not." If she could just talk to her dad, she'd feel a lot better.

Daniel got up and came over to her, the fluid grace of his body impacting her even with all the worries tumbling around in her head about her dad. He stopped in front of her, so close she had to tip her head back to look up at him. She didn't try to mask her worried thoughts, didn't even want to. She'd spent most of her life hiding her weakness from others, but her defenses came crashing down with him.

"I'm worried, Daniel."

"I can see that." He gently pushed against her shoulders until she was lying back on the bed. "You need to let it go." Then he came over her, settling his hips against hers and holding his upper body above her with his arms.

If his plan was to disarm her fears by getting her to focus on him, it was working. She could barely remember her own name, much less what they were talking about.

His dark brown, ultraserious gaze locked with hers. "Everything is going to be okay."

"I want to believe that."

"Then do." He kissed her, and she melted without a second's hesitation.

He took his time about it, nibbling on her lips and exploring her mouth with his tongue. He'd done a lot of that over the last day and a half—kissing her, touching her, pulling her into his lap to cuddle her. Far from ignoring her because she couldn't make love with him, he went out of his way to be affectionate. He pampered her and made her feel as though she was anything but a simple sexual obsession.

Not that she had expected him to dismiss her from his thoughts as if she meant nothing when she wasn't available sexually. They were friends after all, but she knew the nondemand touching excited him. She'd felt the evidence on more than one occasion, and yet he made no effort to protect himself from sexual frustration by sticking with a policy of noncontact. And she'd really liked that.

She'd offered to bring him to a climax with her hand or

her mouth, but he'd refused, saying she was too tired and fragile physically to be worrying about him. The ibuprofen had helped a lot with her cramps, but the exhaustion that accompanied the first twenty-four hours of her period still clung to her.

He finished the kiss with a series of little nibbles down the side of her throat and then rolled onto his side, pulling her with him. He didn't say anything, just rubbed her back, and she felt herself getting drowsy. She didn't fight the sensation because she knew she didn't have to. She was safe with him.

Josie woke feeling totally refreshed to the sound of the shower going in the suite's main bathroom. She smiled to herself. Daniel must have gone for a run or a swim. He wouldn't have wanted to take a mid-afternoon nap with her, but he'd held her until she fell asleep.

That kind of consideration deserved a reward. Besides, she'd dreamt about him, about how it would be to bring him to a climax. She wanted to see if reality matched the experience of her imagination. She considered how best to pursue her goal and was glad for what she'd considered extravagance upon checking in—a secondary half bath off the suite's living room area.

She'd just come back into the bedroom after freshening up when she heard the water cut off. Okay, so a sojourn in the shower was out, but that hadn't been her first choice anyway. She didn't want him to be distracted by anything, including running water.

A few minutes later, he came into the room, a towel slung around his hips and using another to dry his hair. He glanced toward the bed and stopped mid-movement with the towel dangling from his hand.

"*Josette?*" he asked, his voice hoarse.

She'd taken off the clothes she'd put on when the pain meds started working and put his T-shirt back on. It hung down on one shoulder and showed the upper swell of her left breast. She'd meant it to be that way and was very gratified by his response.

"I had a dream."

His hand came down, and the towel dropped from it. "You did?"

"Yes, and it was really nice."

His eyes kindled with heat, and the corners of his lips tilted in a small smile. "I'm glad to hear that, honey. Was I in the dream?"

"Yes."

He started walking toward her. "Do you want to tell me about it?"

"I'd rather show you."

His breathing increased, his expression very interested. "Are you sure you're up to it?"

"Definitely." She put her hand up before he reached her. "Take off your towel and lie down on the bed, Daniel. I want to pleasure you."

If his stillness before had been acute, now it was absolute. "You want to pleasure me?"

"Oh, yes." She nodded. "I want to make you come, and I want to watch you do it." Her dream had been very explicit, and she was still tender in her secret places from it.

She watched with interest as his towel started tenting away from his body.

She smiled, her body suffusing with heat from his obvious arousal. "I guess you like the idea."

"I always like the idea of making love with you."

"This time I want to make love to you—a one-way deal."

His eyes narrowed, the pleasure in them dimming slightly. "It can be mutual."

"But I don't want it to be." She put her hands out, palms up. "Please, Daniel. Touching you is something I want to do . . . very, very, very much . . . but I'm not comfortable with the other."

Concern creased his brow. "If you aren't comfortable . . ."

"I didn't mean physically. I meant mentally."

"Oh." He smiled the pirate's smile she loved so much. "I could make you comfortable."

If any man could, it would be him, but she didn't want to and said so. "I want to show you what I dreamed about. Making love with you the first time outstripped every fantasy I'd ever had, and I want to see if it will be the same like this."

"So, this thing you want to do to me is just a science experiment?"

She laughed, her insides liquefying at his expression. "No. A very special *experience*, not an experiment, and your body is making emphatic statements about what it wants, don't you think?"

He looked down at the towel and back at her. "What you want to do to me is every man's fantasy, and the fact that it's you wanting to do it makes it mine, but—"

"I think we've already established this is something I want, so there should be no barrier to letting me live out my own fantasy," she said, cutting in before he could voice any more objections.

He dropped the towel and stood in a position of complete openness to her. "Whatever you want."

For several seconds, all she wanted to do was look. "You are a magnificent example of the male species." Her throat was dry from excitement, and the words came out husky and inviting.

He was so gorgeous. Even the scars on his body from his years of professional soldiering made him more sexy, giving him a dangerous air that lured women of all types, and he wanted her.

"You could have any woman."

"I want only one."

She barely bit back words of love as his answer penetrated her to the depths of her soul.

"Lie down on the bed," she croaked.

He did, his muscles rippling with movement and his sex jutting out from his body. His maleness, its very difference from her femaleness, fascinated her. He was hard steel sheathed in velvet, and she needed to feel the strength of his erection. She reached out to run a caressing hand down its length.

His breath hitched, and his hips arched toward her hand. "Sweetheart . . ."

"You feel so different from me, not like what I expected a man to feel like."

"What did you expect?" he asked, his expression taut as she ran her fingers over him as if she were playing the scales on a piano.

"Roughness, I don't know . . . not such intense sensitivity."

"Why do you think so many men think with their lower head instead of the one that has a brain? So many nerve centers demand a lot of attention."

"I read somewhere that a woman's clitoris has the highest concentration of nerve endings of anywhere on the body, male or female, but a man's penis head comes in second." She brushed gentle fingertips over the top of his while the clitoris she spoke of throbbed in response to the sensory input of her fingers.

He didn't bother to answer; he groaned instead.

Remembering her dream, she made herself stop touching the most sensitive part of his body for a little while. She wanted it all . . . every nuance of pleasure sensation she could coax from his body. She concentrated on his chest, tracing circles around his nipples and running her short nails down his rib cage while his body jerked with reaction. His stomach was warm, and she caressed it with hands that trembled in exultation at the license he'd given her with his body. He was such a powerful man, and he'd made himself incredibly vulnerable to her.

It was a heady sensation.

His abdominal muscles clenched in response to her touch . . . just like in her dream.

And just like in her dream, she wanted more.

Straddling his thighs, she leaned down and kissed the rock-solid contour of his chest. So good. She loved the scent of his skin, the spicy maleness that she associated only with him. Brushing her lips over his warm skin, she moved her head until her open mouth was over one of his now turgid male nipples. She flicked her tongue out to taste, and remembering how much he liked it, she started to suck.

His fingers dug into her scalp, and she sucked harder, rubbing up and down against his erection with her torso. His big body vibrated under her, the sexual tension buzzing off of him palpable.

"Josette, this is going to get out of hand really fast," he rasped.

She released his nipple from between her teeth and sat up. "No, it's not."

His brow rose, questioning her assertion as did the pulsing erection protruding even more stiffly from his body.

"I'm taking you in hand, not letting you get out of it." She curled her fingers around the evidence of her effect on him, gasping when her fingertips would not quite meet. "You're so aroused."

"You're sitting on top of me wearing my T-shirt, looking sexy as hel—heck, touching me in a way guaranteed to separate me from my sanity. Aroused is a tame word for the storm you've got raging inside me."

His words made her thighs clench in excitement where they straddled his, and she couldn't help rubbing herself against him, frustrated that the layers between them muted the sensation so much.

He made a hoarse sound low in his throat. "Is this part of your dream?"

She squeezed his erection, unable to tell if it was her hand or his penis that was so hot. "What do you think?"

"I think I want to see more of your body."

She peeled the T-shirt off over her head, exposing breasts whose peaks were tight with excitement. He reached up and touched them, cupping her and rubbing his palms over elongated nipples highly sensitized by her monthly hormone changes.

She shivered, pressing herself into his palms, and then she pleasured him.

Using the small bottle of hand lotion the hotel had provided, she stroked up and down his length and over his head until he was bowed off the bed, his expression one of tortured pleasure. She felt as if he was inside her, touching her erogenous zones even though his hands were now fisted in the bedspread. Her lower body throbbed with vicarious pleasure, and her nipples stung with excruciating sensation.

"I'm going to come!" His hoarse shout reverberated in the room.

But he didn't, and she could see the effort it was costing him. Whether he couldn't take that final step and make himself completely vulnerable to her, or he felt some macho need to hold back his own pleasure when he wasn't making it mutual, she didn't know. And she didn't care.

It *was* mutual, and she didn't need him to be inside her to make it that way, but she did need him to orgasm with her hands wrapped around the most intimate part of his body. "Don't try to hold back, Daniel. I want you to come for me."

He looked at her, his expression reflecting conflicting desires, his body so taut with arousal it felt as if he was about to snap like an overextended rubber band.

"Give up control. *Please.*"

"It's hard . . ."

"Do you trust me enough?" she asked, her own body trembling with an excess of feeling.

"Yes!" And he came, shouting her name and ejaculating in powerful surges.

As the warmth of his essence mixed with the hand lotion

over her fingers, she felt contractions start low in her belly, and these contractions didn't hurt. They were pure delight and corresponded to something happening in her heart she could no longer even attempt to deny. A well-spring of consuming love bubbled through her bloodstream like uncorked champagne overflowing its bottle.

She tumbled forward, a special gravity pulling her to him that could never be explained in a physics book. Locking her lips to his, her body convulsed in its own orgasm from the sheer pleasure of the man she loved allowing her to give him one.

His hands settled onto her bottom, and he kneaded her, his mouth voracious under hers. They shook together in aftershocks every bit as intense as any they'd had after full intercourse, only finally relaxing into sated passivity several minutes later.

She rubbed her cheek against the sweat-slick skin of his chest, and words came she did not plan, but had no desire to hold back. "I love you, Daniel."

The silence of his response did not surprise her, nor did it diminish in any way the feelings engulfing her.

Love did not have to be returned to be as deeply embedded in her heart as the roots of an ancient oak in the soil under it.

Chapter 17

Josie stood beside Daniel at the airport's security exit and watched for her father. Daniel had been quiet since she'd told him of her love, but not distant, so she had hope. He wasn't pushing her away for bringing emotion into the equation of their mutual obsession.

He wasn't embracing those emotions, though, either.

She didn't blame him. He'd said all along his feelings for her were not rooted in sentiment, but physical desire. Whether or not he could change his attitude remained to be seen, but she certainly wasn't giving up on him because he hadn't made any declarations.

Several passengers came through the exit as they waited, but none of them were Tyler McCall, and she grew antsy.

"Do you think he missed the flight?" she asked.

Daniel's hand settled on her shoulder, giving the comfort of his touch. "Don't worry about it. Hotwire confirmed Tyler checked in for his seat assignment."

"It could have been a smoke screen." Her dad was tricky like that.

"He'll be here, sweetheart." The hand on her shoulder squeezed and then fell away. "Relax."

A dapper older gentleman, wearing a conservative gray suit and carrying a briefcase, came toward them, and it was only as her dad got within ten feet that Josie recognized him. His military haircut was hidden under what had to have been a wig. It looked like a very real head of graying hair, cut in a typical businessman's style.

He smiled as he reached them, his eyes warm with approval behind the silver-rimmed glasses he wore. "I knew you'd figure the journals out."

With better than perfect eyesight, he'd never worn glasses, but they complemented his alter ego rather well. While one part of her admired his ability to camouflage in any environment, she was pretty frustrated by the whole cloak-and-dagger thing at this point. He could have been hurt while she was busy trying to figure out the clues in his diaries, and she'd spent a lot of unnecessary time in a state of anxiety.

She did not appreciate the added stress. *"Why didn't you just call?"*

"Could have had a bug on your phone. Didn't need the enemy realizing I had lived through their little explosion sooner than they had to."

"I've been worried sick about you."

He looked at her as if she'd lost her mind. "Why?"

"Someone tried to kill you," she reminded him with exasperation. "Why did you leave the hospital?"

Her dad's eyes dimmed. "I'm not sure. I was a little confused. Couldn't remember why I had to get away, just knew that I did. I was halfway here before I remembered why I was headed to Nevada and what had happened. By then, I figured you'd find me through the journals, and like I said, I didn't want to risk your phone being bugged."

He started walking, even his gait that of a businessman, not a soldier. "Come on. I've got a checked bag."

It took several minutes to get his single piece of luggage, and when she asked him why he checked it, he told her it went with the cover.

He picked up the medium-sized suitcase. "Did you bring a car?"

"Yes." Daniel put his arm around Josie's waist and began to lead the way outside.

She raised a startled gaze to him, but he was looking at her dad and asking how the recon mission went. Her father's reply confirmed Daniel had been right in assuming reconnaissance had been her father's objective.

"They've got fifteen soldiers, nine wives and eleven kids in the compound. Four of the soldiers have been through my training camp in the last year. Little pricks thought they could get rid of me after a six-week training course when I've been a soldier longer than most of them have been alive."

They'd reached the car, and Daniel opened the trunk for her dad to drop in his bag. Josie climbed into the backseat and waited for the men to get in.

Once they did, she asked, "Did you get any names?"

"No more than the ones I've already got. I didn't want to risk going in through security until I'd scouted the whole area. When I did go in, I didn't have time to do anything but get some details on the internal structure of the compound I hadn't been able to achieve via long distance observation."

"How's security?" Daniel asked.

"It's all right. Nothing like what you and your friends would have set up. We'll get past it pretty easily."

She'd been afraid of this. "Get past it for what?"

"Not to blow them to kingdom come, if that's what's worrying you, Josie-girl. I don't kill innocent women and children."

"I know that." It was her turn to look at him as if his brains had leaked out through his ears during the flight from Missoula. "However, that doesn't mean whatever else you've got planned won't get you into trouble."

He rolled his eyes and looked at Daniel. "She been worrying like this the whole time?"

"Not all of it," Daniel said noncommittally.

Her dad grimaced. "I guess the feds are already involved?"

"Yes."

"Would be a hell of a lot easier if they weren't, but I figured they would be, what with the Homeland Security Act and the area surrounding my property being national forest."

"They thought you'd set the explosion yourself at first," Josie said, still unable to comprehend what kind of logic had worked that scenario out.

"Idiots."

"Josie's also a suspect. The extremists took out a life insurance policy in your name and named her as beneficiary. Then told the press about it."

She hadn't wanted him to tell her dad that. He was bound to be angry enough as it was.

"They spread the blame around. The press also acted like they'd received tips indicating the responsible parties belonged to ELF," she said by way of getting his attention focused on something else.

"And caused reporters and cameramen to park themselves in Josette's front yard and harass her through the door or in person whenever she went outside."

"You are not helping," she said as her dad slammed his fist against the dashboard.

"Those sons of bitches!"

"My feelings exactly." Daniel sounded only slightly more controlled in his fury than her dad, and it occurred to her that he'd been hiding from her a lot of his reaction to what had happened.

They couldn't afford to dwell on their anger. "The important issue is what you're planning to do about it."

"Take them down."

"How?"

"Break in to their compound, dispose of their armory and weapons, find their records and turn the sons of bitches over to the feds for disposal. If my investigator's research is accurate, and there's no reason to believe it's not, getting documentation of the group's activities to the feds will have several members facing arrest and long-term prison sentences."

"Not to mention the ones responsible for your attempted murder." She wasn't sure how practical his idea of neutralizing their armory and weapons was, but his objectives were way better than she had been expecting. "I assume you have an idea of how to go about doing all this."

"I do, but I'll want some time to put it into mission-briefing form before I present it to you and Daniel. I spent the flight flirting with the woman in the seat next to mine."

Shocked, Josie squeaked, *"Flirting?"*

"Part of my cover, but she was a nice-looking woman. Oriental. Tiny thing, with a voice as soft as an angel's. Gave me her phone number. She only lives about twenty minutes from my house here. Can you believe that?"

She couldn't believe any of it, but before she could think of a way to phrase such a statement diplomatically, Daniel asked, "How did you know the Society of New American Patriots was responsible for the bombing?"

"The man who runs the background checks on my students discovered a connection between a soldier who'd been in my January training camp and one that had just taken the early summer training. He had just figured out that they both were involved in this stupid-ass white supremacist organization when the compound got blown up."

"You knew you had somebody after you, and you didn't say anything?" Josie asked, much more dismayed by this revelation than by her father's apparent attraction to a woman for the first time in her memory.

"I didn't know they were *after me.* I only knew I'd been training domestic terrorists. I was deciding what I wanted to do about it when they tried to kill me."

"You didn't tell me about it," Daniel said.

"It was my problem. They came through the camp before you bought in to it."

"I'm your partner. All problems related to the school are mine, too." There was no give in Daniel's voice, but then she hadn't thought that argument was going to hold water with him.

"Hell, Nitro, you've got enough trouble on your hands courting my daughter. Any idiot could see that."

"He's not *courting* me, Dad. I swear, sometimes you talk like you were born two centuries ago, not a few decades before the new millennium."

Her dad snorted. "Doesn't matter when I was born. Call it what you like. Courting is courting, and I wasn't born yesterday. I can see what's going on right in front of my face."

"You're more perceptive than Josie is. She thought I didn't like her." Daniel sounded amused, and she glared at the back of his head.

Was this some kind of guy thing or just another case of her dad and Daniel being alike? How was she supposed to know that glaring, brooding and general cranky behavior was the male mating call for the modern-day warrior?

Her dad turned around to face her. "I guess you've worked it out different by now?"

"Yes," she clipped, still irritated with both of them for acting so superior.

She didn't repeat the assertion that Daniel wasn't courting her because he hadn't denied it.

There were only a couple of reasons she could think of for that, and the first one she already knew to be false—that he really was interested in marrying her. She remembered what Daniel had said about how her dad had been warning men off of her since she was young. As his new partner, her mercenary lover probably didn't want to start his new working relationship with a huge fight over his desire to bed but not wed the other man's daughter.

Since she wasn't up to a big argument with her dad either, she understood where Daniel was coming from. She didn't know if his present silence on the truth was going to help anything in the long run, however.

"I'm glad you finally got smart," her dad said. "I thought Nitro was going to self-destruct the way you ignored what he felt for you."

"I didn't realize you were aware of it to that extent," Daniel said, his voice now laced with chagrin. "I'm not usually so easily read."

"I notice everything related to my daughter."

He hadn't noticed she craved some level of normal domesticity in her life, but then even the best parents were blind to some things about their children.

Tyler's plane had arrived late evening, so it was dark when Daniel and Josie drove him back to his house. He was tired and wanted to get working on the mission strategy, so they left him and continued to the hotel.

They returned the next morning after breakfast.

Tyler made coffee and served it on the brick patio, having pulled some chairs out of the storage area attached to the back of the house.

"I noticed you didn't stay here while I was gone," he said as he took his seat next to Josie. "I wouldn't have minded."

Josie smiled, looking so sweet Daniel wanted to lick her lips like a lollipop. "We knew that, but we thought staying at a hotel would be better."

"The bed was more comfortable. She'd have had to sleep on top of me in yours," Daniel added, winking at Josie and enjoying the way she choked on her coffee.

She was damn cute when she got embarrassed.

"You've staked a claim on my daughter."

"Yes, sir, I have."

The look Josie gave him was enigmatic, and Daniel wished he knew what she was thinking. She'd said she loved him and given him one of the most amazing experiences of his life, but he didn't know how she felt about the fact he hadn't repeated the words. He couldn't.

He didn't equate the way he felt about her with the way his mother had been devoted to his father in the face of her own compromised safety. He sure as hell didn't see what his father called love as having anything to do with the way Daniel reacted to Josie. He wasn't sure what he did feel about her, except that he had no intention of letting her go.

"So what are your plans for taking the target?" Josie asked in the silence that had stretched after his declaration of intent.

Tyler looked from Daniel to his daughter as if he was trying to gauge what was going on between them. Daniel wished him luck.

With a small frown, the older man shrugged and focused on Josie. "I figured a small force of four to six soldiers would have the best chance of pulling it off. We go in at night when they've got two sentries patrolling the perimeter. The soldiers guarding the compound are pretty much weekend warriors, despite what they might think—even the four that have been through my training camps. They rely heavily on their not-so-incredible security system."

"So, we disarm the system, neutralize the sentries and follow through on our objective uninterrupted? It sounds too easy." And Daniel didn't trust easy on a mission.

"It shouldn't be, but sons of bitches stupid enough to think they can use my training camp to develop domestic terrorism techniques are stupid enough to be brought down without a five-star effort."

Maybe his business partner was right, but Daniel planned to call Wolf and Hotwire in to be two on the team. He wanted the best with him because he knew Josie was going to insist on coming along, and he wasn't going to let her get hurt if he had to stop a bullet with his body.

She was the other half of his soul, and somehow he was

going to have to come to terms with that truth, whatever it meant.

"I'm not sure about your plan to disarm them." Josie wrinkled her nose as if she'd smelled something bad. "That doesn't seem like a simple objective with an organization like this one."

"The armory is kept in an underground storage facility. We weld the doors shut, and it will be days before they can get the supplies in necessary to cut through the two-inch-thick metal. They're a real live-off-the-land type of group, and their transportation in and out of the compound is pretty rudimentary."

"But what about their personal weapons?"

Tyler grimaced. "That's going to take more doing. Everyone in the compound is armed, but they store their weapons in communal rooms when they aren't using them, and as far as I can tell, only the sentries take firearms with them at night. We have to infiltrate the rooms and take out the arms."

"The easiest thing to do would be to put them in the armory before we weld it shut," Josie said musingly as Daniel became more convinced this was one mission she should not go on.

Tyler nodded. "I think so, too."

But Daniel shook his head. "No way."

"Why not?" Josie asked.

"We're good, but no matter how good we are, with the kind of invasive mission objectives your father has outlined, someone is going to wake up and raise the alarm."

"Not if we put a sleeping agent in their evening meal. They all eat from the same supplies. All we have to do is mix it in with the flour the women use to make the bread they serve every night."

"Too risky."

"I got in before; I can do it again."

"There's no way to regulate how much of the agent they

ingest. Enough to knock out an adult could kill a child." And Daniel wasn't willing to take that chance.

"What do you suggest?" Tyler asked.

"Change our objectives."

"To what?"

"The four men who went through your training school are probably the same ones who set the bombs on the mountain. I assume you noted their sleeping quarters. We take them prisoner and deliver them to the FBI, along with copies of the extremists' files. Welding the armory doors shut is doable, but one level of risk higher than I think we should take."

"With the four soldiers gone, won't the others run?" Josie asked.

"Possibly, but with the evidence we'll provide them, the FBI can put a hold on their funds and confiscate the property housing the compound under the Terrorist Act."

"And unlike big-name terrorists, these men don't have a whole lot of financial resources at their disposal," Tyler mused. "The feds will get them eventually. From what my investigator can tell, their alternative identities are pretty thin. Even the suits in Washington should be able to see through them."

Josie nodded, her expression saying she had a lot more confidence in the authorities than her dad did. "And if they don't run, with the inside information you've accumulated, the FBI should be able to infiltrate the camp without allowing a hostage situation to develop with the terrorists' families."

"I don't suppose there's any way I can talk you out of being on the team that goes in to take down the extremists?"

Josie looked critically at the paint job she was giving her toenails. She'd never done this before, but it wasn't all that hard. Not for a woman who had been trained to hit a target before she'd learned how to ride a bike.

The pink nail polish she'd picked up at one of the airport stores while they were waiting for her dad glistened with a pearly shine. She wiggled her toes. Nice. Very feminine.

She raised her gaze to Daniel. "Why would you want to?"

"I don't want you hurt."

"I'm a soldier. This is what I do."

"No, you aren't. You're building a different life for yourself. Maybe you should consider giving that life a chance before taking on a mission like this."

"There isn't going to be another mission like this."

His expression said that wasn't a bad thing.

She went back to painting her toenails, giving them a second coat. "Wow, the color really changes when you add another coat."

"Haven't you worn nail polish before?"

"No. There's tons of stuff I haven't done."

"Like what?"

"I'd never been in a girls' locker room until I joined a health club near my house."

"Did you join so you could go in one?"

She finished her right foot and switched to her left. "Yeah. It probably sounds crazy to you, but there are so many normal life experiences I want to try."

"You can't exactly do stuff like go to dances, pass notes with your friends and have a crush on the most popular boy in school now."

"I didn't go to school at all. The one time I tried in junior high, I felt so out of place I never wanted to go back. I like college, though. Claire and I have even passed notes." Having finished her toenails, she closed the bottle of nail polish and put it on the nightstand beside the bed. "I wonder how long these will take to dry."

"What does the bottle say?"

"It doesn't. I guess they figure women don't need directions for this sort of thing."

He came around the bed and sat down beside her, laying his long legs alongside hers. "I'd give it at least fifteen minutes."

She wiggled her toes again, careful not to let them touch each other. "Sounds good."

"Are you sure you're up to a mission right now?"

She looked sideways at him. "Of course."

"But you're having your woman's thing."

"*Woman's thing?*" she asked and giggled.

That was another thing she hadn't really done before, but her big, bad mercenary was looking distinctly uncomfortable, and she couldn't help herself. Considering how solicitous he'd been of her, this obvious discomfort over discussing her monthly was hilarious.

"Well, men don't have them."

"I guess not, and anyway," she said, dismissing the subject for a more important one, "I've gone on lots of missions during that time of month."

"You were so fragile yesterday morning."

"I'm feeling better now. It's not a problem."

Daniel didn't look as though he trusted her current state of healthiness, but after the day before he couldn't very well argue that she was still in a state of fragility.

"No more excuses. I'm going." She grinned at him, ready to talk about something else again.

She'd said what needed to be said on the subject, which was that there was no reason for her not to go.

"Would you like to hear what else I want to try?" she asked with a wink, making her voice as provocative as possible.

It worked. His eyes narrowed with interest. "Sure."

"I want to be kissed on a first date, preferably by a guy I can't resist." She looked down at her hands, fanning her fingers out. "Do you think I should paint my nails, too? I don't know if it's conventional to paint your toes and your fingernails the same color. Do you suppose the fashion police will get me if I do it?"

He grabbed her shoulders and turned her to face him. He'd been tense about her involvement in the mission, but now he positively vibrated with obvious displeasure. "No way in hell."

"You don't think I should paint my fingernails?"

He clenched his jaw. "No first date. No kissing."

"Why not?" she asked, all innocence.

"You belong to me."

"And that means I can't go out on a first date and get ki—"

"No other man is touching you with his lips or anything else," he growled.

"Did I say another man?"

"You said on a first date."

"Since we've never actually been on a date, is that a problem? Don't you want to go out with me? We could see a movie, or go to a show, or go on a picnic in the park."

"We can go on a date." He sounded as if he was agreeing to take her on a tour of a mushroom farm the day they fertilized.

"That's magnanimous of you."

"I mean, if you want to go out, I'll take you out." His voice was infused with slightly more enthusiasm.

She cocked her head back, giving him her best come-hither look. "And will you kiss me?"

"Are you saying I'm the irresistible guy you were talking about?"

"I haven't been able to resist you yet, have I?"

His eyes dark with the desire that never seemed to diminish, he cupped her face. "Then I think I can take care of this *first* for you, but maybe we should practice a little just in case."

She didn't get a chance to answer because he was already starting.

*   *   *

Later that night Josie was snuggled against Daniel on the verge of sleep when he said, "We'll have to play spin the bottle when your woman's thing is done, too."

That would mean a lot of kissing between them if they were the only ones playing. She smiled around a yawn. "Sounds good."

Curling around her more securely, he settled his hand possessively over one of her breasts. "I bet you never played doctor either."

"No."

"We'll have to get a stethoscope."

"Who gets to be doctor and who gets to be patient?" she asked after another yawn.

"We'll take turns."

She thought of something else that would be fun with him. "Can we have a slumber party where we stay up all night, too?"

"I can guarantee when all this is over that I'll give you an all-nighter you'll never forget."

She wiggled her bottom against him. "Sounds wonderful."

"It will be." He groaned when she wiggled again. "And it can't come soon enough for me."

Chapter 18

Hotwire and Wolf arrived the next day. Lise came with them and gloated when she realized Josie and Daniel were a couple.

"I knew you two had a thing for each other. I told Joshua, but he didn't believe me," Lise crowed to Josie while they dangled their feet in the shallow end of the pool.

The others had checked in to the same hotel as she and Daniel. Over lunch, Hotwire had challenged Wolf and Daniel to a competition to see who could swim the most laps. They were all even at the moment.

"I was as clueless as Wolf," Josie admitted. "I thought Daniel couldn't stand me."

Lise shook her head. "The guy practically spontaneously combusts every time you are around."

"He's volatile, all right."

"Is he really?"

"You mean you haven't noticed?"

"To tell you the truth, no. I've never seen Nitro even come close to losing his cool. Until I saw him around you the first time, I didn't think he had any emotions to speak of."

"Is lust an emotion? I thought it was more like a chemical reaction."

"He feels a lot more for you than mere lust."

Josie watched Daniel slicing through the water, his powerful body rippling with muscle. "I hope so."

"I'm positive. He's so possessive."

"The male animal is sexually possessive, but that doesn't mean his heart is engaged." She'd told Daniel she loved him again that morning when he'd woken her with a tender kiss that made her toes curl with emotion.

He'd kissed her again, but he hadn't said anything.

"Daniel isn't an animal. He's a man, and his heart is engaged or my name is Aunt Fanny," Lise said emphatically, her Texas drawl acute.

"Do you really think so?" Josie wanted to believe Daniel's silence meant more than tolerance of her emotional reaction. "I'm having my period right now, and he's been really affectionate and caring."

"There, you see. That's a great sign."

"I thought so, too, but when I told him I loved him, he didn't say anything back."

"Welcome to the club." Lise smiled wryly. "I told Joshua I loved him over and over again, and he never said a word. I thought he only wanted me for my body, but I was wrong, and I'm sure you are, too. More than any other woman, you should understand how reticent these guys are to admit to any kind of weakness, love included."

"Love doesn't make you weak."

"But it does make you vulnerable to hurt."

Josie couldn't deny it. She had no defenses to hide behind when it came to Daniel. Her love left her heart open to him in a way it had never been to another person, not even her parents.

"What are you two talking about?" Wolf moved to stand beside his wife, his hand automatically making connection with the part of her body he could reach, her head.

Josie hadn't even noticed they'd finished their competition. Daniel and Hotwire were still drying off a few feet away.

Lise looked up at Wolf, her expression wry. "What do you think?"

He responded with a probing look that jumped from Lise to Josie to Daniel and back to Lise. She made a small inclination of her head, and some silent communication passed between them because he heaved a sigh and frowned at Daniel.

"Who swam the most laps?" Josie asked as Wolf lifted Lise from the side of the pool.

"I did." Hotwire tossed his towel in the bin beside the pool and then struck a pose, flexing his biceps. "It's easy to see why, don't you think, ladies?"

"By one lap," Daniel said, coming to stand beside them, and then shoved his friend sideways into the pool.

The resounding splash sent water spraying over Josie, and she shrieked, jumping to her feet.

Daniel grinned at her, his gaze dropping to where her now wet tank top clung to her chest. "Wolf and I were ready to get back to you two."

"I'm always ready to get back to my wife." Wolf caressed Lise's protruding middle, his warrior's eyes reflecting joy and satisfaction. "Pretty soon you're going to be too round to be sitting on the ground."

Lise looked down at where his hand rested against her and grinned. "I'm already there, but as long as I've got you around to hoist me back up, I'm safe."

Hotwire heaved himself out of the pool, no limitation to *his* strength and agility in evidence. "Was that my victory dunking?"

"Watch it or you'll get another one," Wolf warned.

"The element of surprise works only once in an encounter, unless your enemy is stupid, and my mama didn't raise any idiots." Grinning and giving Josie a once-over, he shook himself, and water sprayed all of them again.

Josie jumped back from her second unplanned cold shower and landed right against Daniel. His arm came over her shoulder as a towel landed around her neck, strategically covering parts of her wet tank top. Her gaze shot to her lover's face, and the expression there stunned her. He was looking mean, and he was looking at Hotwire.

She glanced over at the blond Georgian and couldn't see anything in the other man's expression that could have upset Daniel, until she remembered that Hotwire had been looking at her as he deliberately sprayed the water again. Apparently it bothered Daniel that Hotwire had seen her wet tank. She could have told him not to worry. Most men she met did not react to her modest attributes with unbridled desire, but saying so would do no good.

Daniel had gotten extremely territorial since Hotwire showed up. His friend had noticed, making it obvious he delighted in pushing Daniel's buttons.

She was used to being around strong men who jockeyed for position with each other despite close friendship, but she wasn't used to being the target they jockeyed around.

"You afraid she's going to run away if you don't hold on to her all the time?" Hotwire asked, his smile nothing less than a goad.

"I like touching her."

"Do you now?" Hotwire mocked, "I never would have noticed." But the significant look he gave them said otherwise.

Heat that had nothing to do with the summer sun climbed up Josie's neck. She was unfamiliar with being the other half of a couple, particularly around a friend intent on teasing her to death. His target might be Daniel, but she was the one embarrassed. She knew without looking that he wasn't blushing.

She threw out the first verbal sally she could think of to change the direction of the conversation. "And I'm not going anywhere, even if you'd all like me to."

The other two had joined Daniel in trying to convince her to stay behind. It made no sense to her. She was one of the best soldiers they'd ever worked with, and she didn't have to be arrogant to think so. They'd said it. They'd also brought her in on more than one independent mission. Their desire to keep her behind this time baffled her.

"We don't want you gone. I like watching Daniel squirm around you. It humanizes him," Wolf said, proving he could be just as irritating as Hotwire.

Lise elbowed his stomach. "Behave."

He smiled down at her. "If I behaved, you'd be real disappointed, honey."

Lise's gaze went unfocused in a way Josie understood very well. "Yes, I guess I would."

A disgusted sound erupted from Hotwire. "Would you two stop it? You're bad enough back home, but I thought you'd at least try to behave in front of company."

Josie had to smile. Beginning a start-up company around a couple of newlyweds no doubt had its challenges.

"Nitro and Josie aren't company," Wolf said, still looking at his wife with enough heat to singe her.

"Which is precisely why Josie shouldn't be going on this mission," Hotwire said, proving he'd gotten the gist of her words from the get-go.

"That's ridiculous." She'd been friends with the three mercenaries before when they were on missions together.

Wolf transferred his gaze to her, his brown eyes serious and compelling. "No, it's not. Look at how Nitro is with you. A soldier with his focus on anything besides the mission ends up a dead soldier."

Hotwire nodded, his own expression grim. "His first priority is going to be keeping you safe."

"Of course it isn't," she denied.

"He cares about you. That changes things," Wolf said.

"Are you trying to tell me that he tries to baby-sit you two on missions? Because I'll tell you right now, I don't buy it. I've seen the three of you in action. You cannot deny you care about each other, but the mission always comes first."

Hotwire made a choking noise, and Wolf stared at her as if she'd said something rude while Daniel laughed. "We're men."

"And I'm a woman. Are you saying you don't think I'm a good soldier?"

"That's not what this is about."

"Then what is it about?"

"Me not wanting to see you hurt."

The sentiment was nice, but she wasn't accepting it as an excuse to leave her behind. "Ninety-five percent of the jobs you took as mercs included protecting someone, and that never got in the way of your ability to fight or do your job."

"It's not the same thing." Wolf hugged his wife to his side. "There's protecting someone and then there's keeping someone you love safe."

"Which is why you did such a terrible job on your mission to capture Lise's stalker?" she asked tongue-in-cheek.

Wolf had the grace to look uncomfortable. "But it was a lot more stressful than a normal assignment."

Lise glared up at him. "Thanks a lot."

"So, you're saying Daniel's too much of a pansy to handle the stress of worrying about me?"

Both Wolf and Hotwire looked chagrined at that, undoubtedly as aware as she was that such an idea was ludicrous.

"*Not.*" Daniel squeezed her. "This is not about me; it's about you and you staying safe."

"Lise's not going." Wolf said it as if that was some kind of irrefutable proof Josie shouldn't either.

This was getting nuts. "Can we take a reality check here? Lise is an author, a really great author, but definitely not a soldier, and she's pregnant."

"You're having your woman's thing," Daniel announced with a total lack of tact.

"It's not even remotely the same thing, and may I remind

you that even without being pregnant, she is still not a soldier and I am? A darn good one, too."

"I thought you wanted a more normal life."

She rolled her eyes. "That does not mean I'm going to ignore a threat to my dad's life or that I'm going to let you all go in and risk your lives while I stay behind and paint my toenails again."

"Damn it, the job only needs a four-person unit."

Technically it could be done with four people, but five would be better, and he had to know it. "Then one of you stay behind."

"*Nitro . . .* " The censorship in Hotwire's voice would have been funny in other circumstances.

"I'm sorry," Daniel growled. "I'm trying, dam—darn it."

"What are you trying?" Lise asked, her expression saying everything happening right now was great fodder for her imagination.

"Not to swear in front of Josette." Daniel rubbed her shoulders as if apologizing again. "She's a lady, and it's not polite."

Wolf smirked. Hotwire nodded, and Lise smiled. "That's really sweet."

Daniel's expression could have melted the polar ice caps. "I'm not sweet."

"That's a matter of interpretation," Josie said.

The metal-melting glare got turned on her. "When this woman's thing is over, I'll show you how sweet I am."

"I can't wait." She gave him one of the fluttering eyelashes looks she'd perfected and puckered her lips in an air kiss.

"I'm not convinced Nitro is sweet," Wolf said, "but you sure as he—heck are stubborn."

She wouldn't bother denying something she knew to be true, and it was a good thing in her opinion. If she were less sure of herself, these guys would walk right over her. "Did you ask my dad what he thought of leaving me behind?"

"He's worse than you are about it. He figures he's trained you to be the best and there isn't anyone else he'd rather have covering his back." Daniel was still looking plenty irritated.

She smiled triumphantly at all of them. "Well, that's settled then."

"How do you figure that?" Daniel asked in a dangerous tone.

"It's no use trying to argue with both me and my dad, and I think you're all smart enough to realize it."

Josie pulled the black face mask down and adjusted her night-vision goggles.

They'd hiked in and established position after leaving their jeeps parked far enough away that the sound of the running engines wouldn't carry to the compound.

"Ready?" Daniel's almost soundless voice came from right beside her ear.

She nodded once.

"Be careful."

"You, too," she said at a bare whisper.

Then he was gone.

Hotwire would cut the security system while Wolf and Daniel neutralized the guards. Her dad was supposed to neutralize the armory, and she was responsible for getting the files. She had six 256 MB jump drives in her vest pocket— enough to download the pertinent information on several hard drives. While she was getting it, the other four would be collecting the men who had taken her dad's courses.

The plan was to dump them along with the incriminating evidence on the FBI's doorstep. Hotwire had convinced her to leave the stolen laptop where it was so the authorities could come into the compound on the charge of theft. It would allow them to move faster than if they had to accumulate a case based on the documented evidence.

Hotwire gave the signal over the headsets that security was disabled. Three minutes later, Daniel indicated his man was down, and not five seconds later, Wolf signaled the same thing.

She and her dad headed in. She didn't hear him moving, and she knew he couldn't hear her either. Unlike when she'd been a little girl, she now knew how to move silently without leaving a trail behind her in the forest.

The office was exactly where her father had said it was. Only two sleeping quarters were attached to it, and they were at the other end of the long corridor, the mess hall between them and the office. Which meant that with the security system disabled, there was almost no chance her presence in the building would be detected.

Three computers were on different desks in the big office, and one of them was her laptop. She powered each one up. While they were coming on-line she started methodically taking pictures of the files in the cabinets. The memory card on her tiny digital camera could hold over one thousand images, and she had extra memory cards in her vest along with the jump drives.

She'd be able to walk out of there with the entire file system in her pocket.

The ding of Windows finishing its start-up routine indicated at least one of the computers was on-line. She plugged a jump drive into the USB port and started downloading the documents folder before doing a search for encrypted and hidden documents. Using techniques Hotwire had taught her, she found a second documents folder, this one both hidden and encrypted. She set it up to copy to the jump drive when the current application was finished and went back to taking pictures of the paper files.

Hotwire or the FBI could work on decoding it later.

"I'm headed to Position Three." Hotwire's voice came across her headset, indicating he was on his way to help her out. He must have turned his prisoner over to one of the other soldiers.

He arrived a minute later and immediately started working on a second computer. She said nothing, but dropped the remaining jump drives on the desk in front of him so he could complete the downloads.

It amazed her that groups like this one kept copies of incriminating documents. She'd already copied a memo from one of the members of the compound to the leader detailing his suggestion for taking courses from Tyler McCall and then disposing of the older man. She tried not to read the documents as she went, it would go faster that way, but her dad's name had leapt off the page at her.

"Daddy?" The sound of a child's voice in the corridor outside the office froze Josie's blood in her veins even as she headed for the door.

The light in the corridor came on, and Josie came to an abrupt halt at the door, tugging down her night-vision goggles so she could see. It took precious seconds for her eyes to adjust to the light.

"Abel, what are you doing up?" The woman's sleepy words came from the left of the door.

"I wanted to ask Daddy somethin'."

"He's not here. Daddy is on sentry duty tonight."

"I know. I wanted to help him."

That would have been a complication they didn't need, and Josie was glad the child hadn't gone with his father on his nightly rounds. She could see the small body near the doorway to the outside at the office end of the corridor.

"You're too little." The mother sounded less sleepy and a little impatient. Josie could not see her at all, but her voice came from the end of the hallway near the sleeping quarters. "Now, it's time to get back to bed, young man."

"Daddy's in the office, Mama. I wanna ask him."

Josie's heart rate accelerated.

"Don't be silly. Can't you see there are no lights on?" Definite impatience this time. "No one's in there."

"But I saw lights. Little ones. Like Daddy's flashlight."

The quality of the stillness outside the room told Josie all she needed to know about what the mother thought of her son's comments. "Abel, go wake the others. Now."

Josie moved. She whirled into the hallway and sprinted for the boy before he could get out the door to sound the alarm. Hotwire was running for the woman.

The little boy lifted his arm, and it was only then that Josie realized he was carrying a gun.

"I'm going to help my daddy!" She heard the safety disengage and dove to her right as the child fired, but the bullet found its target. Pain that she'd felt once before burst through her thigh, and her legs collapsed beneath her.

"I'm down. Get out," she said into the mouthpiece of her headset, and then blackness overwhelmed her.

Daniel ran toward the building with the office in it faster than he'd ever run in his life. His heart was beating so hard he could hear it. Damn it to hell. Josie had said she was down. They'd all heard the shot over the headsets, and it had sounded like thunder in his ear, but the sound from the building had been muted. The merc part of his brain automatically computed a low probability it had awoken others in the compound.

Hotwire had said he'd neutralized the mother and was headed toward the sleeping quarters at the other end of the building, but a child of approximately five years of age had made it outside. The child was armed.

Daniel saw the small body outlined against the dark buildings. He was wearing light pajamas, but he had a black object in his right hand.

This child had shot Josie.

Daniel approached him at a sprint and grabbed him from behind still in forward momentum mode. He clamped one hand over the boy's mouth, used the other to disarm him and then immobilize him.

Figuring a quick knockout would be less traumatizing for the kid than a drawn-out battle against a bigger foe, he pressed against the carotid artery, and the child went limp against him. Daniel had a minute, maybe less, to get the small shooter tied up before he became conscious again.

He burst through the door to the building and came to a skidding halt in front of Josie.

Her eyes were shut, and her head lolled to one side. Blood was all over the floor under her, and one of her pant legs was soaked with it. The mother was against the opposite wall, her eyes dilated with shock, tears running down her face. She was gagged, but when she saw her son, she squirmed against her restraints and tried to speak.

Daniel used plastic ties to secure the child's hands behind his back and his ankles together. Then he put the little one on his mother's lap. He hated putting the tape over the little boy's mouth, but they couldn't risk him waking and raising the alarm.

When he finished, the mother looked up at him, terror in her eyes.

"Your son is fine." It was all he could take time to say.

And frankly, he didn't see the use of saying anything else. How many women and children had he seen hurt by the fanaticism of the men responsible for their safety? Not that women couldn't be just as fanatic—and dangerous—which was why he did not untie the woman so she could cuddle her son. She might decide to try to finish the job the little boy had started.

Her eyes widened again, the fear that had abated with his words increasing, and he turned to see Hotwire running silently down the hall toward them.

"We're not here to hurt you," Daniel said roughly to the woman before turning away from her and her son.

"The others?"

"Neutralized."

Daniel fell to his knees beside Josie at the same time Hotwire did. The other man already had his knife out, and he slit her pant leg. Daniel put his arm around her, prepared to prevent her from crying out in pain if she woke disoriented from her unnatural sleep.

"Is she still bleeding?" Daniel asked.

"Yes, but it looks like the bullet missed the bone." Hotwire probed the wound, and Josie's body jolted in involuntary reaction. "I'm not sure about her muscle, though. She's going to hurt a fricken long time from this one."

He started binding the wound.

Daniel waited until he was done and then lifted her gently into his arms. Though she did not waken, her face twisted with pain at the movement. He felt helpless and so damn angry he could have killed.

"Take her back to the others. I'm going to finish in there." Hotwire indicated the dark office doorway with an inclination of his head.

"Someone else in the compound might have seen the corridor light before you turned it off. I did."

"I know how to keep my head down. Don't worry about me. Just go."

And Daniel went.

He double-timed it to the meeting place, giving details into his headset as he went.

It was decided that Tyler would take him and Josie to the nearest hospital while Wolf waited for Hotwire with the prisoners. They would bring them out in the second jeep. It would be a tight fit for the four adult male prisoners in the backseat, but Daniel didn't give a rat's ass about those bastards' comfort.

Pain radiated through Josie's body. It seemed to be centered in her thigh, but it was hard to tell. It was all-consuming. The jeep went over a bump, and she groaned.

"It's all right, sweetheart. You're going to be okay. We're taking you to a hospital."

She opened her eyes to darkness, but eventually shapes distinguished themselves before her. The interior of the jeep, her dad's head in the driver's seat. Daniel's face above hers. She couldn't see his expression, but she could feel his concern. His arms were firm around her, but gentle, and his breath was more labored than her own.

"You okay?" she croaked, her mouth dry from the pain.

He tensed, as if he'd just realized she was awake. "That should be my line."

"I hurt."

"I'm sorry, baby."

"Me, too. Screwed up the mission." She grimaced as pain throbbed in her thigh. Definitely her thigh. "Didn't expect the little guy to have a gun."

"It's hell what parents will do to their kids in the name of fanaticism."

"We've seen it before."

"Yeah."

"So, I should have been prepared for it."

"Don't you be blaming yourself, Josie-girl." Her dad's voice was gravelly, as though he was having a hard time getting the words out.

"But the mission . . ."

"Screw the mission!"

"Hotwire stayed behind to finish gathering the evidence, and Wolf was watching over the prisoners. It's all good." Daniel brushed her cheek. "But you getting shot wasn't. I'm sorry about that."

Her heart contracted, and she wanted to cry. She could grit her teeth at the pain in her leg, but knowing that he was taking on another load of guilt because of her hurt in ways she couldn't deal with. "It's not your fault."

"I let you come."

"You're not my commanding officer, and even if you were, I probably would have disobeyed orders. I make my own decisions. It's one of the reasons I never went to formal military. I don't like people telling me what to do." It was hard to get the words out, but she had to make him understand. "You weren't responsible for securing the office. That was my job. None of this is your fault."

He didn't say anything, but his hand caressed her face, and the sense of grim tension surrounding them did not abate.

"Please don't let me become another burden, Daniel. I couldn't stand it."

"You are not a burden to me." His words were low, intense. "I love you, Josette."

She wanted to believe him so badly, but he hadn't said anything when she'd whispered the words to him before, and now he was feeling guilty. Did he think he had to tell her he loved her to make up for her being shot?

"It's not your fault," she said again.

The jeep lurched to a screeching halt as her father cussed out a deer who'd run in the road. Josie's leg got jolted despite Daniel's attempt to prevent it from happening, and another wave of intense pain rushed over her. The darkness around her became absolute as she slipped back into unconsciousness.

Chapter 19

Daniel held grimly to Josie's body, cursing the deer, the pain that had sent her into another faint and his own lousy timing on admitting his love for her. She hadn't believed him. He was sure of it. Rejection of his words had radiated off of her even though she hadn't said anything. Just that it wasn't his fault. It was obvious she thought he had told her he loved her because he felt guilty.

But that wasn't why. It was because he'd finally figured out that the feelings she brought to life in him couldn't have any other name. Not obsession, not desire, not even friendship. Those were all part of what he felt, but none of them were dominant.

What overwhelmed him with her was this absolute knowledge that life without her would be an abyss of solitude and pain.

She brought joy into his life. She made every day better. Spending time with her was the most exciting thing he'd ever done, bar none. He wanted to be a better man with her. He wanted to prove he could live without giving in to the demon of temper, that he was capable of walking a different path in marriage than his father had taken.

If that wasn't love, he didn't know what was.

Now all he had to do was convince Josie. He hoped it didn't take her as long to believe as it had taken him.

She woke one more time on the way to the hospital, and he wished she hadn't. It was obvious she was in terrible pain, but she was soldiering on, trying to hide how bad it was. He knew anyway, and it was killing him.

Josie's mouth tasted as if she'd swallowed sawdust, and her head swam with the effort it took to distinguish the voices whirling around her.

"She's been out for four hours." That was Daniel's voice. "She should have woken up by now."

"It was like this after the first time, too," her father said. "It's the anesthetic. She reacts strongly to it. Last time it took her hours longer to come to than the doctors were expecting."

"And you didn't think you should mention this to the doctors here before they gave her a hefty dose?"

"I did mention it, but they had to give her enough to put her under."

"Can't they do something to wake her up?"

"They don't need to. Sleep is the best thing for the healing process."

"Natural sleep maybe."

"I'm not going to get any sleep, natural or otherwise, with you two arguing over my bed." Her voice came out raspy and weak, but the words were distinguishable, and she was proud of herself.

A hand came softly against her face in a brief caress. Daniel. She would always know his touch. "How do you feel?"

She forced eyelids that felt glued shut to open. He was a blur while her vision focused, but she tried to meet his gaze. "Numb."

"It's the anesthetic."

"My leg?"

"The bullet went through tissue and muscle. No major arteries. No major bones. You should be back to normal in six weeks or less."

Daniel slowly came into sharper focus. He'd made an effort to wash off the black face paint, but smears remained near his temple and on one cheekbone. She wondered if she looked any better. Somehow, she doubted it.

"I'll tell the doctor she's come to," her dad said before leaving the room.

"The mission?" she asked.

"Successful. Hotwire got what we needed. The prisoners and the evidence were delivered to the FBI two hours ago. They plan to move in on the compound immediately."

"Good," she croaked and then grimaced. "Thirsty . . ."

He lifted a cup, putting the straw to her lips, and she sipped at the icy water with real pleasure. When she was done, he took the cup away and settled carefully on the side of her bed away from her injured leg.

He took her hand between his, the warmth in him infusing her with comfort. "I don't like you getting shot."

"I'm not real thrilled about it myself."

"I don't want the mother of my children to work in such a dangerous profession. Too stressful on family life."

She stared up at him. "The drugs are making me hear things. You don't want children."

"I didn't before, but now I do."

"With me?" she asked, just to make sure. She felt too loopy to trust her first interpretation of his words.

"With you." His hands pressed against hers as if he was willing her to listen to him. "I love you, Josette. I know you think it's the guilt talking, but I swear it's not. I need you in my life. Permanently."

"You mean like get married?" She had to be hallucinating.

"And have babies. Yes." He lifted her hand to his face and pressed her palm against his lips so she could feel his words as well as hear them. "Will you marry me, Josette? I'll spend the rest of my life proving I can be a different man than my father."

Tears that had nothing to do with the pain she was in filled her eyes. "You already have."

The nurse and doctor came in with her dad. She was examined, poked and prodded until she didn't feel in the least bit numb. Daniel's tension grew and grew until he told the doctor and nurse to leave her the hell alone. With both her dad and lover there, looking dangerous and none too pleased, the doctor and nurse listened. The doctor gave hurried instructions for her care and left. The nurse injected a pain killer into her I.V. before going.

Josie didn't have enough energy to say thank you, but as she slipped into sleep the knowledge Daniel wanted to marry her did more to anesthetize her pain than the drugs.

The next few days flew by. Josie improved rapidly, and Daniel never left her side, going so far as to sleep on a cot in her hospital room. The staff didn't mention in his hearing that it was against hospital policy since he wasn't a relation, but Josie heard two of the nurses talking about it.

They also mentioned they wouldn't mind having him sleep in their rooms. Josie changed the subject when Daniel asked why she was so cool toward the two women when they came into her room.

Her dad and the others were frequent visitors. Even Lise flew in and came to the hospital to see her. Josie had another visitor, her third day in the hospital.

A pretty woman with troubled eyes came into the room with Daniel after lunch. Clinging to her hand was a small blond boy of five or six. He was looking at Josie with eyes that broke her heart.

They stopped beside her bed.

The woman spoke first. "He needed to see that you were alive. Mr. Black Eagle assured us you wouldn't mind us visiting, but I'll understand if you want us to leave."

Josie looked at the little boy and put her hand out. "I'm alive. Feel."

He tentatively reached out and then touched her hand. His was cold, and she curled her fingers around it.

"You're warm."

"Yes."

Tears started streaming down his cheeks. "Dead is cold. I know 'cuz when the men hunted, the animals they shot was cold when they brought them back."

"I'm warm and I'm alive."

"Does it hurt?"

"Some, but they give me medicine to help with the pain."

"I'm sorry." His lower lip trembled, and then the tears were audible as well as making wet tracks down his cheeks.

His mother dropped to her haunches beside him, and she hugged him to her.

He threw himself into her body, tearing his hand from Josie. "I didn't mean it, Mommy. I didn't mean it."

"It's okay, Abel." She calmed him until the crying had diminished to a few sniffles, and then she looked at Josie over her son's shoulder. "I know why you broke in to the compound. Most of us had no idea the men were involved in things that dangerous. We thought we were making a simpler, better life for our children, and now that life is in shambles, but I'd rather that than raise my son to kill."

She stood up, her son held against her. "I'd never seen a person shot before. When the others talked about fighting for our way of life, it was emotional rhetoric. This is real, and Abel and I will have to live with the memory for the rest of our lives."

"I don't blame your son for shooting me."

The woman's eyes filled with tears. "Thank you."

"Abel," Josie said.

The little boy looked at her.

"I forgive you."

He wriggled down from his mom and came to the bedside.

"Can I hug you? Mommy hugs me when I get hurted and it feels better."

"Sure." She went to reach down, but Daniel was there, lifting the boy to her so she wouldn't put any stress on her wound.

He hugged her tightly around the neck, choking her, but she didn't complain. This little one would live with more trauma from the shooting than she would.

When he let go, he looked at her anxiously. "Do you feel better?"

"Yes. Much. Thank you."

He and his mother came to see her twice more, and each time, Josie reiterated that she was going to be okay and that she forgave Abel. He'd started smiling again, which his mother tearfully thanked her for. There would be more traumas to come with the investigation into the shooting, but both he and his mother were going to make it through.

Josie could tell. The woman was strong, and her attitudes were changing rapidly. She and Abel were just leaving when the doctor arrived on rounds.

He read her chart and then smiled. "You should be able to go home tomorrow." He looked at Daniel. "That is provided she has someone to care for her. I'd like her to stay off that leg for another week and then only mild exercise until the torn muscle has healed."

"I'll make sure she doesn't overdo it."

He hadn't repeated his marriage proposal in the last three days, but his behavior indicated it was on his mind.

"Good." The doctor put the chart back in the pocket on the wall. "I'll draw up discharge orders for tomorrow morning."

"Can I fly?" Josie asked. "I don't want to spend the next five and a half weeks staying in a hotel."

"No. I'm sorry, but plane travel would put a lot of stress on the wound, and a long car trip, even with frequent stops, is out of the question for a while as well."

She understood the doctor's reasoning, but she couldn't mask her disappointment. She wanted the privacy of home.

"What about a personal jet where she could lie down for most of the journey?" Daniel asked.

The doctor's eyes widened. "I can honestly say that's the first time I've been asked that question. If you can arrange such a thing, I don't see any reason for her not to be taken home. Just make sure she has follow-up care on her wound with her local doctor."

"Will do."

The doctor left, and Josie smiled at Daniel. "You think Wolf will fly me back to Portland?"

"No, but he'll fly you to my home."

She'd love to see his house. "Do you think you'll have a better chance of keeping me immobile on your own turf?"

He shook his head, his expression not reflecting her humor back at her. "I think I'll have a better chance of convincing you to marry me."

She wasn't going to need much convincing, but his reasoning intrigued her. "Why?"

"I'm more than a soldier there, and I hope seeing my house will make you realize I can be something other than a warrior."

"I've always known that." She was going to cry again. "I thought you *wanted* to stick with the soldier's life."

"That was before I had a better one to go to."

"Being with me is a better life?"

"Yes."

"This isn't about you feeling guilty because I got shot?" she asked, needing to know, hoping desperately it wasn't.

He sat down on her bed, putting his hands on either side of her and hemming her in so the rest of the hospital ceased to exist for her. "This is about me not wanting to live the rest of my life without you." He took a deep breath and let it out. "I realized you were right about my mom. She chose to stay with Thunder."

"Like I chose to go on a mission."

"If I'd been physically present in either case, I would have done anything I could to prevent you being hurt."

"I know that, but your mom chose to be with your dad, and I chose to go on the mission."

"Will you choose to spend the rest of your life with me?"

Her heart twisted at the emotion in his voice and the warmth in his eyes. "You don't have to give up being a soldier for me. I don't need you to change who you are to want to spend the rest of my life with you. I only have to know you love me."

"I do love you."

"I love you, too, Daniel. The man you are, not a man you think you have to be to make me happy."

"I don't want to raise my daughters to be soldiers. I don't want my sons to feel that's their only alternative in life. I've been a mercenary for a long time, and I'm ready to give you the normal life you want."

She cupped his face, her heart in her eyes. "Life with you will be normal for me."

"I've already talked to your dad. He's ready to shut the school down. He doesn't want to rebuild."

"But what will he do?" Her dad didn't know anything but being a soldier.

"He's going to move to his house in Nevada and get to know that woman on the plane. They've talked on the phone every day since we've been here. She knows more about you than I do. She runs a garden nursery, and your dad has developed a sudden interest in plants and how to grow them."

It was too much to take in all at once, but the idea that her dad might have found something to live for besides training other soldiers was a nice one.

She smiled. "He's not going to get blown up growing flowers."

"I talked to Wolf and Hotwire. I want to do more than design high-level security alternatives. We could work together on some projects, but our businesses would be separate. They think I could make it as an architect."

She knew that like her, he probably had enough money in savings to last a lifetime, but they'd both make lousy lounge lizards. "I know you can."

"So, will you take a chance on me?"

"You were so against marriage, so sure you didn't want kids and all you ever did want was to be a soldier. Are you sure this is what you want?"

"Yes." He kissed her, his mouth warm and possessive on hers. "I needed that. Look, Josette, I spent most of my life afraid that underneath all the self-discipline I was a man just like my father. But then I realized that the self-discipline was what made me different."

"But you're nothing like your dad. Even when you had a temper, you didn't take it out on people smaller than you."

"You're right, but I'd spent so much of my life being told I was the image of him, I had this belief deep down that meant more than just physical appearance."

"But—"

He kissed her again. Quick and hard. "Shh . . . I know. I'm not like him, and I will never hurt you or our children. I've spent too many years learning to control myself, but when that little boy shot you, I knew."

"Because you realized you loved me?"

"Because even though he had hurt the person I loved most in the world, and I was so furious I could have spit nails, I didn't want to hurt him. I didn't want to take my anger out on him."

"Oh, Daniel . . ."

"He's starting trauma counseling, did his mom tell you?"

"Yes."

"Anyway, if I didn't hit that kid, I'll never hit one of my own."

"According to his mom, you were really careful with him."

"He was just a little child, doing what he thought his daddy would want him to."

"His daddy probably did."

Daniel shrugged. "His mom doesn't, and she's the one that's going to be raising him for the next few years. His dad is one of the society's members who is facing a long prison sentence."

"She's got to be hurting so much right now."

"She married the wrong man."

"And now she's paying for it."

"Like my mom did, but, Josette, I'm not the wrong man for you."

She curled her arms around his neck and moved until her lips were brushing his. "I know that, Daniel. I've known that since the night you made me your woman. You were so gentle, so careful not to hurt me and to make it special. I've been in love with you a long time, Daniel, but that night it became irrevocable."

"It took me forever to realize what I felt was love."

"I wasn't that quick on the uptake myself."

"At least you said it."

"So did you."

"But I waited so long, you had a hard time believing me."

"I believe you now."

"I love you, Josette." Then his lips molded hers in a kiss that sealed the words in her heart forever.

They were married four weeks later. Josie finally got to meet Daniel's sergeant major, and she understood why her new husband respected the older man so much. Claire was her single attendant, wearing the first dress Josie had ever seen her in and her grandmother's locket.

Hotwire had found it in a drawer in the office and brought it back to her.

Her dad brought his new wife with him. He'd married the woman he met on the plane a scant week after his return to

Nevada. He'd told Josie he was too old to waste time like Daniel had. She'd laughed, unable to believe the difference in her father since he started training plants instead of soldiers.

But the difference in her own life was even more phenomenal. Daniel had asked her if she wanted to run the business side of his new venture into personal home design, and she had agreed. She was going to finish her degree remotely, and she and Daniel had decided to start a family right away.

She'd thought that staying with Daniel would mean giving up her dreams, but instead he was making each and every one of them come true. She'd given him a new name in the language of his people—Dream Maker, because Angry Warrior did not fit him any longer.

Don't miss Susan Johnson's
sensationally romantic new novel
WHEN YOU LOVE SOMEONE.
Published this month by Brava.

A short time later, Julius and Amanda dismounted before the house and were met at the door by a young man-servant.

"The Marquis of Darley and Lady Bloodworth," Julius said. "Come to see Lord and Lady Grafton."

"I'll see if my lord and lady are in."

"No need. We're old friends," Julius had no intention of being turned away. He gestured the man forward.

The servant had no choice, of course, as Julius well knew.

Moments later, the flunkey opened the drawing room door and announced their names.

Lady Grafton looked up from penning a letter and went pale.

Taking note of their hostess' stunned look, Amanda quickly said, "I thought I'd take the opportunity to call on you, Lady Grafton." Advancing into the drawing room with a warm smile, she added, "My family has a race box in Newmarket. I believe you know the marquis." She glanced at Julius who had followed her in. "I hope we're not intruding."

"No—that is . . . my husband is at the stables. I'll have him summoned." Elspeth turned to her maid as she rose to meet her guests, high color having replaced her pallor. "Sophie, have Lord Grafton called in."

"No need to interrupt his lordship," Amanda smoothly interposed. "We won't stay long. We were out for a ride and found ourselves near your house."

"I'm sure Lord Grafton would like to see you," Elspeth countered, signaling her maid to fetch the earl. She couldn't chance he'd find out later that she'd had guests without his permission. "Would you like tea?" It was impossible not to observe the social graces, although she found herself hoping her visitors might refuse.

"That would be lovely," Amanda replied with a smile.

"Sophie, tea as well," Elspeth ordered, trying to avoid eye contact with the marquis. She could feel her cheeks flushing with embarrassment. Or excitement. Or something else entirely.

"What a lovely view," Amanda exclaimed, walking over to the row of windows overlooking a bucolic vista of green fields and grazing horses. "Do you have a favorite mount you like to ride?"

Whether intentionally or unwittingly, Amanda's words incited an outrageously lewd image. Struggling to displace her wholly inappropriate thoughts, Elspeth found herself at a loss for words.

Aware of Lady Grafton's overlong silence, Julius smoothly interposed, "I've been trying to persuade Lady Grafton to take Skylark out for a ride."

Amanda spun around. "Skylark? You'll absolutely adore him! He's powerful and swift, yet gentle as a lamb. Tell her, Julius, how he took me over ten miles at top speed without even breathing hard."

"He has enormous staying power. It's characteristic of the Atlas Barb breed. You'd enjoy trying him out, Lady Grafton."

Elspeth tried not to misinterpret the marquis's comments. *Get a grip,* she told herself. Everyone was simply discussing horses and she was reacting like an agitated adolescent to the most benign remarks. "If it were possible, I'm sure I'd enjoy riding Skylark, my lord. However, we lead a quiet life since my husband's illness. But thank you for the offer. Won't you sit down," she politely offered when she would have preferred pushing her guests out the door and avoiding any further complications. From her husband and otherwise.

"Oh, look!" Amanda exclaimed, gazing out the window. "The most precious basket of violets! I adore violets!" Contriving a moment alone for Julius, she opened the terrace door and stepped outside to inspect the willow basket on the balustrade.

"Why did you *come?*" Elspeth hissed the second Amanda closed the door behind her. "I'm sorry—how rude . . . please forgive me," she stammered, blushing furiously at her graceless behavior. "I shouldn't have said—I mean . . . I don't know what came—"

"I couldn't stay away." Uncharacteristically blunt words for the marquis who only played at love. And if Grafton wasn't about to appear at any moment, Julius would have taken her in his arms and kissed away her trepidation.

"You *shouldn't* have come. He might—that is . . . you don't understand my . . . situation." Nervously surveying the door to the hallway, Elspeth visibly trembled. "My husband"—she took a sustaining breath—"is very difficult."

"I'm sorry." She was so obviously alarmed he felt a twinge of conscience—a rarity for him. This frightened child was clearly not equipped to undertake any amorous games. He shouldn't have come. "I'll fetch Amanda and we'll be on our way," he offered, moving toward the terrace door.

"No."

It was the merest whisper. His pulse quickened despite his newfound conscience and he turned back.

"God help me—for not having more restraint," she breathed, her hands clasped tightly to still their tremors. "I shouldn't be talking to you or even thinking what I'm thinking or—"

"Will your husband be here soon?"

She nodded, a jerky, skittish movement.

"We'll talk later, then," he calmly said when he wasn't feeling calm in the least. When he was contemplating taking the lovely Lady Grafton to bed and keeping her there until he'd had his fill or couldn't move or both. "Please, sit down." Offering her a chair with a wave of his hand, he swiftly walked to the windows, knocked on a pane and beckoned Amanda in. Turning back, he smiled. "Don't be nervous," he gently said. "Relax. We're just here on a friendly visit. Tell me something about your father's parish. I understand he was a vicar."

The marquis's voice was incredibly soothing, as though they were indeed friends. She felt an instant lessening of her anxiety. "I suppose you do this all the time," she murmured, taking a seat. "Rumor has it, you're—"

"I never do this," he said. In fact, the mindless craving he was experiencing was so outré, he thought he might still be feeling the aftereffects of last night's drink. Taking a seat a respectable distance away, he added with almost an unbecoming brusqueness, "You affect me in a most unusual way."

Have a look at MaryJanice Davidson's
hilariously romantic novella
"Cuffs and Coffee Breaks" in
VALENTINE'S DAY IS KILLING ME.
Available now from Brava.

"Well, this is it." Julie Kay tossed her keys on the kitchen counter. "Home sweet hell."

"It's nice," he commented, glancing around the small house she rented from her brother-in-law. "I used to live in Inver, back when I was a student at the U."

"Yeah, what, six weeks ago?"

"Oh, you're hilarious."

"I hate apartments. I always feel like a bee in a hive. So when my brother-in-law moved into a bigger place, he let me rent this one. It's worked out for everyone."

"Mmm." Scott was prowling around the living room and dining area like a big, brunette panther. "I have an apartment, and I know what you mean. But I'm almost never there."

"Where are you?"

"Work, usually. That's why I was really glad when you decided to go out with me. I mean, I have *no* social life."

"But you're so . . ." Gorgeous. Delicious. Fabulous. Tall. ". . . smart."

He shrugged. "I was always the tallest kid in my class, *and* the skinniest. But I was bad at sports. So who'd want to go out with a big gork like me?"

Oh, I dunno, anyone with half a brain?

"Uh, let me see if I can find something better than my old cardigan." She turned to go into her bedroom, but he came up behind her and put a hand on her shoulder, gently turning her around.

"It's fine," he said. "It's the least of my problems, believe me. What the hell am I going to do about that poor guy at the restaurant?"

"Uh... well, I... uh..." Blue eyes were filling her world, her universe. They were getting closer and closer. There was nothing else: no house, no living room, no cardigan, no dead guy.

She felt his lips on hers and she put her arms around him— she could hardly reach, his shoulders were so broad. Her mouth opened beneath his and his tongue touched hers, tentatively and then with more assurance, licking her teeth and nibbling her lower lip. She pulled and the cardigan was on the floor, and her hands were running across his fine chest, and...

(Dead guy, dead guy!)

... she yanked herself away. "Stop that! This is totally inappropriate!"

"Hey, *you* kissed *me*."

"I did not!" Oh, wait. Maybe she did. "Well, it doesn't matter. This isn't the time or place."

"I *know*. That's why I didn't kiss you. Although, I have to say," he added cheerfully, "I've been dying to all night. But you're right, this isn't the right time. Bad, sweetie."

"Oh, like you were really fighting it!"

"It seemed rude to give you the brush-off," he said, sounding wounded. "You know, me being a guest in your home and all."

"Well, never mind that. Let's stay focused. Put your sweater back on."

"I didn't take it off," he grumbled, but did as she asked.

"Let's figure this out. We have to be back there in fourteen hours. So, if you didn't kill the guy—"

"Charley Ferrin."

She gasped. "You know him?"

"No, no." He held his hands up, palm out. "Calm down, don't have a coronary."

"I'll have one if I damn well please!"

"It's not like that. Detective Hobbes told me his name. I swear, I have no idea who he is. The name meant nothing to me."

"Okay, okay." She forced herself to calm down. He was right, this was no time to burst a blood vessel. "So, if you didn't do it, who did? Who had a motive and could do it quick, and avoid the cops, and stick you with a murder charge?"

"Honey, I got nothin'. I've been trying to figure it out all night. I was minding my own business, waiting for you, and the next thing I know, I'm wearing handcuffs. And not in a good way."

She felt the blood rush to her face as she pictured him cuffed to her headboard. "All right. Did you overhear any arguments? See anybody fighting? Anything weird at all?"

"No."

"Come on. There must be something."

He shook his head. "No. And no, and no. I told the cops all this already."

"Well, now tell *me*," she snapped.

"Don't boss me!"

"I'll boss you if I like! If it wasn't for me, you'd still be rotting in jail!"

"The hell. My lawyer would have vouched for me."

"Yeah, I could tell what a great job he did by the way it took him *hours* and *hours* to *not* show up."

"Listen—mmph!"

She had kissed him again. What was wrong with her?

"Not that I mind," he gasped, extricating himself from her grip, "but, again, don't you think this is a little inappropriate? Given the circumstances?"

She got up to pace. "Of course it's inappropriate—it's nine kinds of inappropriate! What the hell is wrong with me?"

He opened his mouth, but she beat him to the punch. "I'll tell you, it's this fucking holiday! It's killing me! It's making me act in ways I would never normally act! God, I hate it, I hate it, *I hate Valentine's Day!*"

Here's a scintillating peek at Sylvia Day's
"Stolen Pleasures"
in her new anthology
BAD BOYS AHOY.
Available February 2006 from Brava.

British West Indies, February 1813

He'd stolen a bride.

Sebastian Blake gripped his knife with white-knuckled force and kept his face impassive. If the beauty in front of him was to be believed, he'd stolen *his own* bride.

He watched as her chin lifted with defiance and her dark eyes met his without fear. She was tall and slender with blond curls tumbling down from a once-stylish arrangement. Her lovely watered-silk dress was torn at the shoulder, revealing a tempting display of creamy breast. There was a sooty hand-print marring her flesh, and unable to stop himself, Sebastian reached out and rubbed the offending mark away with gentle strokes of his thumb. She stiffened and lifted her bound hands to knock his away. He met her gaze and held it.

"Tell me your name again," he murmured, his hand tingling just from that simple contact with her satin skin.

She licked her bottom lip and his blood heated further. "My name is Olivia Blake, Countess of Merrick. My husband is Sebastian Blake, Earl of Merrick and future Marquis of Dunsmore."

He lifted her hands and stared at her ring finger, noting his crest etched in the simple gold band she wore.

He scrubbed a hand over his face and turned away, striding to the nearest open window for a deep breath of salt-tinged air. Staring out at the water, he spied the debris from her ship bobbing in the waves. "Where is your husband, Lady Merrick?" he asked, keeping his back to her.

Hope tinged her voice. "He awaits me in London."

"I see." But he didn't, not at all. "How long have you been married, my lady?"

"I fail to see—"

"How long?" he barked.

"Nearly two weeks."

His chest expanded with a deep breath. "I remind you that we are in the West Indies, Lady Merrick. It is impossible that you were married only a fortnight ago. Your husband would not be able to await you in England if that were true."

She was silent behind him and finally, he turned to face her again. It was a mistake to have done so. Her beauty hit him with the force of a fist in his gut.

"Would you care to explain?" he prodded, relieved he sounded so unaffected.

For the first time her bravado left her, her cheeks flushing with embarrassment. "We were married by proxy," she confessed. "But I assure you, he will pay whatever ransom you desire despite the unusual circumstances of our marriage."

Sebastian moved toward her. His calloused fingers caressed the elegant curve of her cheekbone and entwined in her hair. Her breath caught, and her lips parted in response to his gentle touch. "I'm certain he would pay a king's ransom for beauty such as yours."

Through the smoky smell that clung to her, he could detect the arousing scent of soft woman, warm and luxurious. He reached for the blade strapped to his thigh and withdrew it.

She flinched it away.

"Easy," he soothed. Sebastian held out his hand and waited patiently for her to step forward again. When she did, he sliced through the rope that tied her hands together and sheathed his knife. He rubbed the marks on her delicate wrists.

"You are a pirate," she murmured.

"Yes."

"You have taken my father's ship and all of its cargo."

"I have."

Her head tilted backward on the slender neck and she gazed up at him with melting chocolate eyes. "Why then are you being so kind to me, if you intended to rape me?"

He caught her fingers and placed them on his signet ring. "Most would say a man cannot rape his own wife."

She glanced down and gasped at the heavy crest that mirrored her own band. Her eyes flew up to his. "Where did you get this? You can't possibly . . ."

He smiled. "According to you, I am."

Olivia stared up into the intense blue eyes and felt certain her heart would burst from her chest. Her mind faltered, stumbling over the shocking revelation that the notorious Captain Phoenix was claiming to be her husband.

She backed away from him in a rush, and he reached to steady her when she would have fallen. A whimper escaped as his touch burned her skin. The day's events had shaken her, but it was the gorgeous face of the infamous pirate that made her weak-kneed.

Tall and broad shouldered, his presence sucked all of the air from the tight confines of the cabin. His black hair was unfashionably long and the darkness of his skin betrayed how much time he spent outdoors. He was wild, untamed—a man of the elements.

She'd watched, fascinated, as he'd swept onto her ship and took command of it within moments. Phoenix had executed the attack with brilliant precision—not one man was seriously injured and no one had been killed. Having spent most of her childhood on her father's ships, Olivia recognized singular skill when she saw it.

The way he'd used his sword and barked commands, the way loose tendrils of his hair had blown across his face, the way his breeches delineated every stretch of his muscular thighs . . . she'd never experienced anything so thrilling. So exciting.

Until he'd touched her.